KILLED
by Mary

NORMA FRASER

Edited by Kriti Tripathi
kriti.tripathi2504@gmail.com

Original cover design by Jonny Liver
noorefiver@gmail.com

Cover design and typesetting by Mary Turner Thomson
www.thebookwhispererscommunity.com

Hardback cover image courtesy of Mantis Dan
www.mantisden.co.uk

Author's Facebook page
www.facebook.com/Surprising-reads

Prologue

No one gives a shit when you're living in a remote village, except every other arsehole that lives there. Always in your fucking business, thinking they know the best. . . Inverie fits perfectly in this. The most exciting thing to do is kicking a plastic bottle around one of the vast fields or laughing at the usual drunk that falls out of the pub door. Boring as fuck! Something definitely needs to change!

"Vicious Circles" are another one of nature's kick in the balls. Living in a small town with no jobs, unable to escape because there's no money to move. It's not like there's any housing available here to get anyway. Even when one waits for the old codgers to take their rightful place in the ground, the selfish bastards pass it onto their ungrateful family members. My situation isn't the worst though. I mean, I'm thirty and still live with my mum—that's shit, but at least I have my own space. Mum is in a wheelchair from the car accident that killed Dad so she can't get up the stairs. Not that she would want to see the fucking mess up here. It's tidy for me but she wouldn't think so. The good news is, that leaves me with the whole of the first floor while she has the ground floor to herself. I've created a nice little space for myself, changing the second bedroom into a cosy living room, having the main bathroom and my bedroom, sorted. I mean what else do you need for a bachelor pad?

Dr Fucking Twathead told me I should get a pet. A fluffy wee garden-shitter for company. No thanks! It's not like he actually cares about my mundane life, but more because his rampant wee shit got out and is pregnant again.

For once in my life, I could agree that he was right. A pet was exactly what I needed and I don't know why I didn't see it before! Mum is definitely not up for a pet, don't know why it might cheer up her miserable puss but what she doesn't know and can't come to check on, won't kill her. Although if she knew what I chose she'd probably die of fright.

As usual, the town's cop is more worried about the five-pound petty cash that went missing from the post office than the actual contents of packages coming in. Bert, "the fantastic specially trained sniffer dog" obviously, would pick anything suspicious up. For a place like Inverie, the government won't care to spend even a penny, so, Bert isn't a trained dog actually. It is another one of the Doc's giveaways that Constable Dobber pretends he has trained to sniff out all sorts of shite.

Well, you missed that one, Bert! The little box that's about to make a massive impact and it passed right under your crap nose!

Opening the package with the utmost care, following all instructions indicated by the breeder, I saw the most beautiful creature and wondered how I went this long "pet free". When we think of pets, what words come to mind first? Fluffy, cuddly, loving. . . NO!

I needed something silent so Mum doesn't hear it or even smell it, as my mum's got a nose that can smell shit being created in your body before it even starts moving down. In fact, she should take over Bert's job! No shite gets past her!

It even cost me a bloody bracelet because "Miss-tell-everyone-everything-because-my-life-is-so-shit" told Mum I'd got a package so I had to tell her that it was a surprise for Mum. That little, loose-mouth, Lizzy will get what's coming to her one day! I don't mean the shitty post office her mum owns! Smiling and waving at everyone. How can someone even pretend to like everyone they meet all the time? It can't be how she actually feels!

"Let me carry that bag for you, Mr..."

"Ow how is your poorly cat, Mrs..."

"You sure you don't want me to wipe your ass for you, Mr..."

It's the most gut retching act to watch.

"She'll make some man very happy one day." That's what Mum always says about her. *Yeah! When she gets up and leaves!*

Another vital feature I needed from a pet was it being low maintenance and the need for very little space. I wasn't having something restrict my space more than it already is and the thought of something being completely dependent on me makes me lose all respect for it. I'll chuck it some food and water but it can piss off if it thinks I'll be spending any of my time giving it attention. That's why my choice was obvious and straightforward.

Although, have you ever tried to find someone willing to sell and send you a highly dangerous weapon in the post? It's not illegal but their liability insurance must be bat shit crazy! It wasn't that simple, though. I had to make some decisions. I think I made the perfect choice and, here she was. Finally home.

Mary!

Just as described online—fluffy, brown-eyed with the look of the devil, beautiful!

One positive thing about no one knowing who you are is. . . the fuckers don't see you coming.

Chapter One:

Planning

My eyes widened when I saw her size. I knew they could be big but she was massive. An absolute beauty! It had been easier than I expected! Faking the necessary license and the research made me sound like an expert. This wasn't just a heated idea. Two years of planning but, that's the fun part. Moreover, perfection takes time.

The biggest decision was making sure Mary was just the right species or it wouldn't work. Black widows are too common and someone might recognise the symptoms, never mind an anti-venom is available in all likeliness.

The Wolf was my initial choice but their little heads and big eyes creeped the shit out of me. . . It wouldn't be easy if I couldn't even look at it.

Then there was the Funnel Web but they're way too aggressive! No point wasting all this time and effort if I got bitten first. Mary was my final choice. She isn't just any species. She's a Red Fang Wandering spider, part of the Phoneutria family meaning "murderess" in Greek. How fitting!

I was actually looking for the Brazilian Wandering one but then this picture popped up. It was so beautiful and exactly what I was looking for. Just as dangerous as the Brazilian but smaller in size. Females are smaller than the male which makes them less likely to eat the males and an expert in hiding. They don't make webs to live in so, no pre-warning there.

Tick, tick, tick, tick! The sound was one of the best music I'd ever heard. She was perfect! As long as she didn't touch me with those massive tomatoes hanging off her face, we would get on great. I could now see why everyone insists that a pet changes our life and makes us very happy.

Obviously, I couldn't just have lots of packages turning up with Lizzy, the-fucking-nosey-bitch, alerting Mum constantly. I managed to fool my mum once but she's a smart cookie so I wasn't pushing my luck! I was hoping to buy everything I needed on one delivery but the only money I had was Amazon vouchers that I'd saved from my birthdays and Christmas and they didn't seem to sell dangerous spiders. *Losers!*

I did however manage to get a lot that I needed from there—a humidity machine, logs, moss, cotton balls, tongs, and little water bowls—lots of good stuff. There's a charity shop in town which I'd always thought of as the most ridiculous thing ever.

I mean, everyone knows who has donated what so one wouldn't want someone shouting "Ah! I'm glad you're enjoying my old clothes. . ." while they're walking down the street.

When I was younger, the boys at my school would play a game of guessing the teachers, or any woman's cup size, and then check who was right in the charity shop when they handed one in. The charity shop also sells the pants that are handed in, like, come on!

There's only one woman in this town that's size twenty-four and she donated the pants! Who the fuck is going to buy them or even want the scent of her sweaty arse soup anywhere near them? Some people just need a punch with a concrete slab.

However, I was walking past one day and saw that they had a fish tank from the window. The tank gave me an idea. I ran home and asked Mum if she'd care if I kept fish in my room and she agreed. By agreed, she actually said, "as long as you don't smash it and flood the place!"

It was pretty much the same. Anyway, did she think I meant a tank big enough to hold a bloody shark? *No, Mum, it'll def not flood the place. Now that's a promise I know I can keep.* It's just a wee twenty-five litre tank and has a proper sturdy lid so it'll do perfectly. Once I filled it with the logs, dirt and some plants then I'm sure Mary would love it.

I decided on her name even before picking her because Mary, Queen of Scots, was someone who had a proper hard shite life too. She deserves recognition. She was apparently a grumpy, stubborn, bitch so, it seemed fitting.

Mary, my new pet, was advertised as a reliable and tough female—very relaxed, but equally just as dangerous. I think Queen Mary would approve if that's how she was described. In all probability, the Queen was less hairy but we can't have everything perfect. I have plans on getting a partner for her and name him, Wallace. Big, strong and brave like William Wallace. What a beautiful match that would be! Never mind, unstoppable.

When I first contacted Mary's breeder, I explained I would like a male and a female to observe the differences in the sex through different stages of their lives. It was he that informed me that males only live for around one to three years. He insisted it would be best to get the female first so I can observe them as adults at the same time. He literally built my excuse for me so I just pretended to agree. I will be getting Wallace, but further down the line. Also, I'll have to raise more funds before I bring him in.

It wasn't cheap getting Mary sent over here. I actually thought the guy was making a joke when he first sent me the invoice but then it wasn't followed by any laughing emojis. The amount it cost me for Mary alone was what I'd gathered would suffice for both. I was actually glad when the breeder said I should wait and not buy two at once. Saved me turning around and asking him if he'd wait till I sell my fucking kidney. No fucking wonder people don't just have them as pets!

If I did everything legally then I'd be paying about a thousand pound every year just for the license to keep them. The money wasn't the reason I didn't go down that route—it's definitely a good reason not to, but it's more about the paper trail. No license, no cheques and harder for them to find me.

I had ordered a couple of different catalogues from expensive aquariums and left them lying around the kitchen to give my mum the impression it wasn't a super cheap hobby. She questioned me about how I planned to fund it but I explained to her, it was easy to sell my old junk online these days and I'd get back to my usual jobs as the season arrived.

The local fields are home to lots of different types of sheep including Jacob, Herdwick, Icelandic and Gotland. There's no lack of jobs once lambing gets under way. From February to May there's always some farm looking for the extra pair of hands. It's not much pay but a good little earner for people willing to get their hands dirty. I had been doing this since I was old enough to be out in the dark alone. Mum used to get the farmer to pick me up at stupid o' clock and "setting me up for the life of hard work". Being the Head teacher at the local school meant she could get there early and the farmer would get me back to school before the first class, so it was free child care.

I was glad of it though, I loved to help the struggling ewes delivering babies and the infant lambs take their first feed. Obviously, it wasn't all happy endings. However, the first time I saw death I didn't feel the fear or upset I initially thought I would. I wasn't happy about it but after watching the ewe struggle and trying to push to stay alive for three hours straight it made me a little relieved when she was finally out of pain. The vet decided to cut the lambs out. There were three in there, and luckily, they all survived. I spent most of my free time at the farm that year helping raise them and giving them the love, they were missing from their mum. There were lots of multiple lamb births that year so, there was no ewe to support with the extra load.

It's mid-January and by helping out this year I should have enough to buy Wallace by June. There's no rush, as Mary has enough of what I need for now. She should hold enough venom for me to test out on a few unsuspecting people before I have the need for a much larger quantity.

I read a lot about milking a spider and bought some chloroform just in case I couldn't get her to produce it naturally. I didn't bother investing in an electric shocking device as I'm sure I'd find some useless piece of junk in my room that I can cut the plug off. Hopefully, that won't be necessary and she'll happily share her magic with me.

I have a sterile cup and cling film but I still need to work out on how to get her to bite that and not me. I considered putting a moth inside the tub so she'd think she's biting that but then the venom would be hairy and hard to use. I'm sure, I'll find a way. I've researched and planned everything but there are minor details to fill in and things that I'll need to find my own way of doing. I needed to work out Mary's temperament before I could decide on certain things.

Things like these can't be rushed. They take time, money and patients which I have bags of. Well, not the money, but the other two. There will be risks along the way that I can't avoid so hopefully for once I'll have luck on my side. I'm not just banking on luck though, as it doesn't often raise its head. Obviously, I'm not a total fucking moron. I'm not just going to try kill all the fucking people in the village that I hate. First, that would take far too much venom and there's only so long before someone would work out that it's me. But, I do need some guinea pigs so I'll have to take a couple.

I feel like Mary! I'm stalking prey, picking carefully, waiting it out, and then I'll strike. Maybe, I was a spider in my past life, all I was missing was the venom! Well, and the fangs, as I wouldn't do very well if I bite down on someone with these human teeth. It might be too noticeable. There are a few different groups of people I've considered but have managed to narrow that down to two.

Nowhere in the world is completely "drug free" but it's not like we've got many junkies plodding about. There's no money in this town to pay for that type of thing. Then, there are the homeless. There aren't many of them too in Inverie, because everyone here has been born here so all of us have families. Not many "Ladies of the night" either, because unless they're happy with incest, they're not going to make money there.

Kids aren't an option and obviously they need their adults to take care of them so they were also out of the picture. The two I'm still trying to decide between are the old fuckers and the annoying twats. The old fuckers are near popping anyway. I could probably just show them a picture of Mary and they will keel over. No one would be massively surprised if they died. The other group is the annoying twats that everyone hates. Would people really care? Would they still investigate it or would they just have an inside party and move on? I know they have family too, but surely, the families must also hate them.

People round like the fucking saying, "anything you want to know you can now just find on that internet, no brain power needed these days."

Well Mate, I'd like to see you google — "best way to kill a fucker with venom" — I can almost guarantee you won't find the answer. Though, what you might find would be thirty cops on your doorstep and a wee comfy jail cell waiting. There's only so much one can find out online without fucking everything up. That's what's wrong with crazy people that want to do bad things.

I admit I'm crazy, but I'm smart-crazy. I'm not stupid to flag my name all over the web and then wonder how'd they catch me. I wouldn't even buy much stuff that may help anyone put two and two together. I'll be gathering the things I can for their tanks and if it means digging up fucking worms to feed them, then I'll do that too.

I discussed with the breeder about wanting to see if a spider like it could survive on our type of land—the heat would be an issue, but I mainly meant the food supply. He agreed that they should be fine with moths and grasshoppers but he doesn't think it's the best diet for them. He suggested I do that for my research but only as part of their diet and still stick with crickets and vitamins. *Yeah! Mr. Money Bags, I see how long I can last first. Thanks.*

I will need to buy other supplies as I go but as long as the purchases are few and far between, I should be alright. Maybe the charity shop will serve me well in the months to come but they can fuck off it they think I'll be giving them anything for free.

I've still got my DVD collection on eBay hoping that it sells soon and I have loads of other shite to put on there too. I need to get Dad's old leather jacket in the wash before Mum sees it or I take pictures. Most of the things I'm selling that are mine are shite, so I have had to pick out a couple things from my dad's stuff to sell too. I'm sure he wouldn't mind and really it all belongs to me now. Mum was going to give the charity shop a lot of Dad's clothes when he died but when she thought about it, she couldn't imagine other people walking about wearing them and reminding her of him. She said I can keep them, being sure I'll grow into them. *Yeah! Because I'm going to grow from five-foot-five to fucking six-foot-three overnight!*

I love Mum but the shit that comes out of her mouth sometimes, seems to drive me crazy. She kept babbling that "I'll grow into them", which I never will so I've decided to sell some of them instead. He didn't have anything too fancy but he had some suits that would do someone good, some nice jackets, funky heavy belts with buckles and a couple pair of nice shoes. There are also about nine waist coats he got from Grandad when he died. I loved Grandad as he was wacky as fuck, even sometimes wore a monocle and a pocket watch. *Detective Poirot, eat your fucking heart out.*

I would def get a few pennies for them online, had even considered contacting that eccentric guy from the chateau but forgot how wee Grandad was until I tried to put one on. I'm sure there are loads of wee hippy guys in the big cities that'll want them.

Then there's the records. I know they could bring in a pretty penny but I'm not ready to let go of them just yet. Good to know I have back up supplies, just in case. It does however mean that I'll have to explain Lizzy what I'm posting and why, but the fish tank stuff isn't cheap after all. Or maybe I'll grow a set of balls and tell her to mind her own fucking business. I'm not worried of her response but she'll def tell Mum that one. Whatever I need to do to accomplish my plans, no matter how hard, I'll do it.

Obviously, I haven't told anyone what I'm planning. Whenever two people pair up and work together as a team trying to accomplish their nasty plans, they always get fucking caught. One always turns on the other.

How do they even start that shit? Do they just turn to a friend one day and say, "Hey here's what I fancy doing, you wanna join?"

Even if they didn't just turn their ass in right away then what that crazy fucker replies, "yeah sure!"

I live in a place where it's absolutely fuck all to do and still I don't think I could find anyone to join. God knows what those city folk are all about. It's not because they are true friends or have a close relationship; it's because they're being thick as fuck, usually always dropped on their heads as babies. *If you're determined to do something the only person you can truly trust is yourself.*

I don't need to tell anyone or brag, I'll get all the satisfaction I need from being successful. I don't give a shit about what people think about me, I know me and I know why I'm doing it, and that's all that matters.

The best thing about my plan is that no one refuses a free gift— that special package that turns up from a secret admirer, the free promo from the new business trying to find its legs. The truth is that most people in this world are greedy. They don't stop and wonder why they have received that gift. Try and think back if they actually ever gave their details to that new company. Meh! What does it matter if it's free? One wouldn't kick a gift horse in the mouth, would they?

People make it far too easy to be caught out. They feel like they are admired and worthy, so how could they be surprised that someone spent their own time and effort into sending a lovely gesture? If a gift turned up at my door I'd want to know why, where it's from and who it's from. It shows the divide between us and them. I know nothing in life is free. I've never had anything handed to me on a plate. I know life is hard and that I've to work just as hard as it is to stay alive. If one is willing to accept something for free with no questions asked, then they fucking deserve what they're about to receive.

Chapter Two:

Awaited arrival

Following the instructions mentioned on the Care Leaflet inside, I removed the newspaper protecting the little plastic tub. I then removed the heat pack and gently lifted the tub onto a flat surface. It was the first time I laid my eyes on her. I didn't want to put her in her cage right away because she'd most likely hide and I wanted to take some time to admire her. Her fangs are much brighter than I expected and her long slender legs are perfectly symmetrical on each side. Her eyes are tiny, dark and direct. Her gaze seems like she's looking into my soul. She was standing in the shape of a star, holding four legs directly in front of her, one outward on each side and pointing two of them back. I was a little worried that she might be dead with how still she stayed, like a rock statue. I gently nudged the tub and, in a blink, she changed the formation of her legs. I jumped at how fast she moved! It was quick as a flash but, at least, I knew she was alive.

They say that spiders are more scared of us than we are of them but, I'd like to see them say that while standing in front of this little beauty. I've learnt loads about spiders during my research and was surprised about how little I actually knew. Spiders only suck out their prey's liquids. Arachnid means spider. All spiders build webs. All have eight eyes. . . All of this, is a pile of bull shit.

Spiders can eat solids. Scorpions are Arachnids. All make silk but don't necessarily build a web and all don't have eight eyes. So

13

even if this plan doesn't work, which I hardly doubt to fail, I could maybe get a job as some spider expert somewhere. Not very sure what I'd do in that kind of job but sounds like a solid investment anyway. Or maybe, this is just the beginning of something bigger. I'd branch out into the world of unusual pets, open a unique pet shop. I'd most definitely have to move to a city to manage that one though, can't imagine wee Mrs Murphy down the road looking to buy a massive snake or fast running lizard.

I realised I was lost into a world of my own again and Mary was still in her tub. I quickly took a sketch of the markings on her back. It'd make for a sick tattoo one day, and then I started prepping up for her release. Tank lid off, water bowl full, humidity levels good, tongs at the ready. . . *WAIT! How the fuck was I meant to open the lid without her catching me?*

Fumbling about for the instructions from the package, I couldn't see them anywhere. It was like God himself had fucking taken them so he could sit back and laugh. To be fair, I needed to tidy my room up. I couldn't find a place to sit in here never mind, a wee scrap bit of paper. *Right, I can work this out, I'm logical. Think! think!*

There had to be a special catch on the tub or something? I tried checking it up, but there was absolutely nothing there. I looked upwards and said out loud, "Keep laughing up there, big man. I'll show you."

I clicked the computer on and found out that the wi-fi was down again. *For fuck's sake, woman!* I've told her to set up the bloody direct debit so it doesn't get paid late but she'd always reply "Oh No! Direct debits are just for giving others control over your money."

Give me strength! You're literally about to kill your son just because you're scared of a wee shitty £12 direct debit. I shouted down to her but she couldn't hear me from the Eastenders' tune blaring away. It's only 5 p.m. but Mum likes to watch Eastenders while having dinner so she makes sure it's recorded for the next day. Recorded on the sky box that she never "forgets" to pay on time, I might add! Just because she didn't see the point in the "web", no one else should have to bloody suffer. I hope she fucking chokes on that battered sausage she's munching away on. Serves her right for buying it instead of paying the internet bill. *I'll remind her to sort the internet tomorrow, right now I've got to get Mary free.*

I didn't recall being that scared. My hands won't stop shaking and sweating like that drippy comedian who's on the TV. I'd like to see how he'd cope in this situation, probably he'd accidently drown himself. *Right! Get a grip man, this is the day we've been waiting for, grow hairs on your balls and get her out!* OMG! what was the bloody point in oven gloves? I couldn't get hold of the little tub, in fact, I couldn't even think when I'd been able to get hold of an oven tray with these bloody things. "Still laughing, big man?"

I need to calm myself down. I'm pretty sure Mary can smell the fear she's installing in me and is loving every inch of it.

I shake the glove off and decide to just go for it. I place the little tub in the bottom of the tank and try to slowly clip the lid off. Mary is watching me intently but still holding her ground and not moving. I can't work out if she is following me with her eyes or not as she's like one of those creepy pictures that just look like they are always staring at you. Hopefully she's in sleep mode and I can get this lid off without freaking her out.

Right! I heard the pop of the lid coming and pulled my hand out fast, dropping the lid back in as I recoiled. I would get that with the tongs later. Mary didn't seem to care, she just sat there like she was invisible, gutsy wee fucker. I waited a couple seconds to see if she made a move but ended up having to gently nudge her with a paper straw that was lying on the floor.

Paper straws are a pain! At least I've found a bloody use for this one. If I wanted to drink soggy paper, I'd have ordered it as a drink. As soon as you pop the straw in the juice, the countdown timer starts! I get the point of them because I've seen what plastic can do to animals. I saw a cat walking backwards on the beach once with its head stuck in a crisps packet. I couldn't stop laughing until

I realised it was about to walk backwards off the rocks and into the water so I helped it. I still laugh at that image when I think about it but I don't like to see an animal getting hurt.

Mary slowly wandered over to a large piece of log I put tilted for her so she'd have a place to hide but she stopped before entering. I thought she'd run off and hide right away but she was either a cool cat or she was trying to work out the gangly man in front of her. I remembered the instructions mentioning she wasn't likely to eat for the first day or two but I couldn't hold my excitement any longer. I hadn't ordered any crickets because I didn't want my mum hearing them so I hoped she'd enjoy the field findings I caught for her this morning.

Took me ages to catch that big fat moth. I didn't think it was going to fit in the little Playdough tub I took with me but I managed to squeeze it in. I emptied the tub into Mary's tank—the poor little guy's wings were clearly broken but Mary must be tired from her travels so she'll probably appreciate the easier catch. She makes a little move from the moth falling in and turns to face it but just stops still again. "It's ok little one, it's just dinner being served."

Twenty minutes later, the moth walks about the place like it's his new little crib. "Don't get too comfy, little guy."

I turned off all the lights except my lava lamp hoping she'd make her move but clearly, she has got more patience than me. I've never been able to stand feeling hungry, luckily, nor can Mum so there's always a snack to grab. I'm grateful she's not one of these healthy eating freaks and bought enough chocolate and crisps to keep the titanic going for a week. Obviously, before the accident.

I lay my head on the desk watching her intently, knowing she'll attack and I definitely didn't want to miss it.

It was 4 a.m. and she still hadn't moved. Even the poor moth was just sitting still in the corner. Maybe it saw her and was dead from fright either way, I didn't see her wanting that half dead thing now.

I head downstairs and find Mum passed out in her chair in front of the TV. She really struggles to get to bed these days so I've to put her to bed more and more. The eight cans of Strongbow's not helping her agility much but we all have to find happiness somewhere. I tuck her in, set her hoist next to her bed and park the wheelchair right up against it. I fill her cup with a big ladle of coffee and set her Teasmade to go off at 10. After she's had a good night's sleep and her morning black coffee, she manages to get back in her wheels fine. I placed one of the dumbbells that I bought three years ago, adamant that I was going to get fit but then couldn't be bothered, on top of Mary's cage and hop into bed.

I knew I wouldn't get much sleep from the excitement for the day, but lying down beat sitting on the floor. I tossed and turned and finally fall asleep.

.oOo.

When I opened my eyes, I was surprised to see it was only 6 a.m. but felt like I'd slept for a week. I wondered if I could go and try to get Mary's breakfast before Mum wakes. I crept to the kitchen and found one of Mum's milkshake cups with the screw on lids. She won't notice it's gone as she stopped all that shite when Dad died. I grabbed a torch and a white pillow case from the cupboard downstairs and slid quietly out the back door. It was still pitch black and I almost lost my footing at the end of the ramp. I hung the pillowcase on the washing like and shine with the torch behind it. My plan worked a treat!

I wished I'd thought about that earlier instead of spending so much time in that field trying to chase them. I quickly swooped the cup around and jammed the torch in the opening to stop the moth getting back out and remove the pillow case from the washing line. Perfect! As long as I could keep the little guy going until the night falls, I was sure Mary would enjoy it. It wasn't as big as the previous but sure was feistier, battering itself against the side of the cup. Once I got back upstairs, I quickly moved the pillowcase and

17

carefully balanced my racket on top of the cup, so the moth could breathe, but not escape. I had to wait a few minutes for it to stop jumping about, in case, it knocked the racket off. It finally settled and I turned my attention back to Mary. She had finally decided that she'd had enough of my ugly mug and climbed into the gap under the log. I took the opportunity to remove the dead moth, lid and tub that were still lying about at the bottom. I checked the temperature of the tank and decided to try to get some more sleep.

I was aroused by Mum screaming, "Rab, Rab!" She must have been at the bottom of the stairs. "Why the hell are there muddy footprints all over the stair carpet?"

Shit! In my rush to get the moth upstairs I forgot to take my shoes off.

"Sorry, Mum!" I shouted back. There was no point arguing with her or trying to tell her she made them, I probably would've gotten a slap for that one. At least, she already called and got the internet put back on so I checked for any emails, not like I usually get anything but spam, then clicked over to my favourite Facebook page "Scottish (Slightly Insane) Reptile and Invertebrates fans".

I loved that page—one gets exactly what it says on the tin! No pissy arguments about someone buying a broken second-hand toaster or complaints against the "very normal" Scottish weather. I found this page when I was looking about spiders online and was actually shocked by how many people in Scotland actually own crazy pets. There were people with like twenty or thirty snakes, maddos with scorpions and even poisonous frogs. I think, I might get one of the frogs some time, although they're maybe too cute to give that dangerous feeling. I read about a guy's snake that accidentally ate his daughter's pet rabbit and a guy's video on sexing snakes. I saw people with lots of spiders on there but none of them were like Mary. I never actually comment on the group, in case, I'm outed for illegally having her, but they are a really good entertaining bunch.

I couldn't concentrate on reading the words as my belly was shouting at me for food. For once, I'd actually not noticed how hungry I was. I scoured the cupboards and finally resigned myself to a waggon wheel, a packet of monster munch and a can of coke. I really could have done with a proper cooked breakfast but Mum was too hungover to bother. I sat on my bed watching some shite on the TV about global warming thinking she was talking piss with how cold it was out in the garden—someone clearly got too much money for heating! Mary wasn't likely to venture out until the night, so I decided to head into town to pass some time but as soon as I was about to head out the door my phone beeped.

YUS! The DVDs were sold! Not as much as I would've liked and not meaning to steal anyone's punch line but every little thing helps. I eagerly tipped out the contents of a box I found under my bed and packed up the DVDs wondering if I'd manage to get through the trip to the post office without punching Lizzy in the face. I pumped up my bike tyre and managed to get there in a record time.

Lizzy was nowhere to be seen. *Were my prayers answered?*

Nope. My seconds of joy diminished as I saw the room to the back open.

"Good afternoon, Robert. Twice in two days? What gives me the honour?"

I fucking hate that she calls me Robert, has she not noticed that no one else does? She claims to know everything but can't even get my fucking name right.

She was invading my personal space again, stinking up the place like I'd walked into a perfume shop. I coughed and backed off.

"Oooo... what have you got in there?"

I wanted to tell her I'd ten grams of cocaine and see if she called the pigs but decided against it as Mum would slap me for being a cheeky bastard.

"DVDs." I said, "Raising money for a better pump for the tank."

She wattled on for ages about how she loved watching fish swimming about, fish I'd never heard of and places online I could buy some. There's no pet shop here, it's just the local shop with dog, cat and fish food and she informed me, depending on the fish I kept, I might need to buy their food online. I gritted my teeth in an attempt of a smile and put the package on the scales. I couldn't even pretend I was in a rush as she knew I'd absolutely nothing going on in my miserable life so a job that should have taken two minutes, lasted thirty-five! I gave out a massive sigh of relief as I made it back out the door and hopped onto my bike before she could follow.

At 1 a.m. Mary finally wandered out. She moved super slowly and I remembered about the moth in the cup. I lifted the little feeding hatch and dropped the moth in. She didn't seem as startled this time but she still froze. The moth started going crazy and dashed all over the tin. I started to think that he'd be too fast for her to catch but he soon settled down. In the videos I saw online, I often saw spiders either lifting their legs quite high or running really quickly. Mary did none of these things—she gently crept forward with tiny little steps. Maybe all that traveling over the last few days had left her body a bit sore. I laid still watching her, not wanting to put the TV on, in case, the light scared her back into her hiding. Sluggishly and with utmost care, she inspected her new surroundings. Tapping her legs gently on the glass before moving forward and checking the next bit. It was like she was checking to see if there were any spaces in the glass she could escape from. Thankfully for me, there weren't. The moth didn't seem to notice her presence in the tank, it just stayed at the corner mesmerised by the lava lamp.

Again, I wondered if Mary would be interested in not having the hunt before the kill but if I'd turned the lamp off, I wouldn't have been able to see. A quick search on my phone informed me that moths couldn't see red lights, so with just a couple clicks I secured a red bulb and decided Mary wouldn't mind the current situation for a couple more days and I kept the lava lamp on.

It happened in a blink of an eye! It took me a couple seconds to even realise it had happened. Somehow, Mary had managed to get halfway across the tank and grabbed the moth without me actually seeing her move. Two small flutters of the wings were all the moth had time for. What had changed? Did the moth give out a signal I missed? What made her choose that moment after so many hours of waiting? I needed to find out if I was ever going to be able to milk her. She didn't seem in a rush to eat though and just sat there with the moth limply hanging from her fangs. Was she waiting to see if it moved? Slowly she started to dismember her victim.

First, tearing off the wings and legs and still holding on to it tightly with her fangs. It was too dark and I was too far away to see exactly what she was doing but I could see her making very small movements at the front. I desperately wanted to get closer but also didn't want to disturb her first meal since her arrival. I couldn't decide if I was disappointed at what an anti-climax it was. After thinking so long about the hunt, stalk and fight, I didn't even get to see it properly, but her efficiency gave me much more confidence for the events to come. She waited and picked the perfect time, definitely the surprise I was after.

The next morning I removed the tiny pieces that were the remains of the moth with the tongs and refilled her water bowl with a large syringe— I was certainly not putting my hands in there after what I witnessed last night. She didn't venture out to see what I was doing but I could see a couple of her eyes directed out into the tank. I could see now why people needed licences and training to be allowed to keep a pet like this. One tip onto the floor and I doubt I'd be able to find her again. Her dark colour not only helps her camouflage with the surroundings, but her ability to remain a perfect statue would make spotting her a near impossible task.

I made sure to return the dumbbell back onto the lid every time I close it again so there was no way she could get out. I also added brown tape to the feeding hatch as the clip seemed to be temperamental. *Can't be too careful when you're responsible for something that can not only kill you but every other person in her path.*

It wasn't until a few days later that I woke in the middle of the night to see her perched up at the top corner of the tank. I knew it was possible for her to climb glass but I couldn't see how she could be choosing that over the comfort of that mud. I left her be and returned to bed deciding I'd need to find another way to secure the lid and hatch.

.oOo.

It had been four weeks since Mary arrived and we were settling into our routine very nicely. She tended to eat my catch most days and spent all day in her hiding space. I found myself talking to her more and more often and have to keep trying to stop so my mum doesn't think I'm talking to myself. Mum had asked many times about if I'd actually set up the tank yet or if I'd added any real fish. I explained that it takes time for the tank to settle but I'd order a fish soon.

I hoped she wasn't getting too interested and asked to see any of them when they arrive. I doubt she might, though, as she'd never been a big fan of animals, especially pointless things swimming round and round in a bowl.

"Tomato face", as I'd affectionately started calling her, was proving to be a very relaxed soul. I'd put my hands in her cage a couple times now to lift out her water bowl or to sort some of the plants and she'd never even venture out to see what I was doing. She happily wandered about her cage at night even with my face right up to the glass. I think she'd got used to me now and I've definitely become more settled around her. Sometimes, I even have to remind myself of the danger and to stay cautious.

I upgraded the dumbbell with a chain that clips onto the lip at the bottom of the tank at both sides which doubles up by holding the feeding hatch down. At first, it kept shocking her and disturbing her while I removed it to feed her but now, she's used to the noise and it's more of a dinner bell for her. I managed to catch her a grasshopper a couple days ago and she seemed to really enjoy it, even if it did kick her in the face a couple times before she whizzed it up into a little package and just sat watching it for hours. I'd been learning so much from her that I'd not even thought about before. Like spiders don't blink because they don't have eyelids. I love to sit and watch her intricately clean herself after each meal, rubbing her legs together like Mr Burns from the Simpsons. The way she moves each leg so carefully and independently, never fumbling or tripping up over her other legs. I suppose if we had eight legs, we'd get used to it but, I can't imagine trying to control them all. I tripped myself up a few times in my years, even got a scar on my forehead when I once face-planked the floor just walking to the loo. Two legs are enough for me to handle.

I think she enjoys our chats in the wee hours, sometimes I even make up a voice for her in my head with the responses she might give. I'd ask her, "what's that wee lesbo Lizzy been going on about today then? She's fucking late for a how to be a bitch meeting?"

And Mary's made-up voice would reassure me, "Don't worry Da, I'll bite that nosey wee twat for you!"

It isn't like she fucking smiles or claps for me anytime but she doesn't seem fazed and continues to trot around the tank as I talk. I told Mum I'd got a little black fish since I accidently referred to Mary one day whilst grabbing a snack. She seemed really confused as to why I named the fish but I told her that it was what her type was called and it wasn't in an affectionate way. *Got to be more careful next time.*

The worst thing about slipping up wasn't trying to make up a story but having to catch myself in front of Mum. But much worse than that was two days later when I opened the front door to find Lizzy standing there. She ventured out too far this time! She was standing there with a Cheshire cat grin on her face and hands behind her back.

"Can I help you, Lizzy?" I managed to say without sounding too annoyed by her presence.

She whipped her hand round and produced a bag of water with a little goldfish swimming around inside. I was really confused for a second until she explained why she was there. "I brought you this," she said staring at my confusion and replicating it. "Your mum said your tank was finally ready and you had started getting fish, isn't that right?"

"Oh yes!" I said finally catching on to what was unfolding.

"Well, I told your mum that as soon as it was ready, I'd get you a fish from my Pops as he has loads. I hope you like the one I've picked."

"Yeah, it... eh... looks great." I realised I was being rude but I took the fish from her outreached arm and closed the door with a direct thanks! What the fuck was I meant to do with this?

My mum was straight in there with, "that was really nice of her. Did you not invite her in to let her see you putting it in the tank?"

Yeah, mum! Let's invite the crazy bitch in to watch her little fish be thrown to a killing machine. "No," I retorted. "She seemed busy so let her be, maybe another time."

I popped the fish in the toilet sink upstairs while I tried to think what the hell I'd do with it.

When I logged onto my computer, I had an e-mail from Amazon showing me there was yet another sale but before I hit the delete button, something caught my eye. A reptile tank. I didn't believe the shite about "half price for 3 more hours only" but it seemed like a decent price so I bought it.

I'd got just enough left off my amazon vouchers and the next week I would be helping with the lambing so it should be fine with the funds. I laughed to myself thinking at least it solved the problem of the wee arsehole making me have to wash my hands in the bath. I'd to actually buy some of that fish flake shite from the local shop. *When one thinks of surprising someone with a live animal one must at least provide some food with it!*

Well, it helped my made-up reality anyway. I kept standing over the toilet going to flush the wee thing but didn't have the heart, and then decided to chuck it in the water down the road. But the poor little bugger would probably freeze to death in there. The fish tank was to be free very soon, so I decided to keep the fish. I might even go get some stones from the water's edge and make it a bit more homely for it.

The tank arrived just two days later and I was ready with fresh dirt and stuff. I'd been so excited when I saw the sale on the tank that I hadn't actually worked out how I was going to change her over. There was no way I could lift her current tank and just tip her in, not only could that hurt her but it would have been incredibly stupid. All it would take is one jump and before I know it, she'd be on the floor.

I was already worried that my search history online was becoming too spider related so I couldn't take the chance of googling it. I finally came up with an idea but it was going to take another trip to the charity shop and a whole lot of guts. I dashed down wishing that they had what I needed. I'd a list of objects that would do, but the sturdier it was, the better.

A dryer hose—okay, that might do but keep looking. A plumbing pipe—at first, I thought it would be perfect but then realised I couldn't see through it so it wasn't probably a great idea.

On the shelf at the back, I found a clear large plastic measuring jug with a big crack in its bottom. BINGO!

I was surprised by the man's response when I tried to buy the item. "You know, this has a crack in it, son. Eh…Yeah, well how are you going to use a jug if it's got a crack in the bottom?"

More to the point, prickhead. Why the fuck do you have it on the shelf if you're not willing to sell it?

"It's ok," I said to him, "it's just to hold some tools for my fish tank so it doesn't need to hold any liquid."

"Ahhh!" He exclaimed. "We have some boxes over there that you might prefer?"

"No...no," I tried to justify, "the boxes are too big so the jug will be the better option. It has a handle. It will help to get the items in and out of the small gap easier."

He finally agreed to let me purchase it.

.oOo.

I couldn't actually believe I was doing that. Poor Mum! She couldn't come up and find me if something goes wrong. It was a good thing but I still hated to think of the worry it'd cause her. I pinched the washing up liquid from the kitchen sink, worried that Mum would catch me for it but I just didn't have the time to deal with Lizzy. I decided to be careful not to use too much. I finished taking the lid off Mary's tank and tried removing as much of the wood, foliage, and dirt, as possible while leaving Mary hidden. Finally, I removed the piece she was hiding under and exposed her. She looked at me confused and I told her, "it's ok. I will be as careful as possible."

She just sat there waiting like she understood. Slowly and cautiously, I lifted the tank, letting the dirt fall down and giving Mary a chance to adjust herself. It took some time but finally the case was on its side and Mary didn't seem bothered. I threw a towel over the cage to keep it dark while I went away to set up the rest. I took the washing up liquid and washed my hands. I smeared it round all the sides of the bath, checked the plug hole was in and the shower pipe was tucked behind the taps instead of draping in the bath.

I carried through the new cage and put it at the bottom of the bath slop so I could have clear access and then, I opened one door. Carrying Mary through in her tank, I prayed to God for the plan to work. I sat her tank in the bath on its side with the lid facing the new one. Before I started, I cut the bottom of the jug off leaving just the circular shape and the handle with the large bread knife from the kitchen. I had to do all the preparation while Mum was out so that everything was back in place, including the washing up liquid which I replaced straight after I used it, before she got back. The problem now was that Mum had returned. I didn't worry her coming upstairs to check up on me, but what if I screamed? What if, she called on me at a specific second that makes me jump and Mary kills me? But, yet again, it was just another risk I had to take.

Garden gloves on, which felt as pointless as putting on a burst condom but, at that moment anything was better than going in bare. I started to unclip Mary's lid. It would have been a whole lot easier if I had three bloody hands! I kept sliding it up slowly until I could fit the jug over the opening, the base of the jug resting in the gap of the open door of the new tank. It was going good until then, but I didn't have time to relax. I jammed the jug in place, carefully chaining the tank lid back on so the only main gap she could escape from was the top of the other open door. I took the towel I used before and draped it over the new tank trying to make it dark and appealing.

I used a bobble to tighten the towel over the door to prevent Mary climbing out of it. *Okay, nearly there! Why the fuck did I decide to buy a new tank again?*

Opening the feeding hatch on the original tank, I inserted the tongs. Come on baby! Into the tunnel. There's a lovely little place on the other side.

Again, Mary seemed completely unfazed and relaxed. She wasn't defensive and gently walked forwards as I nudged her. Before long, she was through to the new cage and I waited for her to retreat under the log before daring to remove everything and shutting the door. She was stalling and I decided to lift half the towel off to let the light in and it encouraged her to go into hiding. In a moment, but with extreme precaution, I took everything out the way and the door was closed. Finally, I could relax. Mary had a number of opportunities to get me but she seems to actually like me. Other than Mum, I think she's the first female I could say that about. I hoped she liked her new home and it was worth the drama.

I carried her back and spent the next three hours cleaning up the mess and setting up the tank for the fish. By the time I was finished, I'd made two new homes for the pets. The bath was cleaner than ever before even if it was going to be a bubble bath for a wee while and I was absolutely exhausted. Thankfully, I'd enough time for a nap before dinner, maybe even a shower.

Chapter Three:

Testing the Venom

I was struggling to find a way of getting the pot to Mary's fangs without my hand actually being there too. I tried tapping it to the end of the broom but it was too rigid to get the pot in place. I tried using a larger tub but it meant the opening of the tub was far too big to get in close enough. I managed to ruin and break many things in my room trying it, but then just gave up!

I watched lots of videos online but there were only two ways, or two types of people! The crazy fuckers that just got their hand right in there and the rich fuckers that could afford all the fancy safe equipment! I was neither. I fell into the third type—the poor mother fucker than didn't want to get munched by his spider!

Of course, I had the antivenom, but My God, that cost a bomb! Not like I could just order a new one each time I needed to milk her. The magic saving serum was as expensive as Mary herself. I initially planned to buy two, one for my mum as well, but when the shopkeeper told me the price, I thought, "Fuck that!"

She never comes up here anyway, what are the chances of her being a victim?

"Nah! I just needed the one. I'd save myself then make sure the cage was locked. No point wasting money I didn't have."

I decided to go for a walk to try to rid myself of some frustration and ended up back outside the charity shop. I decided to go in and look around. *Who actually buys this crap?* There was an actual mug there with a crack in it! *Have some fucking self-respect and chuck it in the bin. Just because someone has donated it doesn't mean you need to try sell it.*

A few minutes in, I knew that it wasn't the place for me to calm my anger. As I turned to leave, I kicked a bin of old bits and bobs and scurried to tidy it up before someone comes and starts talking to me. There were bolts, thimbles and loads of other tat that clearly no one wanted but then, I'd found it. I wasn't sure why, but it looked perfect! It was basically a long metal doughnut with an arm reaching out of the centre of its side and finished with a flat end with two little holes. I raced my brain to think what it could be for in case I was about to walk up and pay for a BDSM toy without realising it. That would become the talk of the town, "not only that Rob is a loner but also he's taken to abusing himself". Well, it wasn't like there was anyone around there to pay to do it for me! I couldn't think what it was used for but I found a second one and now I needed to buy them.

I took them up to the old man at the till and he begged them without blinking. I asked if he might know why I was buying such an item, and he looked at me confused and suspicious as if it was a trick question. "You need to hang a curtain pole?"

"Oh! Yes, of course I do, just upgrading the bachelor's den and ridding myself off the broken blind." *OMG! Did I actually just say that?*

He looked at me sympathetically and pointed in the direction of the curtains. He gave me a wee wink and told me he could give me a wee discount if there was a pair I liked but was just out of my price range. I assured him I'd a pair at home but thanked him for the kind gesture. *How the hell am I going to explain that away if Mum catches?* Wind was beyond me, and I was hoping that the man was as embarrassed as me, so he didn't want to relive the encounter.

By the time I got home Mum was away for lunch with the other old codgers from up the street. Her sitting there and listening to their actual mouth drool, was a talent in itself. I suppose when you're stuck in the house all the time then you take a wee outing where you can find it. She better not bring any of them back again tonight for a wee cider—bloody let an OAP have anything but a nip of brandy and you're asking for trouble! Last time, I ended up violated but Mum was adamant she was just being friendly. Well, if friendliness is nipping someone's arse, then she can count me out. Got to hand it to the old bag though, she had some strength in those bony wrinkly fingers. I'd a bruise there for more than a week!

I head upstairs excited to get my contraption ready for tonight. Poor Mary. I didn't give her dinner last night but I had a nice juicy cricket for her after she'd given me what I need. Mary preferred the grasshoppers but trying to catch them was like finding a needle in a haystack! I started back at the farm in a couple days so I'd make the effort to go a little earlier to try to catch some before I'm due to start. With all those fields, surely, they have plenty.

I tried entertaining myself until I knew she'd be up and waiting for food. 1 a.m. seemed like her preferred time.

Facebook can only entertain you so long, especially when your only friends on there are your Aunts that live just out of town and have as shit a life as you do. I decided to go see if Mum made dinner but just as I dreaded she was sitting round the table with a couple coffin dodgers drinking. She slipped me some money and told me to get fish suppers all round. I was grateful for the getaway but do I look like a fucking delivery boy? Huffing and grumbling like I used to when she'd tell me to clean my room, I tied up my laces and headed out on my bike. It was actually quite pleasant that night and not as cold as I expected. The face lashing wind was still there, but at least I could feel my fingers and toes when I reached the chippy. I probably looked a bit like Mary with my helmet hair on show.

As I reached there, I read the name and disgust filled me. "The Fry". How very original it was! Other than the name, the place was pretty decent. The food was good and cheap. The guys behind the counter took your order and then went out, no chin wagging. They were more than happy to ignore the customers even if they have to stand there for twenty minutes while the customer waited for five fish to be fried. I like that. Some people complained that they were rude but I appreciated their "couldn't-give-a-fuck-what-you-think" attitude. If someone's unhappy with the service, they could go to that another chippy, fourteen miles down the road. I popped my money on the counter, nodded at the guy and my transaction was complete. Everywhere should be like that! I heard Lizzy complaining to Mum before about how she endlessly tried to be friendly but they just didn't want to talk. Poor bastards had to listen to that, I hoped they burnt and spat in her food! No doubt she'd return though as she was too polite to complain.

When I returned, I had hoped to just put the food on the table and run upstairs but no! They couldn't just say "thanks". "Can you just get the plates? And some forks? May as well top up our glasses while you're at it? Oh you are a good boy! You sure you don't want to sit with us to eat? We don't bite". No thanks I'd rather put a gun to my head! In fact, I'd rather be upstairs with a known killer.

I cheered up when I saw it was near 7 p.m. as I knew that the old granny bus would be here at 8 to pick them up. Getting rid of the hunger always made things seem better. I told Mum I was going to have a couple Jacks tonight so got her to pick me up a bag of ice. The truth was, I didn't want to be intoxicated before risking my life! I didn't drink much these days. I don't mind and don't have a problem with others drinking but it's different with Dad gone. Friday nights were for staying up late, watching a scary movie with a bottle to share, so I don't really see the point anymore.

Last time it just made me feel sad about Dad and then angry that it happened in the first place. A tree fallen on the road isn't something people tend to notice and inform others if not many cars travel on it. Dad always took the bike but got a lift to work that morning so Mum could collect him after and they could go have a romantic night away for their anniversary. I wish I hadn't been so grossed out by the idea and had properly said goodbye to him that morning. I wished I'd let him give me a hug before he left.

I know my actions won't make him proud by why the fuck should it only be our family that is chewed and spat out, left to live in a broken ignored society with no funds to escape?

He made this place worth living in and could make all the dull seem fun. I know Mum blames herself for driving that night, she was excited and said she wasn't paying much attention to the road. At first, I thought that it truly was the end as the scars on Mum's arms increased. They say time's a healer but really, it's not. She hasn't stopped trying because she misses him less or found a purpose in life. She has just stopped because the fuckers at the hospital won't let her die and she's determined not to be sectioned again. Then life just became an endless routine of staying alive until you're allowed to die.

I was lost in my own world when I heard Mum shouting, "Rab, you have any Jack left to share?"

I shouted back, "I don't," trying to sound drunk. Those greedy bastards had already cleaned out the cider and two bottles of cheap dessert wine. I wasn't wasting my stash on people that are selfish enough to still be using the oxygen.

They say when your time comes it won't miss you. Well, either these knee creakers had made a pact with the Devil or Mum and I had the power to see ghosts.

I heard the bus finally arrive and the poor driver fighting off the feisty bunch. The poor guy clearly dealt with this a lot and I bet he didn't get paid much for it. I'd rather stick my head up a cow's arse than be to them what the backstreet boys are to school girls—a piece of meat!

Finally, it was quiet and I heard Mum sticking the telly on. No way was she missing the Eastenders episode before bed!

.oOo.

Finally, the clock hands turned to 1 a.m. The last half an hour felt longer than a full day! Mary was up and leisurely strolling about waiting for me to drop in the favourite part of her day. I removed the plastic lid of the tank by taking out the tiny screw and holding onto the large screws I attached to the holes, lowering the contraption down. If Mary had still been in her old tank this would have been easier. I had been trying to work out how I was going to approach this and decided that it would be safer to take the top of the tank off rather than having the full front glass doors open.

I had the lid in my other hand ready to be slammed back on if she tried to get out. At first, she moved back and seemed confused, but then she put her front legs on it like she was trying to give it a hug. I panicked that she was going to run up the arm so I dropped it. It might have frightened her too and she bit down hard. I slammed the lid back on and sat the dumbbell in place knowing I'd still need to retrieve the goods before screwing it back together. I was relieved I got what I needed, but *Holy Shite! I couldn't get my heart to slow down.*

I dropped the grasshopper into the other side of the tank and waited for her to move. She was standing her ground today and feeling all around the tub. I hoped she didn't damage the film and let the venom drip out. There was nothing I could do, I needed to get it out and onto the ice but was I supposed to get my hand inside just yet. I waited for another hour and she finally moved away. I waited until she caught the hopper and I slowly reached for it retrieving the tub. I screwed the tub lid on tight and placed it in the sink under the bag of ice. My heart was still playing a tune against my ribs, I was shattered so I secured the tank back up and collapsed into bed. Out like a light!

I'd ordered syringes and needles from Amazon that were for refilling ink cartridges and hadn't really thought to check how thick the needle would be. I milked Mary three more times over the next ten days, replacing the ice often to prevent the venom going off. I divided the small amount into three of the syringes and popped the little caps over the top to protect my leg and popped them in my pocket.

I knew Lizzy was giving Paul a lift to the farm each morning so if I could get to the shop for opening then I should be able to get in and out before she returned. I arrived at the shop at 5:54 a.m. and I was glad to see Lizzy's Mum already inside hugging her coffee mug and staring at the little portable TV. I didn't mind Lizzy's mum. She didn't talk much, probably because Lizzy didn't let her get a word in edgeways. Her mum just sits there minding her own business unless you begin a conversation first. I walked round the shop jumping out my skin every time I heard the bell telling me someone else has entered the shop. I stood trying to regain my composure and raked my mind to try and remember what items I had decided upon. A large orange, a bio yogurt drink that I could very slightly open and press back down hard so it wasn't very noticeable, and a sausage roll. I wanted to see if the items had a different effect on each person, showing me what things to avoid or use.

I grabbed the orange and with Lizzy's mum giggling away at Kyle on the T.V., I quickly injected the orange and emptied the contents. I was just replacing the lid properly onto the little white yogurt tub when the bell went again. I put them back on the shelf and darted to the magazines pretending I was reading while the other customer grabbed the items she was looking for. I recognised the voice of Mrs Barbed right away and I knew I had enough time now to inject the third item. Another talker. Lizzy's mum just contributed with acknowledging noises and perfectly placed giggles every now and then.

It was hard to concentrate with this type of fog horn in the shop and I got engaged to listening to the conversation too, well, it wasn't like I really had a choice. Poor Mr Barbed had the dentist that morning, finally getting that screw put in to replace his front tooth. It sounded dreadful how they did it but as usual he was pretending like he was going for a spa day, not a care in the world. He said he needed his smile as he'd not got much else going for him now. He could say that! I don't think I remember the last time his body was up to the job!

They both laughed loudly and I realised I haven't got long left before Lizzy would be back. I became a bit frantic in my search but couldn't find any sausage rolls. I panicked and grabbed a lone jam doughnut and plunged the needle in.

"Hey, you! Rab!"

I turned to see Mrs Barbed gaining on me. *Oh Fuck! I'm caught.* I placed the doughnut back on the shelf and slipped the needle up my sleeve but I knew it wasn't of any use. I'd been caught and fucked!

"Yes you, Rab, what have you got there?"

I squeak out a reply of "nothing" and I could feel I was on the verge of bursting out crying or running. After everything, I was caught before I could even begin. I looked at the door and saw Lizzy parking up. What should I do? Should I run? Where the hell would I hide? It was not like I could just jump on a bus and head north. I could feel the sweat starting to run down my forehead.

"Are you alright, Rab?"

I turned back to see Mrs Barbed looking concerned.

"Eh...Yeah," I managed it out of my mouth.

"It's just you've gone awful pale son, hope you're not feeling poorly."

I nodded my head but nothing came out when I tried to speak.

Mrs Barbed continued, "It's just I seen you eyeing up that jam doughnut and it's Mr Barbed favourite treat. No matter how tough he sounds, he's going to want a wee cheering up and some TLC when he gets back. I know it's the only one and you saw it first but would you be a pet and let me have it today? I'll buy you one back when they get more in."

I didn't know what to say. I felt the colour coming back and my heart restarting. I nodded at her, "Of course."

"Thank you, pet. He'll be chuffed when he sees I'd got him one." She walked off and I nearly vomited on the floor.

Lizzy was now in front of me asking if I felt ok and I explained her, "I'm just running late, trying to grab something for lunch before heading to the farm."

She offered, "You need a lift?"

"No, I prefer the cycle. I'd need it to calm myself down before arriving at the farm."

She shrugged, "okay," and handed me a sandwich, crisps and a bottle of juice. "On me," she said and I headed for the door thanking her in a crackled voice.

I let the syringe fall out of my sleeve into the bin and covered it with the newspaper already in there. I jumped on my bike and cycled as fast as my wobbly legs would go. I stopped the bike and sat down in the long grass. I needed to get a grip of myself.

I couldn't believe how close I was to being caught. How sure I'd been of myself when really that could have been my undoing. What would have I said it was? Extra syrup? I tried to calm myself by the thought that I'd make sure to be extra careful next time. I tried to rejoice in the fact that at least, I'd been successful in my task. I always knew there would be risks involved and the excitement made me forget that—I decided it won't happen again.

I start panicking about Mum. What if she buys one of those contaminated items? What if in my stupidity, I actually kill the one person I don't want to? Stop! I commanded myself.

There was a reason I picked those particular items. Mum wouldn't ever buy something healthy and can't stand the mess it made eating a sausage roll. She'd have bought the doughnut, but I saw Mrs Barbed buy it with my own eyes, so that was definitely gone.

I gave myself another couple minutes and tried to think of how far I'd come. It wasn't long ago that I was sitting in a field just like this when I began plotting my revenge. I'd come far and even though there was still a lot of work to do, I felt proud of myself.

My heartbeat returned to normal by the time I parked my bike against the farm wall and was grateful for the heat off the lambs' lamps. My first job of the day was feeding the little orphans before heading over to the pregnant ewes' barn to see what help was needed. The noise of all the new babies bleeping was extra loud that day but I also found it comforting. All those very strong little lives that'd keep the town going over the next year. The first rule we're told is to never pick a favourite and never get attached, but it happens anyway.

It's pretty much impossible not to when you've spent a good ten minutes rubbing and blowing on something to see it take its first breath. I don't give them names anymore, not because I care less but because it's better to just refer to them as the numbers sprayed on their sides. The farmer is really good at ensuring that we're not here when the killer trucks come collecting them. With different types of sheep, they tend to lamb at different times so you arrive to see the first sets gone but at least you don't have to watch them leave. "Take tomorrow off son," is all the farmer usually says and we all know what it means.

It must take a strong stomach for him to load them on but he informed me when I enquired, "I watched my dad do it forever, it kind of helps. It's just always a part of life—you pull them out, feed them up then send them off. To continue to care for the ones you've kept and there's not much time to sit and stew in the choices you've made."

Well, I just feel glad that it's him and not me.

It's always busy on the farm so the day flies by. When I finally got home dinner was ready and the Eastenders tune had begun. I didn't realise how hungry I was until I started eating and helped myself to another ladle of *stovies*. Mum had always been a good cook but she just couldn't be bothered these days. She tried making an effort when I was lambing as she said it made her happy seeing me doing some good in the world. Regardless of the comments, I was grateful for the gesture. I'd been trying to catch a couple of hoppers and moths each time I went out now so that I could just fall into my bed when I get home.

Each time, I wake up at 1 a.m. on the dot to feed Mary and I find her already sitting, waiting. I used to put a vibrating alarm on my phone and hide it under my pillow but that's not needed anymore. Mary and my body are tuned into the routine. Which is for the best because trying to rely on a phone that's like a century old isn't great. It just holds enough battery to check the time now and then and often dies before the alarm begins. Suppose, beggars can't be choosers and it does the job.

My eyes were opened with a judder, my skin soaked by the sweat. I had a nightmare that Mary had got out her cage and had placed me in it. It was like our roles were reversed and I was trapped in the little glass box while she began a killing spree. A giant moth just sat beside me, watching and waiting too. I was terrified but at the same time I knew Mary wasn't going to hurt me or Mum.

I glanced over and saw the tank was locked and Mary sitting there up on the glass in the corner, as still as usual. For like the fifth time today, I tried to calm myself down. I felt like I'd aged ten years in one day, no wonder nutty scientists always looked about ninety, even if they are only like twenty-five. I'd only got an hour before I had to be up again so I just laid down listening to the wind squeezing through the crack at my window sill. I didn't dare tell mum there was a draft because she'd have someone over in a shot. Since Dad died, the only repair man we had now is the weirdo at the end of the street. He is a creeper than Mary so most people try to fix broken things themselves.

For the next twenty-four hours, there was no news of anyone dying in the town. *I don't get it!* I appreciate the orange and yogurt drink might not have been purchased yet or consumed but that jam donut was a definite. She herself said he wouldn't be able to resist it, so how was there are no shouts about someone finding him dead? You can't fart in this town without everyone finding it out within an hour so, no way, could he have popped his clogs secretly. Maybe they shared it and both were lying in bed waiting for someone to visit. It was more likely and we'd probably find them in a day or two.

I decided that from now on, I was going to buy the items beforehand. I'd then inject them, and sneak them back into the shop. I still might get caught but it was a lot easier to explain that I've changed my mind rather than why I am standing there with a massive needle. I should have enough in another two weeks to try again, this time picking items that perish quicker so I don't wait months for someone to buy it.

I write off the yogurt drink but kept my hopes raised for the donut and orange. There was no way I could go back and check if either of them had been sold because even a smart dude would probably find it difficult to recognise an orange from a pile when he had only glanced at it for mere seconds.

Another day flew by passed on the farm and I raced home to hear of any news of a surprise corpse or two. I was in absolute shock when I walked in to find my mum on the landline laughing harder than I'd ever seen her do so before. If it was the news I was waiting for, then she was being very disrespectful which just isn't her. I waited patiently for her to get off the phone and share the joke, disappointed that it was not going to be what I wanted to hear. She struggled to tell me through the laughter and I felt myself becoming a little annoyed. "Mr Barbed has been rushed to hospital."

I spun back around, "what?" Wait? Did it finally happen? "Wait, why the hell are you laughing then?"

I looked at her in a daze of confusion, as she tried to speak again. "Yeah, Mrs Barbed had called the doctor out and he had summoned an ambulance."

I was straining to make out her words but I stayed quiet waiting for what she might say next. They didn't know why it was happening but I did! Mum continued, "That dirty Mrs Barbed got too excited for once and popped more of those little blue pills in his tea than necessary."

"Eh? You think Mrs Barbed tried to poison him?"

Mum regained her composure and took a big gulp of water. "No, no, don't be silly, Rab! He's been rushed in because for two days straight he hasn't been able to stop the sailor from saluting..." She winked at me, "You know. . ."

She might have seen the confusion and irritation on my face so finally she gave it to me plainly. "His Dick! He's had an erection for two days now and apparently is close to tears," she burst into laughter again, "you'd think it should be Mrs Barbed crying from the pain."

"Oh! Mum," I said walking off and heading upstairs. I could still hear her bursting into another bout of laughter every few minutes.

I didn't understand! Was that why he didn't eat the donut? Too pilled out on his nut by Mrs Barbed? I shudder at the thought. It was not really something one would want to think about when they come face to face with those people most days. The frustration took hold of me and I buried my face in the pillow to stop Mum hearing my scream. I thought that donut was a definite win. I mean, she bought it right away and seemed like he was super eager to eat it. I mean, if he wasn't up for eating his favourite treat then I don't see why he would be up for that other type of activity.

It served me right for putting all my eggs in one basket, well three baskets, but you know what I mean. I whirled the computer on and type erection by spider poison, and there it is. He'd eaten the donut after all. I hadn't put enough in, unless he just dipped his dick in it. You can never tell with a weirdo like him. *Actually, what a piece of shit for complaining! It was almost transparent he'd not managed to put a smile on Mrs Barbed's face for a while so he could have been a little-more-bloody-grateful!*

I concluded that next time I needed to add a lot more venom and to aim for something bigger. Something that more people would eat. *Pizza? Ice cream? No wait, I have it! A cake!*

The town fair was happening soon and most people baked for the occasion, even Mum made a cake or two. It was perfect! I didn't need to go to the shop too, as Mum always chose other people's bakes over hers because, she is not great at baking. I felt the excitement coming back. Three weeks. That was all I had and I needed to gather as much venom as possible. It couldn't be any more perfect. The whole village would be there and if I could convince Mum to make a couple cakes then I should be able to hit a good few of them. *No one will suspect anything!* People would be dropping like flies after an event where nearly everyone makes something, and the evidence would be all eaten. There'd be no trail to lead back to me or anyone for that matter. I'd make sure I offer Lizzy a large piece first.

I start giving Mary a moth and a hopper at night. She'd need more strength if I was going to be milking her every three days. Most days she only ate one but now and again, she might eat both.

I didn't get much from each milking but my supply gradually started to grow, but so does the question of why I was always buying so much ice. Mum was convinced I'd got a drinking habit even though she'd never seen me drunk. The weather was too warm now to keep it outside so I took the massive risk of hiding it in the freezer. The freezers are always full of stuff we never seem to eat, but Mum keeps buying the same shit anyway. I found a half-used bag of cauliflower, which surprised me as I couldn't remember the last time she used that for anything. I popped the little tub in the bag. I was scared Mum would find it but I decided I'd tell her it was some sort of food for the fish.

Lizzy often asked how the fish were getting on and if I'd added anything else to my tank but everyone else had pretty much lost all interest. I told Lizzy "no" every single time she asked, and it seemed like she was losing interest too.

Milking Mary had become quite easy now. She seemed to see the tub and knew what was expected of her. She did her trick and then I gave the treat. With time, I had calmed down a lot whilst doing it, which seemed to help further. Thankfully she'd never gone for my hand or tried to get at me in any way. I'm not stupid enough to think she never will and still use my milking contraption but am grateful she's just happy being compliant for now. I'm looking forward to getting her Wallace, and it won't be long now. I think she'd be happy with another one of her kind for company. Well, if we can class staring into another tank beside you, company. It would be like looking into the mirror for her. Well, it would probably be better than nothing, and I expect maybe they could learn to communicate with each other through some sort of sign/body language. Double the amount of venom for me is all that matters.

Chapter Four:

The day of the Fair

I was a wee lad when I felt this excited for the fair, the last time. Filling my face with sweets and cake and seeing how long I could jump on the bouncy castle for. That obviously ended up with me vomiting everywhere and Mum having to take me home. You'd think I must have learnt my lesson but I never did. Year after year, I did the same until I got too old for the bouncy castle. I still enjoyed going for the baked goods and other games. When I got older, I could join my dad at the drinking table playing card games and bowls. It was always a great day no matter the weather. How I wish things hadn't changed so much!

You can be shat on and lie in the gutter or you can man up and show those fuckers on their pedestals that they aren't untouchable. Some innocent bystanders would get hurt on the way without knowing that they're sacrificing their lives for a bigger purpose.

Mum had been busy in the kitchen over the last three days making cakes and brownies. I thought the brownies would be the best thing to use with it having a gooey centre but Mum burnt them so that was out of question. She made one Victoria sponge and one lemon drizzle cake—not the most appetizing in my eyes, but they'd have to do.

When I woke up at 1 a.m. to feed Mary I snuck down to the kitchen while Mum slept. Both cakes felt quite hard so I decided

I'd need to mix it in with the filling. I scraped the jam out first into another container then did the same with the lemon curd. Dividing the venom up equally into both fillings, I stirred hard until it looked combined and spread them back on the cake being very careful to put them back on the right cake using different spoons. I quietly washed the containers and spoons trying to not wake Mum, dried them and placed them back in the cupboard from where I'd took them. I replaced the tin foil over the cakes and creeped back to bed. The best thing about Mum being in a chair was she couldn't just sneak up on me because I always heard her coming. Regardless if she saw what I was doing, waking her would create unwanted questions.

I was up and dressed super early but couldn't go down stairs as Mum would have become suspicious. I've hated the fair since Dad died. Mum usually has to fight with me just to attend for five minutes so I couldn't let her see my excitement. I dither about my room trying to make enough noise to wake her but not enough for her to realise I was up and dressed... I tripped over a book and crashed it to the floor, thinking that would wake Mum.

"What the fuck are you doing up there?" A grumbly voice comes up from downstairs.

"Sorry Mum, I fell out of bed," I replied, not wanting to tell her that my room was an actual shithole.

"A clear room, a clear mind" as mum always says to me. Yeah, sure mum, clean the house and it will make everything fucking amazing!

I picked up the book, The Unabomber Manifesto. I'd never been a keen reader but this book was a must read. I know he was a "bad guy" but I'm always struggling to understand why. Killing people always causes uproar but the guy had his reasons, I guess. It's crazy to think that after everything he did, they still didn't listen to him or try to understand his reasoning. Just chuck him in the jail and forget about him. Was that not exactly not listening that caused him to do this in the first place? *People need to be listened to and understood regardless of how crazy their thoughts and beliefs are, otherwise they will fight back.*

I placed it on the unit next to Mary's cage as I could do with re-reading it.

The village was starting to wake and one could hear people loading foldable tables and chairs into their vehicles. The old bag home brings extra for people like Mum so she doesn't have to worry about trying to balance it on her chair. I needed to be super careful this year! Last year while pushing Mum I hit a crack in the pavement and she dropped the cupcakes. We still took them but they were completely squashed and had lost one-third of their frosting. It was fair to say that most still remained by the end of the day so definitely I didn't want a repeat this year.

I came up with a solution though. I tore some flaps off a cardboard box and pushed it into the bottom of a plastic bag, creating somewhat of a protection to stop the cake from getting broken. I then added another flap on top and placed the second cake in. With this, I could hang them off the chairs handles without the worry of them being bent in half or Mum dropping them. I chucked the brownies in another bag and hung them from the other handle—they were like bricks so I didn't want them bashing the cakes.

I did my usual moaning and grumping about going to town to avoid Mum getting suspicious ignoring her shite about not meeting "that special person" or "making some actual friends if I always just hide away in my room". And then came her usual dialogue, "I want to see you settled down before I leave this world..."

Why do people feel you need to "settle down"? I'm fine with my own company. I can't imagine always having someone else there, going through my stuff, moaning about the mess, etc. No, thanks, I don't want it.

We turned the corner and Mum lifted her hand telling me to stop. I thought she was going to give me another lecture about being polite and at least pretending to have a good time. To my

45

utter surprise, she burst out laughing. When I glanced across the road, I knew why.

There was Mr and Mrs Barbed heading into the fair. I rolled my eyes and shook my head. "Mum, Grow up. Honestly, I wonder who is the parent sometimes." Luckily, the rest of the streets were dead so no one else caught her acting like this.

She said, with her cheeks red and her eyes watery with laughter, "I just need to compose myself."

I didn't see the point in her spending too much time trying to "compose" herself because as soon as someone would say anything it would have set her off again.

When we finally reached the fair, she didn't even last a full five mins.

"Mrs Barbed, I'm sorry to hear Mr Barbed was poorly," she just managed the last words and went up roaring again with laughter, tears streaming down her face.

Mrs Barbed couldn't help herself and joined in which even set me off. I supposed, those old codgers were alright. Well, their sense of humour was.

I helped Mum into a folding chair and put the cakes on the table. I used to wonder why people in a wheelchair would get out of their seat just to sit on another chair but since Mum got her chair, I realised how uncomfortable it can be. I plonked myself on the grass and watched others arriving.

I like watching people. You don't get many chances to do so. I could sit at my window for hours and only see one or two people pass by. It was funny how they all have their own little quirks, like Miss Parker who always swipes her hair behind her ear when she goes to speak to someone even if it's already behind it. And, Mr Gardener who checks out all women that pass, regardless of their age, and one couldn't help mentioning Mr Farrows who's always itching his leg with his other foot. Mum says the poor man is riddled with psoriasis but I think it's a nervous response.

I turned my head just in time to see Lizzy swaying about trying to carry four stacked boxes and bags hanging off her arms. I knew what was coming so I started to stand up.

"Rab! Go help!" Mum shouted. Not like there wasn't anyone else around to do it.

I tried curbing my annoyance as she opened her mouth—Little Lizzy in her fucking dreamland. I could actually see her running about the fields with flowers in her hair like those idiotic hair adds on TV. *One day her world will come crashing down, in fact, that day will be today. Not long, and most of these irritating arseholes around me will become silent, here's hoping it even stops the fair happening each year.*

We heard the mayor ringing his bell down the street to signal the beginning of the Fair. He was followed by three little girls, all wearing puffy dresses and hair neatly in place. *Same shit every year!* One of them gets picked and crowned "Little Ms Inverie", and she swears her promises of doing the village proud. The next day, all her promises are forgotten by everyone.

Daisy, last year's winner, did everything she could to keep it up. Out picking litter from the street, packing people's bags at the shop, pretending to be a lolly-pop lady and helping people cross the road. She really went for it but even she gave up after two months. I don't like kids but certainly wouldn't see one hurt as it wasn't their fault. They too were, stuck in this life. It becomes their fault when they're old enough to take their own decisions. No kid would go near my mum's cakes though—they are not polite enough to pretend to like it. There were lots of sweets, a chocolate fountain and Mr Bread with his ice cream cart to keep them happy.

The smell of burgers, hot dogs and sugar fills the air. It reminded me that from all my excitement, I'd forgotten to eat. Offering Mum a hotdog, I found myself taking an order for five. Did I look like a fucking octopus? How did they expect me to carry all of them covered in ketchup and mustard? I wished I hadn't opened my mouth as Lizzy joined me to help.

Fine! I thought, I'll pack my face with my hotdog on the way back so I don't have to speak to her. Not like you get a chance to do it, anyway.

I was surprised to find out that she didn't have much to say at all. She looked concerned and busy with her thoughts. I knew I'd be kicking myself later but I asked her, "everything's alright?"

She explained, "My Dad's in a bad way and the Doc doesn't think he'll be around much longer."

Dad?

Hold on, I haven't ever seen her dad! Well, not in the last three years, just assumed he had popped his clogs then.

It turned out I was wrong and he was still very much alive. Well, alive as in, breathing. He was at the old folks home even though he wasn't much past sixty. She explained how he was diagnosed with something called Huntington's disease and now it was a full blown dementia. He couldn't really move or speak so just kept lying on the bed with a feeding tube and drip. *Wow! That really is fucked up! Poor guy, just shows how selfish she really is expecting him to continue like that.*

"Come on Lizzy, you never know what will happen." I pulled in my highest sympathetic voice but I think I didn't manage it. *He might even outlive you.* Knowing my plans, I was hoping she won't live to see tomorrow. "Try to forget about that just now and enjoy the day ahead."

She thanked me and tried to give me a hug. I stepped back raising my hands reminding her my hands were full. *Thank fuck for all those hot dogs.*

I lied down in the grass listening to the music being pumped out from an amplifier a couple tables up. I could hear chatting and laughter—it gave me a strange comforting feeling which then made me feel a little uneasy but I decided to fuck it and just enjoy it anyway.

It was always nice to be nudged awake by a kick to the legs.

"Rab, does this look like a bed to you? Jesus Christ son, what's been keeping you up because I know it's not skirt."

Billy, or Uncle Billy, as my mum used to make me call him, was my Dad's supposed best friend. Although, he was around to help pick up the fucking pieces when he died, I still hated him! *He'd have some of the cake.* The greedy bastard would lick the floor if anything was dropped.

"Brenda, you been keeping him up with one of your wild parties?"

Mum gives a little giggle. The rage this man causes in me is indescribable. About a year after Dad died, he kept coming over asking Mum if there was anything he could do, if anything needed fixing or if she'd like to have dinner. It became apparent that this "best friend" couldn't give two shits about Dad, he was just trying on his wife before his side of the bed even got cold. I swore that day I'd kill the fucker and hopefully Dad will kick his arse in the next life too. Prick! Mum couldn't stand the pervy bastard either and politely just nodded or gave out a little laugh. If you know Mum, then you know she's a talker so I couldn't see why Billy didn't notice the coldness coming off her.

Mum always said that Dad was and will be the only man for her, never has she even looked at another guy, never mind, this ugly fucker. Thankfully, Lizzy is good at reading people and she diverted Billy away from Mum before she lost the act and we both gave a sigh of relief. For once, I thought, *Well done! Lizzy, doing something is actually helpful for a change.*

The alcohol was flowing, music blaring and a couple kids vomited beside the bouncy castle, I felt like giving them a high five. Everyone was cheerful and relaxed and it was nearly time for the cake. As a ritual, the Mayor used to look over all the bakes and tried any he liked then picks the winner. Unsurprisingly, Mum never won this or even came in the top ten.

I was disheartened when he decided to not even try Mum's but I supposed there was not enough for everyone so, I had to let that one go. Once the winner has been picked and a picture with the Mayor and cake is complete then everyone's welcome to come enjoy the cakes.

I could see Mum slipping out the chair, can in hand and pissed as a fart. I take this as an excuse to leave, not wanting Mum to have to see what was about to unfold. When you've seen one man die you don't really need to see others just dropping like flies in the street. Hopefully, she settled quickly so I could head back down and watch it unfold.

The walk back home gave Mum another lease of life and she was moaning that I'd brought her home. I fetched her another can and popped her in front of the TV. She was demanding I took her back but I eventually convinced her that it was late, cold and most people had started to head off anyway. She asked if people liked her cake and I nodded hoping inside that it was magically delicious and everyone wanted some. That was definitely not what it will be like but if I got at least ten people then I'd be happy.

We started to talk about how Dad loved the fair and how a couple of times he had won the baking competition. He might have been a builder but when it came to baking, he had the touch of an angel. Unfortunately, Mum just enjoyed them and never actually stopped to learn; it wouldn't have been the same anyway. I think that was why people ate Mum's cakes. Not because they actually enjoyed them but more out of respect for Dad. Well, this year it would definitely be memorable.

I realised two hours had passed and I still couldn't hear sirens or people running about panicking. Did I manage to get the copper, the paramedics and all emergency service workers? Surely there should be some sort of commotion.

I left Mum passed out in the chair afraid that she would wake when I try to move her to bed. I rushed out the door, jumped on my bike and started imagining the scene I was about to find.

Will there just be people lying about on the street? Will those who didn't eat the cake be trying to rescue them? I wondered if they were scared that it might catch them too and ran off leaving the greedy bastards to suffer alone. I was picturing eyes full of fear and blood streaming from their noses but in all honesty, I didn't know what to expect. I knew the venom would shut down their organs but didn't know if anything would be noticeable on the outside, other than them being dead. I was about to find out when I whizzed round the corner.

What the actual fuck! No dead bodies, just a couple stragglers left finishing off the food and drinks. WHAT THE HELL! I just wanted to scream! Why had nothing happened? I rushed over to the bake table and confirmed that Mum's cake was eaten. They didn't just throw it in the dustbin, since there were chunks of left-overs and scores on the cards kept underneath. *Does it take longer because the body has to digest it?*

I thought ten minutes would be the longest they could last but I supposed I'd never checked to see how long it took to kill if it was eaten. *Ok!* I calmed myself, *It's probably that and by morning there will be results. I'll go back, feed Mary and await the news in the morning.*

.oOo.

I tried to sleep but I was too frustrated! Mary too, wasn't interested in her dinner.

It was one of the most poisonous substances you can get, how the hell has it done nothing! It was like getting a drunk person to cross the world's busiest motorway, yet all the cars dodge him. People definitely ate the cake, why were there no casualties yet? Did I live in a village full of venom resistant arseholes? Something had to have happened, they might have just headed home as soon as they felt ill, but then there would still be others there and they'd see them die.

Something was not right!

I saw a flash of green light and dived to the window. It was the Doctor's car speeding to town. Finally! It had to be due to the venom, the Doc didn't come out for any little thing.

Oh! The excitement was too much. I wanted to run after the car to see what had happened but I didn't dare. I wondered who it was? I wondered that poor unsuspecting neighbours not only suffered Mum's baking but were now dead because of it.

It worked! I knew it worked. I needed to sleep but it was how it used to be on Christmas eve. I wanted to sleep for it to be morning but couldn't shut my eyes close from the excitement of what the next day would bring.

I didn't even feel tired, instead I lied on the bed trying to guess who and how many I'd managed to knock off. The clock was moving slow. I checked the brick of a phone in case my clock has stopped. It hadn't, because it was only 4:36 a.m. The green light flashed by again, and I was about to throw up from the excitement.

I didn't have to wait too long for the phone to ring. It never rang at that time so it had to be something big. I waited for Mum to pick up the receiver by her bed before lifting mine so I could listen but didn't have to speak.

It was the Doctor's voice on the other end, "Brenda, I'm sorry for calling so early but was wondering of how you and Rab are feeling? I've got six people in the hospital and two others ill at home. I'm trying to find the source but first need to see how many are ill."

Mum was a little shocked and sleepy but reassured the doctor, "I'm feeling fine and Rab seemed his normal self before bed."

The truth was she won't remember chatting to me before bed but no doubt she'd check on me after the call.

"Brenda, I must ask that you and Rab stay in the house today unless you need to leave for a necessity. I need to make sure it's not catching. The hospital has never had this many admissions at once before so I'd be grateful if everyone could stay at home for now."

Mum agreed and both said their Goodbyes. I waited until she hung up first then put the receiver back in its holder. I could hear her hoist buzzing away and tried to calm my voice. Before long, she was at the bottom of the stairs shouting. I waited until she shouted for me a couple times to give the impression that she'd just woke me. I then headed out the room acting sleepy to see what she wanted.

"Rab, you ok?"

"Well, I was until you woke me."

"No, I mean how do you feel? Do you feel sick or hot?"

"No, I'm fine." I was about to ask her why but then realised I wouldn't be able to hold this act for long so I gave her a weird look portraying I was confused by her questions, and came back in my room.

I got dressed and headed down stairs not wanting to miss out on any other news that might come in. I put the TV on—I knew we were a small village but when a large number of residents from the same place die in one night surely, it was main news worthy. There was nothing on there, but that was ok.

I'd done what I set out to achieve and the less publicity it got, the better. After all, this was just the test run.

The phone rang again. I could only hear a little of the conversation but knew it was not a positive call from the look on Mum's face.

She said on the phone, "It's ok, I'm sure he's fine. He's in the best place."

I moved to the seat closer to her and heard some of the conversation.

I could hear the voice from the other end, "he was violently vomiting and couldn't stop. It was coming out both ends and he was as white as a sheet. I tried to get him to drink some water but he couldn't manage to swallow it before more sickness came. They have sent me home and said I'm not allowed to be at the hospital in case it's contagious."

I couldn't work out who it was but Mum ushered me away to make her a coffee while she tried to reassure the caller.

I was happy to get out of the room as I couldn't hide the smile for much longer.

I did it. I actually bloody fucking did it.

I felt like I wanted to dance and shout but Mum would have heard. I took her coffee through and she was still on the phone so I managed to slip away and headed back upstairs. I wanted to lift the receiver but I couldn't have stayed silent or stopped my heavy breathing. I threw myself on my bed and tensed my whole body, screaming with joy on the inside. I didn't even care who it was, I didn't have a set target in mind. I just needed to know it worked. I wanted to pick Mary's tank up and dance around but realised that was a stupid idea. I should've put some music on or tidy my room or. . . *Forget it, I couldn't do anything in this overwhelming state.*

All that time of planning, selling my stuff, spending so much money, was all worth it. I wouldn't actually believe I had done it. I froze for a minute realising the hospital will do a test and probably find it was poison but then that couldn't even diminish this feeling. *So what? Who cares? Even if they do find out then where are they going to start looking?* I never made anything so I wouldn't be on the list for a start. Also, I was at home with Mum, both of us tucked up in bed, completely innocent. The phone rang again and I didn't need to lift it. I could sense the panic and fear in the village and just lied down relishing in it. *You're getting a massive hopper tonight, Mary! You deserve it!*

Around 6 p.m. the phone went again, and I decided to listen in as I haven't had an update in hours. It was the doctor again. I was glad they couldn't see the massive grin spread across my face and I tried hard to remain silent.

"Brenda, just calling you to let you know all is well and you don't have to stay indoors anymore."

Eh? Ah! They must know it's not catching! I listened on.

"Seems that something must have been off or not cooked properly yesterday, bad case of food poisoning all round." The Doctor continued.

I froze stopping myself from shouting a big "no". I put the receiver down before I blew my cover and found something to throw. *Food poisoning? Fucking food poisoning!* I felt like getting a gun and physically taking all the fuckers out. This however wouldn't have helped my plan going forward. I nearly knocked the computer over by pressing so hard on the power button.

I needed to know what went wrong. I felt sick from anger and tried hard not to just lift the fucking keyboard and smash it against the wall. *Breathe, Rab!* I could hardly type and jumped up, throwing my chair over while I tried to gain back some control. My hands were sore from the tightness of my fists and they found a yellow pages book to try to tear in half. That was not possible but it released some of the pressure.

I finally gauged some sort of composure and returned to the computer. I was struggling to even decide what to type. After a few failed searches of death by eating venom, I found what I was looking for. *How the fuck did I miss that? All my research and careful planning and I had missed out one very important part!*

Turned out the fuckers needed to be bitten!

Injecting it straight into their bloodstream was important to cause death.

Three clicks later, I was done. Wallace was ordered. New plan created. And this time it wasn't going to fail!

Chapter Five:

Long John Silver, not Wallace

I had learnt my lesson about how close I came to death while releasing Mary. I told the breeder this time to send it in a deeper tub so my fingers wouldn't be so close. He kept trying to argue that the spider wouldn't be as safe but I think he finally got the point when I said, "the spider being a wee bit more bruised is not as important as being able to fucking kill me the minute I take the lid off."

Anyways, it was agreed and Wallace was soon on his way. I remembered the first time I saw Mary and knowing the males were bigger I couldn't wait to see how big Wallace is. I was still gutted about how the fair went but as the saying goes, you've got to stumble a few times before you learn to walk, so I decided to write it off as trial and error. I wouldn't be making the same mistake this time though. It was going to take a couple attempts to redefine it, but other than that, my new plan was fool proof. Nothing would get in the way. I came to the part that I could not even give a shit about Lizzy enquiring about what the package contained or telling Mum. Fish tank stuff is what I'd say and they'd just have to be satisfied with that.

I was conscious of my depleting funds and with lambing over for another year I needed to make sure I was careful. I had a good bit left but Wallace cost about a third of my savings so I was watching what I spent. I stayed up late to win a listing on eBay for another reptile tank. It was second hand and looked pretty old but would do the job intended. It was bigger than Mary's cage and depending on Wallace's size it should suit him perfectly. I contacted the seller and paid him an extra five to send it on next day delivery, which was usually about two days to here, but I needed it to arrive before Wallace.

I was watching another listing ending tonight so hopefully I'd have the extra tank I needed but not in a rush for that one. The humidifier had an attachment for another tube so I managed to cut Mary's tube in half and created a bit for Wallace.

I planned to go to the fields at night and gather mud, sticks and moss when I was catching more meals for Mary. The hoppers were getting harder and harder to catch. I managed to collect six and tried to get them to breed but it never happened and two ended up dying in the process. I didn't do anything to help or encourage it. I just left them to get on with it so I wasn't really surprised when it failed.

After spending two hours in the field and only catching one moth, I gave up. I needed to get home for the other tank I wanted to buy. I decided I was going to need to buy crickets, I couldn't rely on the fields with winter approaching. Not only that but I've been caught a couple times and now had the town thinking my fish liked to eat moths floating on the surface of her water. I was so glad no one really cared about pet fish round here because they would have smelt bull shit the minute that sentence came out my mouth. I felt glad sometimes that I was surrounded by idiots, even if they were the nosey gossiping type. The auction had forty-seven minutes left to go and I was glad to see it hadn't gone up much at all.

It was just a large glass box with a slide in acrylic lid with holes and slot in acrylic dividers. Exactly what I needed. It would be the crickets' tank once I had made another few adjustments. I had ruled out the idea of getting crickets when I thought of the extra expense, the noise they make, having to feed and keep them alive, but I was super surprised when I looked into it.

You're able to get a tub of 175 brown SILENT large crickets for two pounds fifty, a large bag of insect gut load for six pound and I already had a temperature thermostat that came with Mary's tank. Apparently, as long as they had fresh water, heat and light then they would pretty much happily breed within weeks. I got it. The tank, twenty-four pound and fifty-one pence, three ninety-nine for delivery but now I had all the tanks I needed.

Even though they are called silent crickets, I couldn't take any risks. The unit Mary sat on was just an old, deep, three-shelf bookcase which I took from the living room downstairs when we were renovating to make more room for Mum's chair. Just like everything else in my room it was full of shite.

How ironic that there were probably beasties in there I could have fed to Mary! I was dreading cleaning it out but it was a perfect place for the crickets. I grabbed a black bag from downstairs and pinched Mum's marigolds from under the sink. I'd never thought I'd ever see myself putting these on but the thought of putting my bare hand in there was worse. In fact, I might be safer sticking my hand in Mary's cage. Who knew what those shelves had been hiding over the past few years? There was nothing I could think of that I'd needed over the time so I decided it must all be crap and I was just going to swipe it all into the bin bag.

Top shelf done! Middle shelf done! But when I got to the last shelf, I saw the corner of a photo, and I pulled it out. It was a picture of Dad, Mum, me and that fucking Billy! I'd taken a pen to his face so hard it had created a hole. I'd not got the time or energy to think about that prick for now but couldn't stand binning a photo of Dad so, I place it on top of the wardrobe.

The shelves were clean and I moved Mary's tank off the top to prevent it falling on me. The unit was just a wee cheap shite thing and though I'd have to smash the shelf to get them out but upon inspection, I realised they were just held up by those little metal hooks. I removed the middle shelf to create a larger gap to the bottom and move the other shelf up to four dots from the top. I made sure it was a big enough gap to hold the crickets' food, vitamins and the little tubs I would need but not much else. I took the shelf out and drew around the red bulb so I knew the size I needed to cut. Mum was out with the coffin dodgers again so I knew I had at least an hour before she returned. It was more than enough time for what I needed to do, as long as I got the noisy jobs out the way. I could always tidy up later, it wasn't like she was going to see it through the floor.

I headed to the hut at the side of the house where Dad's tools have remained untouched this whole time. I coughed from the dust and then recoiled once I noticed the spider webs. I knew it was stupid. For someone that owns a large spider people think that I shouldn't mind the little ones, but in reality, I never really liked spiders and still hated the idea of one touching me.

I sucked it up and started to remove the boxes to look inside. It took a while but finally I found the tool I was after. I didn't have a clue what it was called and the hard plastic carrier that held it gave nothing away. I found the attachment for the size of hole I needed and carefully took them inside, trying hard not to drop any old sawdust on the floor. If I was smart, I would have brought a plastic bag! I did that when I brought it back out. I couldn't use it outside as the neighbours would hear and see me but the mess it was going to make was a concern too. I didn't mind the mess but it was something that reminded me of Dad so I didn't like the idea of having to look at it day after day. I didn't know if you have ever had to clean up sawdust out of a carpet but I could tell you that you're more likely to succeed in teaching a chicken to speak English! Even after all that time, I still saw bits from when Dad was around.

I decided it was going to be much easier to clean it all up off the tiles so I pulled the extension cord into the bathroom and placed both shelves in the bath. I only needed one of them to have the hole but Dad taught me well and I remembered if I wanted a clean edge and not a hole in the bath then I needed to put another piece of wood under. The noise echoed so loud when I turned on the machine that I straight turned it back off to let my ears adjust. The hole itself took seconds. Then I carefully placed the cutter into a plastic bag and grabbed the hand-held hoover I brought up with me and started clearing the bits that have blown onto the floor and the side of the bath. I needed to take the shower head down and remove the remaining amount.

I took the tool back to the shed remembering to remove it from the back and place it back in its case. Once I'd got everything back in the hut I went inside and took off my clothes in the kitchen. I popped them in the wash and cleaned out the hand-held hoover. I was not worried about the inside too much. Mum used it if she made a little mess as she couldn't get round with the hoover so I did that every couple of days and because she couldn't reach the bin outside, it was my job to empty it too. With my third lucky find from the charity shop—an old lamp the I'd taken apart to just keep the wire from the plug to the connector that held the bulb, I placed it under the hole and pulled it through until it was in tight. A little bit of glue and a wiggle to get the shelf back in place and it was done. There was already a hole at the back of the unit for the wire to be plugged into the wall. I bought the bulb for Mary but she'd come to enjoy the lava lamp so I decided to keep using that.

An e-mail came through from the breeder saying there had been a slight delay on his end so instead of Wallace arriving tomorrow he had gotten confirmation that he'd be with me the day after. I felt a pang of disappointment but one more day wasn't going to be too much after the time I'd waited. I told Mary about the delay but promised her that he'll be here soon. I actually felt a little relieved because his tank was coming tomorrow so it saved me running about trying to get it ready for him.

.oOo.

The next day, Lizzy wasn't at the post office so I picked up my parcel and was back home super quick. The dirt and branches I'd collected a few nights ago were in a bucket in my sitting area so not long after, the tank was all set up. It was kept right next to

60

Mary's with the sides of the glass touching so they could be close to one another.

I had to move the lava lamp further back but I should be able to see what was going on. After all the work I'd done catching food, preparing for Wallace, researching for the crickets and staying up late trying to catch a bargain, I finally felt how exhausted I was. I decided, for once, I was going to pop Mary's dinner in early and head to bed. No doubt, I'd had to wake back up for one but then I couldn't either just watch from the bed or go back to sleep. It didn't take me long to go to sleep and at 1 a.m. I only woke up long enough to see Mary sitting in her favourite spot watching the moth.

It was already 10 a.m. by the time I finally was awake again and I felt like a new man. My body definitely needed that. The breeder informed my delivery should arrive between about two and three so I'd plenty of time. Usually, people would arrange for delivery companies to come straight to their house but after numerous responses of "undelivered", "could not find address" I decided it was easier just to get it delivered to the post office.

Something caught my eyes and I looked over to Mary's tank. Why the hell is she still up and the moth is still sitting in the tank too?

I panicked and raced over. To my absolute relief, I realise it was just a skin she'd shed. She'd never done that before, clearly wanting to have a fresh new coat on to meet Wallace. I took it out of the tank and popped it in a tub to admire later.

From the second I'd opened my eyes it was apparent that I needed a shower. The shower was refreshing and completed the task of waking me up completely. I refrained from slipping on the same clothes as I usually did and pulled a clean pair of jeans and hoodie from my drawers. My day just kept getting better! Opening the cupboard, I found a new box of pop tarts and a fresh pot of coffee sitting on the worktop. *What a woman my mum is!* I never understood people that are desperate to "fly the nest". Nah! My nest is warm and comfy, I was not giving this shit up for anyone.

I sat listening to Mum waffle on about the argument two of the oldies were having the other day when she was out. I couldn't help but laugh when she said she thought it was going to break into a physical fight. Mum couldn't help laughing too when she realised what she'd said. I enjoyed sitting chatting with my mum. She's full of absolute shite but it's nice just listening to her voice. I asked her if she needed anything from town as my new pump for the fish tank was being delivered and she told me to pick up a treat for after dinner. *Toad in the hole tonight, Yus!*

I looked at the kitchen clock. It was only half past twelve so I decide to walk to town instead of cycling there. The bike tyre was flat again and I keep forgetting to repair the slow puncture, besides I didn't want it to have a bumpy ride back after poor Wallace has already been in transit for three days.

I grabbed my backpack to carry the items back from the shop and to keep my hands free for my package. I decided to pick up some cola too and have a drink with Mum over dinner. Wallace will be tucked up in his tank by then so I'd have it as a wee celebration. I decided to walk a little further than normal to get the shopping from the other grocery store instead of the post office. People think the other one is bigger than the first one, but in reality, it is only as big as a corner shop, not like those massive shops we used to go to on holiday. I knew they did those red balls of chocolates my mum loved so I decided that could be her treat. I couldn't remember the last time she had them so it should put a massive smile on her face.

I arrived back at the post office just in time to see the DPD guy was leaving the shop. I raced inside and before Lizzy's Mum had a chance to book the parcel in, I was there waiting to take it from her. She'd got quite a few parcels so I said just to give her two minutes and she'd find mine. While I waited, I realised Lizzy was not there again, it felt nice but something didn't seem right.

When Lizzy's mum returned, I asked if she'd killed Lizzy and put her under the floorboards, thinking she'd be surprised at my words, which she was and then she started laughing.

"Never knew you were a funny boy, Rab." She laughed, "Nah, she's at the home again spending time with her dad. She'd been there every day, for the last eight days because they said he hasn't got much time left."

I thought hard on how I'd ask my next question without sounding like a massive dick but there was no need. It was like she'd read my mind. Poor woman must have been used to the questions that come next.

She sighed, "There's no point in me being there. He doesn't have a clue who I am and the man I married isn't there anymore. It might seem selfish but the hurt of someone you've been with for over 30 years just forgetting who you are is a painful thing to see. I'd rather hold the memories I have of him instead of filling them when the man he is now." Her eyes went watery, when she continued, "Lizzy was angry with me at first but since he can't remember who she is now, I think she understands. I'll tell her you said 'hi' when she returns this evening."

I forced a smile, and took my package before thanking her and leaving.

I actually felt quite sorry for Lizzy. Regardless of the person she is, I know how hard it is to lose your old man. At least she'll get to say her "goodbye" and will be there until the end. I couldn't decide what was a better way to go. Dying suddenly so it was like plaster being ripped off then rebuilding things from there or getting to prepare for it but then having to watch your Dad suffer?

It started to make me feel a little upset and I tried to forget about it. I hated Lizzy but I somehow could feel her pain.

To take my mind off, I concentrated on what was in my hand and felt excited that the day had finally arrived. I got the chocs for my mum, cola for myself and even bought her some flowers, trying carefully not to crush them as I walked. It was a good day and for once I couldn't let the emotion for Dad ruin it. There's always tomorrow and every day after to think about him.

I heard some music as I got closer to the house and realised it was coming from mine. I quietly opened the door to find Mum waving around a whisk and singing alone. It was a rare sight those days so I close the door and made a noise showing I was back so she didn't feel embarrassed. I gave her the flowers and chocolate and told her I'd got a couple things to do on the computer and needed to set up the new pump so would be back down in an hour or two. It would have given her time to enjoy her tunes.

I picked up Wallace whom I'd left at the bottom step and gently carried him upstairs. I was really excited to see him but also worried that what if I opened it and found him dead. The extra deep tub and the extra day in transit would have put a much bigger pressure on the heat pad which wouldn't have lasted that long. I grabbed the toe nail scissors that I found lying on the floor and carefully sliced along the brown tape. I was filled with joy and fright when I removed the top paper and something started darting around.

OMG! He's a feisty little fucking.

Even though I knew he couldn't bite me through the tub it was still scary lifting him out as he has his legs raised showing he was ready for a fight.

I was grateful for the breeder for sending a tub that had clips on each side this time. It was much easier to release them than just nudging the lid off.

Wallace wasn't backing down and I could see he was in a bad way.

I tried calming him down, "Don't worry little man, let's get you out that box and into your nice new tank and you can chill."

I put my hand on the other end of the tub so he was not facing me but he spinned around, legs still raised. I popped the tub in the tank and slowly clicked open each clip. Wallace jumped with the sound of each one. I was worried at how fast and aggressive he was being. I knew I couldn't lift the lid with the front glass open. I closed over one door and only left the second one open enough for me to fit a pen through. I slightly poked the lid off and quickly pulled the pen back locking the door right away. Wallace went crazy, tipping the tub over and darting around the tank. *Thank fuck, I closed the door.*

Within seconds, he'd found a place under a log and I decide to give us both a few minutes to calm down. The lid of the pen had come off and dropped in the tank as I had pulled it back so I needed to retrieve that too. I turned off all the lights, closed the curtains and put the lava lamp on, hoping that would reassure him a bit more.

It had been an hour since I put Wallace in the tank so I decided I should be slightly safer to remove all the tub pieces and the lid. I didn't want to risk leaving it in there and him climbing back in. Again, opening one door ever so slightly, I slid the tongs through and tapped the tub gently to see if Wallace would attack.

He didn't move or come out so I opened the door, removing the items out. We could both completely relax now. I wouldn't be opening his cage again today.

I jumped when I looked down at the tub. There was something in there.

I think it is another spider in there and I threw the tub across the room. In an absolute panic, I jumped on the bed and my whole body started shaking. *Did he accidentally send two? What the hell! Is he trying to kill me?*

I stared at the tub waiting to see if anything moves, I couldn't just leave it to get out and kill me later. I creeped over and with my heart in my mouth and a shoe in my hand I gently nudged the tub. Something fell out and again I was on the bed, my pants slightly wetter than before. I was freaking out, I didn't know what to do. Still holding the shoe like it was the last thing on earth, I stared at the thing that was dropped on the floor. *It's not moving. It is hairy but really thin and long. Could a spider hold that type of position?*

I lifted a bit of junk off the floor which turned out to be an empty coke bottle and threw at it to see what it did. The bottle actually hit it but it still didn't move. I was going to have to go over there! I should have listened to Mum when she told me to go for an eye check! I was so frightened that the shoe was actually slipping due to the sweat from my hand.

I crept a tiny bit slower, ready to race back to the bed again if it moved. I wanted to look around for something to poke it with but I didn't want to risk taking my eyes off it. As I got closer, I felt a huge sigh of relief. It was not a spider—well, not a full one anyway. It was just a leg.

I picked the leg and the tub up carefully placing it back in. The leg was massive. It felt so much thicker and sturdy than they looked. I could hold it at the top and carefully push it down so I could get the knee to bend without it snapping. I popped Mary's mounted skin in with it and secured the lid back on and place it on the little shelf I'd made in the unit underneath. I knew they were just body parts but felt better with them being locked up safe.

I was worried about Wallace, but if the leg was his then he'd grow it back eventually. I had a little chuckle at how scared I had been and went to the toilet to let the rest of my piss out. Not a lot came out in my pants, so there was no need to get changed.

Thinking about William Wallace, there was no way he would have let himself get that hurt during battle and decided the name didn't seem as fitting. I couldn't give him that name now, it wouldn't have been right against William.

I giggled as the name came to me. That will work! Silver! As in Long John Silver.

I knew the leg would eventually grow back but it was too good to miss. I thought Mary would have approved. The end of the leg showed a clean break but it wouldn't have known the damage until Silver decided to wander out. Hopefully a leg was all he'd lost.

Chapter Six:

Love at first sight

Dinner was absolutely delicious. So, I was grateful Mum had made extra and I refilled my plate again eagerly. I saw Mum smile, watching me enjoy the food and offered me a drink. It'd been so long since we had dinner together but it felt right and Mum seemed to feel it too.

No need for a conversation of why we were, just a feeling like we had turned a corner in life and we were both happy to just let it play out. We used to always eat dinner together but after the crash it was like we felt guilty to eat so preferred to do it alone. Mum in front of Eastenders and me in my room. It was not something we had discussed or agreed on—it just became the norm, never once trying to impose on the other.

I teased Mum that she might be missing a breaking storyline on Eastenders but she told me she had watched it before I came down and we both laughed.

It's easy to forget small things in life. I heard Mum laugh often with people but not the natural, genuine laughter she was making right now. I started to feel guilty that we'd lost what we had before but I could see it was still there and we were heading in the right direction. It might seem like I was going soft but in reality, the more love I felt for my mum, the angrier I got that we were just left broken and had to struggle to survive. Not only did we lose Dad but Mum ended up losing her job because of her disability and

67

even though they said they would wait for her to get better, before long, they had a new head teacher and just stopped contacting. To be fair, I didn't even think Mum noticed or cared when her "P45" fell on to the mat one day, it was just another thing to not have to live for.

It was getting late and I noticed Mum wasn't very drunk. Seemed like she was staying relatively sober to enjoy every minute and I didn't think either of us wanted it to end.

By midnight, I started to make my excuses as I knew Mary had to be fed and didn't want to miss the opportunity of checking Silver over. A few yawns later we decided to call it a night. I helped Mum into bed, setting up the usual things she'd need in the morning and handed her the remote for the little TV. I laughed that even though she was like a hundred years older than me her eyesight was definitely better than mine because it was just a glowing blur I could see. I agreed to book an eye test the next day and gave her a kiss good night. The night couldn't have gone any better.

When I reached upstairs, I popped a large moth into both cages and saw Mary already starting to stir. Silver, on the other hand, still hadn't moved from his original spot. I tried not to worry of him being dead as I'd learnt that lesson with Mary. A spider can stay still for so long and attack at the blink of an eye. Mary enjoyed her dinner and wandered about finally settling in her favourite place on the glass not seeming to notice anything new. I waited eagerly for Silver to come up and watched as the moth creeped around the enclosure. After waiting an hour, I couldn't keep my eyes open any longer and Silver never came out.

It had been a long day for him so I was sure he just needed a little more time to settle in. Poor wee guy must have been hungry by now but the breeder said he'd put in some food and the tub was empty so I assumed he at least had that one meal on his journey. I couldn't imagine what it would be like having to go through our postal service!

The next morning, I was surprised to see Silver's moth gone. I could still see a little bit of his legs showing. He was still in his hideout so I looked all around the tank but the moth was definitely not anywhere to be seen. I guessed, he might have come out last night after all, which was great as it showed he was calmed down, or was starving. Either way, he must have got around ok on seven legs. I was desperate to get a proper look at him yet I had no choice but to be patient because I wasn't opening his cage again until I saw he did not want to eat me anymore. If I gave him a hopper tonight, it might lure him out quicker. I only had one though, so it meant Mary had to have a moth.

I got a notification on my phone that the tank I bought for the crickets was dispatched, but I was waiting until it arrived before ordering the crickets as they did next day delivery. Mary and Silver would have to do with what I had caught for now. It was still warm outside so I guessed, I'd be able to catch a couple more hoppers before winter creeps in. I decided to head to the field right then, as I'd nothing else to do. I thought if I could catch a few then they should last me until I get the crickets. I felt glad that I didn't have to catch those bloody bugs any more.

Four hours in the field, but I hit the jackpot! Eight hoppers and four large moths. Plenty to keep them both going. I hoped Silver liked hoppers as the breeder said he was quite fussy when it came to food but he ate the moth so I doubt he'd turn his nose up to these guys. There was a pot noodle and a couple of cooked sausages waiting for me on the worktop when I got back. Mum was already deep into her Eastenders so I filled the pot noodle and took the plate upstairs. I put the TV on and found the least shit program I could.

I finished my food and moved to my living room. I'd been putting off tending to the fish tank because I couldn't be arsed. Fish are too much work and I didn't even want it. Lizzy fucking ruined my day without even being here. I should have just given her the fish back. I couldn't bring myself to hurt an animal so couldn't flush it but realised it was not having a great time in the tank either. I finally changed her water and cleaned the stone to make the place more habitable for her.

I'd go to the charity shop tomorrow and see if they have any cheap ornaments to maybe stimulate the little guy a bit. I know I should buy another to give it company but then I'd have to look after two. Fuck you, Lizzy!

It was only ten o' clock when I saw movement in Silver's cage. He was out. I sneaked over to the cage and he immediately raised his legs, making his face look like a red fanny. *Either he's a crazy mother fucker or he just hates me.*

I sat still and eventually he settled back down. I finally got a good look at him. He looked a lot different to Mary. Unlike Mary, who just had red eyes, his full face was the tomato red colour, except for his fangs. The markers on his back were darker and his eyes seemed a lot bigger. He slowly turned and I could see it was his second last leg that came off but there was no apparent wound and he didn't seem very bothered. I knew the name will suit him well when I noticed one of his side eyes was also damaged. It would be cool if I could get him a little eye patch but no way would I be trying to strap one to his body. I turned my head to see if Mary was about but Silver went nuts again and battered his body off the glass causing me to fall off my seat. I hoped he calmed down soon as I didn't think I could deal with something actually trying to kill me every time I came closer. My heart couldn't handle much more fright. I couldn't open the front glass, in case, he threw himself at it again. Thus, I unscrewed the lid and slightly lifted it to drop in a hopper. I didn't think it even hit the floor and he had it. Maybe he thought it was my hand or maybe he was just hangry. *That's ok wee man, the same happens to me when I've not eaten for a bit.*

Not long later, Mary strolled out of her bed but then seemed to realise something was different. I think they could smell each other.

She ignored the hopper and sat staring in Silver's direction. There was no way with her sight that she could see him from there but maybe she could just see that it was something bigger than her moving around. "It's ok baby. It's Silver, well, Wallace. But I've changed his name to Silver."

Silver slowly moved to the edge of his tank, very gentle, but Mary stood her ground. She stood there for another hour before coming one step closer. "It's ok Mary. There's two pieces of glass between you guys so you'll be ok."

It was like she was listening to my voice and moved even closer. Silver hadn't moved, he was just sitting at the glass facing Mary. His face was so red, it looked like he was blushing. Mary came another step forward then stopped again. It took about three hours for her to reach the glass. Silver didn't move a hair and I was grateful that he wasn't fucking banging off the walls and scaring her.

Mary lifted her front leg up on to the glass which Silvers copied. It was like their folding hands. *I know this was a good decision, it's clearly love at first sight!*

.oOo.

I went to bed all giddy and leaving the love birds with some privacy. I wished I could know what they were thinking or that they spoke so I could listen in. I decided I'd just have to make my own dialogue.

Silver must have said, "Oh what beautiful stranger have I just encountered?"

Mary might have blushed a little before responding, "you're not so bad yourself son! If this fucking glass wisnay here I'd have you."

Even though they came from the same breeder for some reason, I saw Silver with a French accent and Mary as a rough Scot. It was cool though as I didn't think they will care. I humoured myself this way for a bit longer but it was hard to continue it when neither of them even moved.

I settled down to sleep and when I woke up at 5 a.m., they were still both in the same spot. Mary opted not to sit in her favourite place on the glass. I was ecstatic at how the first meeting has gone and that they didn't just throw themselves against the glass trying

71

to kill each other. I had a bit of cardboard to slide in between the tanks if that happened. Mary made the first move and wandered, somewhat seductively, back to her hideout as Silver watched on. Once she had completely disappeared from sight, he lifted his legs like hers trying to follow her. "It's very cute but no way in hell are you meeting her any time soon."

It was not anywhere near mating time so I knew it would just end in a fight.

I continued talking to Silver, "Losing one leg should be enough drama for anything without looking to lose more. I would place all my money on Mary winning too. You might be a crazy mother fucker but man to man, women are evil as fuck! The only woman you should ever love is your mother and even then, I think it's because they have invested too much into you to just kill you when they realise you've grown up to be a useless twat."

It took him a while but he finally got the hint and headed back to his bed, managing to walk past me without going berserk. I think, that's the best outcome I could have hoped for, Silver chilling the fuck out at just the right moment. Mary hadn't eaten tonight but I think she had her eyes on a bigger prize. She was usually a really good eater so pretty man or not I don't think she'd be wasting tomorrow's meal.

I fall back in bed for a couple hours since the shops won't have been open this early and I wanted to try and go at the busiest time, better yet I'd take mum.

.oOo.

Mum agreed to come into town with me as she had some things she wanted to get from the shop. I told her I was happy to push her to the further away one, but she said that the postie was fine.

Just my blood luck, maybe Lizzy won't be there again and we could get out with our ears intact. We went to the charity shop first and had a nosey about for any fish tank items. I was looking

72

for something tall that could swim in and out of but still fit in the tank. Mum found a sponge bob standing behind a chest. I was not amused but decided to buy it anyway, if anything hopefully the colours will give it something to look at.

I wasn't even sure if fish could see colours though, but it was worth a shot. I turned around for one second and Mum got away blabbing with some other scorned woman, so I continued the search on my own. I remembered the box with the plumbing pipe and clicked a couple pieces together. *Perfect! That will do the job I want it to.*

They were just three small pieces, two bends and a small straight but it was a small tank and it could swim in and out if it wanted. Mum started questioning me about the tank and I knew it was my opportunity to make everything seem real.

She reminded me, "You shouldn't be keeping lots of fish in such a small tank."

"Mum, I only have the one."

She looked appalled with my response. *Make up your bloody mind woman!* Then I realised, my first black fish and the one Lizzy gave me made two. I was fallen at the first hurdle. I quickly added, "the one Lizzy gave me died after just a couple weeks from something called white spot." I didn't for the life of me know where the hell I pulled that one from but I was chuffed with myself. *Great!* I thought, *saved my ass there, even if I did put myself in it in the first place.*

We arrived at the post office and at first, I thanked God that Lizzy was not there. Nice and quiet—the way I liked it. Well other than Mum, that will have a wee natter. I couldn't stand listening otherwise I'd end up getting pulled into it so I decided to take a wander round the shop. It was as soon as I turned the corner, I saw Lizzy. She was checking the dates on the cheesy pasta boxes near the bottom shelf, in silence.

I considered reversing but I knew she would have already seen me.

"Alright, Lizzy?" I spoke.

She just nodded.

"How's your dad getting on?"

Why the fuck did I ask that? I shouldn't be allowed to be left alone with people when they are in a delicate state. I saw the tears pour down her cheeks as she sobbed, "he passed away yesterday."

"Would you like me to bring you a tissue?"

She sobbed, "it's fine," and used her sleeve. *Classy girl!*

"Should you not take a couple days off?" I suggested.

She explained, "I'd rather stay busy and keep my mind occupied."

I didn't know what else to say. For once, I was having to lead the conversation and this was worse than her not shutting up. I gently placed my hand on her shoulder and before I knew the words had come out. "It's ok, my fish died too."

Like what the actual fuck, Rab! Go, buy a gun, and put yourself out of this misery. I heard a sarcastic clapping in my head. It was too late though; the words were out and there was no going back. I stumbled over words trying to apologize, but only managed yet another stupid sentence. Mum always says, 'I open my mouth and let my belly rumble sometimes.' I couldn't sink any lower. Oh! Fuck, I'd made her proper cry now.

I looked at her face and saw that she was actually laughing. Tears and snotty nose still present, but she was laughing. "Oh! Rab, thank you for cheering me up."

My God, man! Buy a fucking lottery ticket! If I'd managed to get out of that one, then luck was definitely on my side. Once she stopped laughing, she started to apologize about my fish and we both shared another giggle. Mum shouted she was ready to go and I nodded goodbye to Lizzy.

"Thank you." She yelled as I was leaving the aisle.

I wasn't quite sure what happened there. I still hated her when I thought about her but, I did feel sorry for her just now. I was not going soft and still had my plan concreted in my head but I supposed, I'd have to let that go as it was clearly just because of how I felt about losing Dad and had nothing to do with Lizzy.

My mouth should have glued itself but I asked Mum, "Did Lizzy's mum give you the news?"

Maybe Mary had already bit me because at that moment, I was spitting out all manners of shit. Or, maybe I should put my hand in her tank when I get back, better yet, Silver's tank. Thanks to my one enquiry, Mum managed to get upset, calm herself, laugh, then get upset again all within the twenty minutes of getting home. Luckily, when we got inside she said to me, "you best go sort your tank."

I knew she wanted some time alone and that was actually what I needed too. *Son of the year award ain't stopping at my door.*

I decided to stay upstairs for the rest of the day since clearly, I shouldn't be trusted around any other humans just now. Turned out, I shouldn't be around animals either.

When I tried to put the pipe in the fish tank the wee bugger decided to just jump out, flapping around the floor. I quickly scooped it up and put back into the tank.

"Suicidal wee man?" I asked it. "Well, I'm sorry but you're not dying today on my watch, it's been shite enough as it is. I've got you some new things so give them a wee shot and see if they make you feel better." I put in some extra food. "There you go, maybe some comfort eating will help."

I sat down watching the wee man as he looked at the tubes. Poor wee thing didn't seem to care and just wanted to jump back out the tank. I ask it again, "I'll get you a wee play mate, will that make you happy?" The banging on the door interrupted me. I waited a while, but since Mum had her Eastenders on, she ignored the noise. I grumbled a little before going downstairs to open the door. I was confused when I saw Lizzy standing on the doorstep. It was a *deja vu*.

She handed me the bag and I looked inside to see another fish.

"Are you stealing these wee guys or are you a secret breeder?" I asked, not intentionally trying to be funny but it just came out.

Giggling hard Lizzy took a minute to reply, "I felt bad for the last one dying so asked my pops if I could have another to give you."

I replied, "there's absolutely no need. . ."

She cut me mid-sentence, "its's really a thanks for earlier."

Before I could respond, she continued, "I have deliveries coming in early tomorrow morning so I need to get home to bed."

I offered, "You need a backy? On my bike?"

Without saying anything, she denied and pointed over to her car. She said, "good night, Rab," and headed off.

Well, at least the wee one upstairs might stop feeling suicidal.

The perfect way to top off a nightmare of a day was to have an actual nightmare when you sleep!

Lizzy was Mary and I was Silver!

I couldn't bring myself to say any more than that.

Chapter Seven:

Strange Happenings

I decided the best course of action was to not see Lizzy for a few days. By then everything would have blown over and I'd be back to my usual self. I guessed, the love between Mary and Silver has gone to my head! No doubt Lizzy would soon be back to being an absolute irritating twat and I'd feel relieved in the rage that returns. I couldn't write her off now! Not that I cared for her or that she didn't deserve it but the hurt it would cause to her mum. Losing the only two important people within the same year might send her over the edge and I didn't want that blood on my hands. God knows, they will be drenched already. I could see the effects that would have on Mum too. With our Mums being good friends, there was no doubt she would step in and offer some support. The only thing it would do will be causing Mum to relive her experience and I couldn't do that to her. In reality, the only reason Lizzy will live is because of my love for Mum.

There was a strange atmosphere down the stairs and I found myself trying to be quiet while gathering breakfast. Mum was just sitting in her chair at the window, with her coffee cup in hand but not speaking. I thought it was because of yesterday, it would have brough a lot of memories back and she probably just needed a bit of head space but it was worrying that she didn't even greet me with a "good morning".

It dragged me back to the time when we'd both just sit there like zombies, with nothing to say but also not wanting to be alone. Struggling to even make eye contact as that would just let the feelings escape again. No days or nights seemed to pass back then; it was just one massive blur. Even looking back now, I cannot quite work out the timeline. I can't remember who made dinner or if I even ate in those days. Unless you have been in that type of situation you just really can't understand it. Even the necessary things that you know you must have done, like drinking a glass of water or going to the toilet, you don't have even one ounce of memory of it. If it wasn't for the nurses that had to come a few times a day I think, we would have just gladly wasted away.

At different times of the day, some nurse would come to either help Mum have a shower, get dressed, help her cook or even do the shopping. Most of the time, I didn't even notice them coming or going, but Mum grew angrier each time. It was the bathing of dressing she had a problem with, she kind of just resigned herself to them and let it happen but the poor little guy that had to keep coming to help her do her physio really took the burn of it. He eventually gave up asking mum if she had been practicing and decided he would just have to up his visits instead. This was too much for Mum, she screamed about why the fuck did she have to do stupid physio? Her legs were done and so was her desire of anything else. She didn't care how strong her arms were, how big a pot she could hold or that her fingers all even worked when her brain told them not to.

I know she didn't mean it the way it sounded, like she didn't care for me, though I felt the same. Some people can say what they want about how that's an utterly selfish thing to say when you still have a son that needs you.

First, I wasn't a child that would end up being adopted or spend his life in the care system. I was an adult and, in some ways, she had already done her job and I could take care of myself. Second, how can you say its selfishness when she could have as easily died that day too? If she hadn't made it out of that crash or the four months she spent in hospital then, would you still think that of her?

The most important point to make though is there is no way in this world it can be selfish because for you to be able to feel it, you need to have feelings. We were just numb! Like an anaesthetic to the heart there were no feelings to be judged on. We weren't sad, happy, lonely, grateful, nothing. We felt nothing, so it was completely impossible.

I took Mum's cup of coffee from the sill in front of her and started to make her a fresh one. The cup was still full but it would have been warmer sitting in the fridge. I carried the new cup of coffee over to her and reminded her it's hot. It was stupid of me, I know. But it's just something you say.

She didn't even look at me.

I cleared my throat a bit before speaking to her. "I'm sorry for yesterday. I had just assumed that Lizzy's mum must have told you."

She exhaled a breath, "it's fine."

"It is not fine, Mum. I don't want you having to relive the past or remember the pain."

"It's fine son. Honestly, it's not because of that."

I actually felt myself becoming a bit angry. The advances we had made in our relationship just over the last few weeks were massive and all of a sudden, I felt the fear of it all crashing down again. "Mum, you don't need to hide your feelings from me. I don't blame you for feeling this way."

"Rab, I'm asking you to stop. I don't want to talk about it."

"But then it will all start again, not talking one day turns into two, then three. . ."

She sounded annoyed this time, "Rab, please just go away and leave me the fuck alone."

"No! I'm here this time and won't let us undo all the work we have done."

"Rab, it's fucking nothing to do with Lizzy's dad, your comments or even you dad. It's...It's..."

79

"Well, what the fuck is it then mum? Huh?"

I heard her voice and could see that her lips did move but there was no way my brain had translated the words correctly. We both stared at each other, confused and feeling like one of us has just spoken another language.

"You, what?"

"I know it sounds crazy, Rab. In fact, it sounds impossible. I don't think I'm going mad though. Well, I hope not. It has happened a few times now and seems to be happening more often and getting stronger."

I was still standing there looking at her like she had Chinese subtitles playing below and had lost all ability to talk. I dropped into the chair behind me, not even stopping to check if there was even one there but I was grateful there was.

"Mum, sorry. Mum, wait. I don't understand. I don't think I picked up what you said. I mean, I just can't see how that could be possible, could it?"

"I don't know Rab. I've been asking myself the same questions, putting it down to my imagination but it's got to the stage I don't think I can brush it off anymore."

"I'll call the doctor Mum. He'll know."

She didn't stop me so I knew she was serious.

The doctor called me into Mum's room once he had finished his examination.

Mum still looked completely shocked and let the Doc do all the talking. "I must admit, that when you first called me, I was expecting to explain how the brain can play some nasty tricks on you, but I was wrong. I'm going to refer your mum up to the hospital for some further tests before we get ahead of ourselves but it does seem plausible. Is there someone who could give you a lift or would you like me to organise an ambulance?"

"There's no need for the ambulance, I will sort her getting there." Mum absolutely hates ambulances so she seemed a little relieved when I said that. The doctor was definitely hitting his own supply of pills because he explained how it wouldn't be advisable to try to take Mum up on the back of the bike. I burst out laughing but he stood there waiting for a reply.

I reassured him, "I will find someone with a car." I didn't intend in trying to balance a disabled woman on the back of my bike regardless of the severity. He actually seemed relieved. Thank fuck my mum was getting a second opinion as he was clearly off his rocker!

He explained, "I will phone ahead and arrange for her to be admitted at 4 p.m." He headed out the door. He could have fucking offered to give us a lift if he was that worried about my bike.

I was trying to think of who in the village I could ask to help. I turned to Mum, "I'll go sort it and will be back soon."

Our neighbour seemed to be out and the other doesn't drive. There's Derek, the mechanic but he has an MOT coming in at half three so wouldn't be able to. I chapped at the door of a couple other people in the neighbourhood but so far, everyone was either busy, had a broken car or just not in. One neighbour, Fanny Craddock, not a joke, that's her actual name! I couldn't get over it either! Her mum needed a right old pat on the back for that name, fucking legend!

Her car was the one going in for the MOT at Derek's so she couldn't help but asked me to send mMm her love. Hahahaha maw, Fanny sends her love!

Even she giggled every time I told her that.

I called the old folks' home from the next residents' home and asked if their mini bus would be available but thanks to the shellfish wee arseholes booking a cribbage competition, it was a no from them too. I tried to think of anyone else at all that I could ask before I resigned myself to the fact, I was going to have to ask Lizzy. So much for keeping my distance!

It was for Mum so I needed to just suck it up. As usual, I found her in the post office. She seemed a little more cheerful today but still not really herself.

"Lizzy," I tried to say in nicely realising I was asking a favour here. "Mum's got an appointment at the Hospital later and I can't find anyone able to give us a lift."

"Charming!" I was confused at her response. She continued, "Coming to me last? Thanks for that."

"Oh, I didn't mean it that way. I just meant that I knew you would be busy..." stumbling for an excuse.

I looked up to see Lizzy giggling. "I'm just messing with you! My mum will be back in an hour so she can watch the shop. I'll head up as soon as she's back. That ok?"

"Great, thanks." I exclaimed bumping into the guy behind me as I back out of the shop.

Just a little after three the doorbell went, and I heard Mum inviting Lizzy in. I headed down stairs to find Lizzy having a large box with her. *She does realise I asked if she could give us a lift somewhere? Not an offer to fucking move in!*

"This came for you," she said. "I remembered and tried to catch you when you left the shop earlier but you must have not heard me calling. Decided it would be easier to bring it up in the car anyway than you struggling with it all the way home."

"Thanks." I wasn't very sure what else to say. It was obvious they were both staring at me waiting to hear what it is. *Ah see that's her nosey shit side coming back!*

"It says tank on the side of the box." Mum said gesturing towards it.

Well, give that woman a bloody golden star! I said, "Nothing gets past you mum!"

Lizzy giggled.

"It is a new tank for the fish as it seems cruel to keep them in such a small space." I sounded like a fucking scale rubbing fish lover, but it did the job and it shut them up. I ushered them out the door saying we couldn't be late but on the inside I was panicking, in case, Lizzy asked to see the fish.

Mum and Lizzy chatted the whole way to the hospital leaving me in the back to enjoy the scenery. Just field after field after field, wee river or burn now and again but nothing very exciting. I thought about that program I'd seen a few times on TV. "Hunted", I think it was called. Where all people had to do was hide for a while and not get caught. Well, all they won't have to do is come here and pitch a green tent over one of the hills, ain't no fucker going to be prepared to walk all over that looking for you. That show is so damn stupid, I actually watched as one person thought that the best way to hide was to get on a fucking main stream train for like four hours. Yeah! Pal, they are not going to be just waiting for you on the other side.

We thanked Lizzy and said goodbye since there was no point in her waiting for us. If you have been to any hospital, massive or tiny, you may as well pack like you're going on holiday. Even a blood test takes about four hours these days. Yes, Mum had to be there for a specific time but just because they liked to have people sitting about to make the place look busy. It is called free health care but you pay with your own time, keeping the seats warm and keeping the floor free from lying dust as you pace over them for hours.

Mum got her wheelchair and crossword book so she didn't mind too much but I had to sit on that plastic-fucking-trick-seat that nipped my arse every time I leaned forward! *Causing more NHS work there!* It might have been comfier sitting on some nails because at least they won't have kept surprising me with a sharp nip!

I knew they were struggling with funds but would it actually kill the bank to just buy some new chairs? I was pretty sure I'd seen homeless people on TV with comfier seating! I wanted to put it down on the feedback forms that were sitting on the table but very conveniently there was no pens. No point in asking Mum for hers because she'd tell me to stop being so grumpy.

For a second, I thought I'd brought mum to a primary school instead of the hospital. *Is it fucking dress up day?* There was a lad about twelve standing in front of Mum pretending to be the doctor. I thought child labour in the UK was illegal.

Mum, less reluctant than me, or less capable, because before I knew it he was off down the corridor with her. I heard of kidnap but fuck knows what this was called! I was glad I didn't plan on sneaking up on him to catch him out because it would be quite difficult with the squeak, squawk, squeak noise that my footsteps were making. *Were the floors designed to make your feet sound like that to stop your running or if to show the doctor you're poor so he doesn't start to offer information on things you can buy to help your condition?*

The arrogant wee prick waited until I was in the doorway before telling me mum was being sent up for scans so I'd have to return to the waiting area. *Oh! Sorry, did I fucking surprise you turning up at the door? Did I creep here like a ninja?* He could have saved me at least half that walk of shame.

It only took two hours and ten minutes for Mum to return. I hoped they have scanned every fucking bit of her body in that time. Or maybe, it was one of those Ikea jobs where they had to work out how to build the thing first. We didn't have an Ikea anywhere near us but we'd seen the stories and read the reviews. I just don't get why people keep going back if it takes a degree in engineering and a course in a new language to build what they buy. If they actually stop buying there, then maybe they would improve some of their manuals. Nah! They won't stop going there, where's the fun in that? What are you going to fill your social media news feed with if you're no longer being scorned by Ikea? Heard they do some tasty meatballs though!

I think we were finally getting ready to leave but Mum informed me that we had to wait for another doctor to chat through the results before we could go. *Great! I'm trying to think if it was actually a worse idea to have to stay in the car and return with Lizzy.*

Finally, a lad that looked a lot like the previous doctor's older brother showed up. Well, at least this one had some hair on his chin. *I'm not getting fooled this time, no way mate! Your wee brother played that trick on me last time!*

Surprisingly, he stopped and turned after just a couple steps. "You're welcome to come if your mother wants you to."

My mum nods and I felt easier this time because I could pretend the noise was coming from his shoes.

We all took a seat, except for Mum, who already had one. The doctor brought up some crazy indecipherable images on the screen. He looked like he was going to talk us through it but we made it clear by our expressions that we didn't have any idea of what we were being shown.

He decided instead to tilt his chair to face us more and just left the image there to act as some sort of art. I was hoping he was going to make this simple otherwise I might need him to repeat it over and over. To be fair, unlike the last guy he didn't look like a pompous twat that read a dictionary on his lunch breaks. *Maybe he will cut all the crap and just give it to us straight?*

At this point, regardless of the outcome, I thought about taking a wee nap in one of the beds next doors. My nerves were never designed to take so much pressure, it surely wasn't good for my body. After what seemed like a lifetime, the Doctor finally looked up from his notes and began to talk. I reached over and held Mum's hand. Never mind what I was feeling I couldn't imagine what was going through her mind. I gave her a wink, to let her know that regardless of the outcome, she'll always have me. Whether she liked it or not, I might add.

"We've taken scans of your body from the waist down, ran some small electric shocks and tested the automatic responses in your joint."

Not being funny mate but I think she fucking knows that. She was there, after all. Cut the crap and get to the part that's actually news to us. I didn't say this out loud. Yet, I screamed it so loud in my head that the people back in the waiting room might have heard it.

"We have compared these to the test we ran a few years back to see how much has changed. I don't have to give this news out very often so I'm sure you can forgive me trying to find the right words."

NO! No, we can't, stop fucking with us and just tell us!

"On the matter in which you were referred to us does in fact seem to be correct. I'm not sure I can explain right now on how it has happened but I can confirm that we seem to agree with what you're describing. The tests done lie so it does appear that you have regained slight feelings in some of your toes."

The rest of his words became a blur. Mum and I looked at each other. I heard the dreaded word Physiotherapy but this time Mum didn't seem to mind it. It was like we were connected telepathically. *You go mum! Well done! You dance those fucking socks off!*

It was late so we opted for a taxi, not wanting to have to discuss the results with anyone else. It was the best news Mum had heard in years and for just a little bit we wanted to hold it close and between us. We didn't care right now if all her ability would come back. Right now, it felt like we were finally getting some good luck and what was to follow could just wait. I helped Mum into bed and just gave her a smile. There were no words needed. We both felt the same.

She gave me an old-style proper smile and I gently shut her bedroom door. We'd be sleeping like a log tonight after the day we've had but finally I could say it in a good way.

I tripped over the box at the bottom of the stairs that I had completely forgotten about—the cricket tank. I quickly log onto the computer and finalised my order for the crickets, vitamins and some insect fuel. I chucked a hopper in each tank and collapsed on my bed. I didn't have the strength to even undress. I was out! For the first time in a while, I didn't even wake up at one.

It was 11 a.m. and clearly Mum had slept in too. Instead of waking her I decided to get the cricket tank set up. It was not a huge amount of work. It slid perfectly into the space I created in the unit and I filled each section with dirt, a little water bowl and a couple sticks. The crickets were actually really cheap but I couldn't stop having nightmares about Mum hearing them and me never being able to sleep again from the noise. I decided to invest a bit more money into how I contained them.

I spent fourteen pounds extra for some sound proof foam and used it all the way around and under the tank. I couldn't cover the top because then they wouldn't get the light or be able to breath but I was satisfied that should do the job.

I forgot that the tank lid slid off so when Mum would be busy next, I'd need to sew a slice in the side of the unit to be able to open and close the tank. Mum had got bingo at four in the evening I decided to get it done then. It would be plenty time since the crickets were going to now take two days! I was yet to find a company that managed the "next day delivery" to here. It was all good though as I had a couple hoppers left. They were looking a little worse than before, but sure, they'd have sufficed for Mary and Silver. They could now live in this new tank instead of the takeaway tub they were currently sitting in. That should give them the will to live another couple of days, well, really just until tomorrow night

Chapter Eight:

Building my army

Christmas seemed to rush in this year with everything going on with Mum. Physio was up to three times a week and for once, mum was not complaining. She could now feel all of her left foot and half of her right. I was really confused by it all though. I mean if she could feel down to her arse and her feet then how come nothing in between? You could think she'd feel the top of her leg then her knee and moving down. How can it skip a massive part then feel the rest?

I asked the Doctors this a couple times but then they just confused me even more so I decided to put it down to "a miracle". Not that I believed in God or that but I couldn't understand the medical science, so I'd rather just accept that. In fact, I didn't even know if Mum could actually feel her arse? I dared not to ever ask her or even wonder. I just assumed she could because she didn't have a piss bag or that and never fell off the loo. Since being in her chair, I'd always thought Mum must feel like a Weeble. I mean if she can feel her arse but no legs then that's basically what she is. I told her once over dinner and she choked on her food from laughing.

Not to praise myself by my own mouth too much, but I thought I did proper good with her gifts this year. I got her cosy socks, as one downfall from all this was, she now felt the cold and I was constantly having to put the blanket back over her foot. A foot spa, which she liked but not on the big vibrating settings. She says she can feel it in her hips and it makes her back sore, not like she complains much about anything! Lastly, a plug-in foot warmer that's lined with soft fluffy material. The Doctor said anything to make her want to move her toes is great. *See, I do listen Mum!*

So, I thought these would give her different feelings. She loves feeling the water between her toes and feeling like a teddy bear is hugging her feet. I might fucking get that best son award this year after all. As usual, she got me new clothes and an Amazon voucher. Pretty sure, we were keeping that place afloat. Overall though, it was a super good day and four months later I was still chuffed about it.

This year seemed like it might be the best one yet since Dad died, not just with Mum but also any day now, Silver should show the signs that he was ready to be a Daddy.

Most tarantulas mate near October time but the species I chose was perfect. They mate between now and June. I have researched on how you tell if a female is ready but until you put the male in, there's really not any signs. Silver, on the other hand, made it much more obvious.

I was waiting on him building a web. Not the type of web you expect from a spider but a sperm web! How cool does that sound! The web isn't made of sperm. But because they couldn't just hop on like the wild cats, they have to get creative. To be fair, I didn't think I'd want to stick around very long with a female like Mary. Give her it, run away... That was definitely a better plan! So, they make a little web, out of their arse as normal, then they lay a little package of sperm. The guy picks this up and then pops this in the female's ready bits and be on their way. No need to hang around long or worry about if size matters. I think they have it sussed really, well, apart from the maybe getting eaten afterwards.

Silver had really calmed down lately, using his rage and speed on his dinner instead of me through the glass. He still lifted his legs now and again if I approached too quick but I think he just tries to give me a double high five. The initial thought of how I was going to get him into Mary's tank and out again was really daunting but I decided to use the bath method again.

I was more ready this time and I was not prepared to give Silver as much chances as I did with Mary. There was a hamster cage attachment thing in my new favourite shop. The charity shop of the town.

It has a long tube with a little clear tub on the end. It's not very big or long and should easily sit in their cages. I planned to try coax him in with gentle nudges and taking away his wood hiding holes, hoping to hell he chooses to go in his self, then covering the exit with a lid from one of my takeaway meals. Putting all the plastic cage in Mary's tank and wait.

I couldn't go away or go to bed or that. No, no, no, it was far too risky. I was going to watch every moment then when he would be done with the deed, I needed to get him back in the tub and back to the safety of his cage. There was probably no benefit of me doing this in the bath but made me feel a bit safer. I even bought my own washing up liquid for this time. I'd need to keep the lid mainly open to stop Mary going in the tube too and to be ready to save him. It wasn't as common tarantulas to eat the male but I wasn't willing to take any chances.

Every day, I jumped out of bed and checked all of Silver's tank for any signs of a web but there was nothing so far. The days were starting to really drag, but there was nothing I could do.

I had the patience, though. No point spending all this time getting to this point then serving him up like a fucking steak dinner to Mary. Besides, I couldn't afford to buy another. Night after night, when I dropped in a cricket I told him, "Right son, I'm doing my part so it's your turn now."

Not only had I been giving them a cricket every night but also I kept mealworms in their tanks too. I didn't know if they were hungrier than usual as I'd never done it before. Some nights, they were eating the cricket and the two meal worms I was putting in. I hoped this wasn't normal because I could hardly afford to giving them three meals each night. However, I didn't want to starve the poor little buggers too.

My research alleged that during mating times they tended to eat more so I was hoping it was just because of that. I only ordered one food order for them every month, but this month itself, I'd to go with a second. I would catch more hoppers if I had to, because I couldn't have more parcels coming in with the "live animal" sticker on them. Mum thinks I've got five fish now!

I might actually have to set up a full filled tank if she was going to start being able to come up the stairs. I still have the lock on my bedroom door from when I was a teenager so at least, she wouldn't be able to get in there without warning.

When Silver first arrived, he would start wandering out his hiding hole around ten o' clock at night and Mary stuck to her till 1 a.m... But now that it was lighter in the evening, he waited until midnight to come out. I had to stay up even later to be able to watch them.

It never bores me, watching them dine. They are two very different hunters. Silver acts like he hasn't been fed in weeks and lunges at it within ten minutes. Whereas Mary might leave her prey for hours before putting it out its misery.

See, women are just fucking cruel, finding utter joy in messing with the heads of everything they meet.

Even Silver gets impatient for her to eat it. Twice he had launched at the glass trying to kill it for her, thinking the movement of it puts him on edge. *Maybe, she is being even more of a mind fuck that I thought and waiting until he gets hungry again and thinks he's going to get it then she eats it. You never know with these "split arsed" sex.*

.oOo.

Mum and I have been having dinner together more and more these past few months. It was really nice and great that we were starting to enjoy each other's company again. It would never be like it was before, but I like the new way. She'd got her coffin dodgers bingo today so we were having them over for dinner after. She asked me to join them, which I cringed at the thought of, but then she said they always have lots of questions about physiotherapy and what her specialist has said and I can answer some things she can't explain.

Yeah, me! The one that has had to reside to believing in miracles because I didn't have a fucking clue of what is actually going on. She says "please" a second time before I have the chance to say "no", so I better do it.

That's the thing with Mums. They do so much for us so sometimes you have to give back! Even if I would rather stick a hot poker up my own arse and dance the pole after. I suggested to get a chippy again because she'd be out all day and I was not cooking for the toothless twats! What could I even make them? Mash taties for main and jelly for after? Nah, fuck that! I'll go to the chippy; means I can get away from them too.

"Ok Mum. In fact, I'll even go and get us all a chippy, how does that sound?"

"That sounds great! Thanks son! Just don't forget to get everyone a pickle" she said beaming with happiness.

She heads off and then I realise my mistake. Fuck! She thinks because I've offered, then I must be paying as well! Fuck's sake Rab! Next time make sure you say "I'll go for you"!

It was actually putting me off my food. All of them gummy radges sitting with battered sausages hanging out their gums or spitting bits of fish everywhere, every time they spoke. Suddenly, my haggis supper doesn't seem as appealing.

However, for being fucking ancient and not being able to eat properly, they couldn't half get the cider down them. Maybe they needed the moisture to break down the food but twenty-four cans gone! It was already nine fifty p.m. when Mum asked me to go to the shop for more.

"Oh! Aye hun, did I forget to mention I had joined team GB in the cycling event? I'm not getting down there that fast."

She slaps me on the arm for my cheek but was unable to hold back from laughing.

She manages to speak once her drunken laughter settles. "Call Lizzy. She'll sort it out."

Aww fucking fab! Not only am I a bloody waiter but let's phone "fucking chew your ears off" Lizzy to get you more drink. Instead, I decided to give up a bottle of Jack. I'd got three. Well, two and a half. But if it avoided me calling Lizzy then, it was worth it. Even though it had been a few months, I was still trying to avoid her. I couldn't feel the hatred and anger back that I used to get around her, so I was just staying clear.

I didn't know how the wrinkles did it but they managed to convince that poor wee minibus driver to let them stay till midnight! They said it was a celebration or Mum so was allowed. Hope he got his fucking groped loads tonight! I couldn't even have a drink because what if I had to do mating introductions in the morning? No way in hell I was doing that hung over!

Silver would just need to keep his excitement to himself as I was not willing for him to taste me! Sometimes, I wished he was more relaxed like Mary but then I must admit he was much more exciting to watch at dinner times. *Can't have your cake and eat it I suppose. He's a good egg though!*

He no longer tried to give himself brain damage against the glass no matter how fast I came close and I was able to open the front of the tank most of the time without fearing he'd jump straight for my face. It still didn't mean I'd take any bloody chances with him though! He'd get me the first opportunity he got, make no mistakes. I think he's more interested in biting me than reproducing with Mary!

It was fucking twenty to one! Where the hell was the lover boy? I wanted those old arse holes out so I could go to bed. They drank that whole bottle and had the cheek to ask for more. How? How is that possible? I mean if the lining of their liver is as thin as their skin, then surely it should be burst by now? Maybe I should give them more, give the poor lad a night off and phone the undertaker instead. I always thought that when you get older and frailer you were much more reserved? NUTS! These women were fucking nuts! I wouldn't have believed it if I hadn't seen it myself but one of them tried to climb on the table to dance saying she always wanted to crowd surf.

Crowd surf? There is me, a fucking cripple and three other sag bags! Who's going to catch you?

I imagined catching her would have been like pelted with slime—the skin keeps going until you hit something sturdy. *Nah, Pal! Get your arse back on that seat as I'll be happy to let you fall!*

The door finally banged and I opened it while shouting out 'about fucking time". I nearly drop dead when I saw it was Lizzy on the door. I shout out, "No fucking way! I don't care who called you, what they are paying you or what order they have put in, they have had enough!"

She looked at me confused.

I spoke through gritted teeth, "no more alcohol for this lot please, they are practically acting feral!"

Lizzy gave out a snort from laughing so hard. "I'm not here to delivery alcohol, I'm here to take them home. I volunteer at the home and when I heard Nigel was having problems with the bus and has been towed back, I suggested I pick them up."

"Oh! Ok, that makes more sense, I mean it is nearly 1 a.m. Thanks!" I said and move to the side to let her pass.

"Right ladies, bags and jackets please. Let's get you home before the vampires come out to play."

Aye, because they would fucking pick them to bite!

I'd actually like to see if I could pay one to do it. Taking one look at their turkey neck and they would stake themselves!

Lizzy finally got them out the door and into the car. Thank fuck! I would have thrown myself out the window if it was high enough to kill me.

I got Mum to bed and literally threw myself on mine. I then realised I hadn't fed the troops so had to get back up.

Wait! No! Really! The one time I could do with just going to bed you, you prick, Silver! Sitting in your sperm web looking all fucking proud.

Why did I think I'd see it in the morning? Of course, it would be at night! Well, at least Mum was basically in an induced coma so she was not going to wake. Still, I couldn't risk trying to clash them into the bath. I decided to let them do it on the floor, so I could use my bed as like a safely island.

I couldn't find the Tupperware lids so chose a spatula instead. This might actually be better as I can hold it above them so if they jumped, they won't get very high. My heart was beating faster than the beat to the song "blow my whistle baby" and I felt a little sick. I was excited, scared, happy, sweaty. It was happening but I'd just be happy to get out of this alive. I think Silver probably felt the same. At least I was not having to deliver the package to a male eating, demented bitch. I think it was like working for Domino's and getting a delivery to Maleficent. Not happening, pal!

Ok, I've got this!

I lifted both the cages on to the floor then unscrewed the lids. I lifted Silver's just enough to fit the hamster cage bit in and lowered it with the tongs. Silver was in the corner trying to high five me but this was no time for pleasantries. The bit was in and I put the lid back down giving myself a minute to breathe again.

If I had two brain cells to rub together, I would have done this a few days ago so he would treat it as his normal bed but obviously I was thinking of that right then, when it was too late. I took another deep breath and lifted the lid.

I slid the tongs in and slowly pulled up his wood, removing his current hiding place so he didn't run in there. I put the wood on the floor far away from me. I prodded at it and lifted it up looking all around. Not sure why. I could see Silver right there and it was not like he would have been harbouring a wee baby or that but it was still scary even though I knew nothing was inside it.

Once I removed the second piece of wood, all that was left was the water bowl, small sticks, moss and the hamster cage part. I tore off a bit of material from one of my holly t-shirts and draped it over the box as best I could try to make it dark inside. Surprisingly, Silver was actually cooperating for once!

I nudged him lightly towards the tube entrance and he slowly got closer. The problem was, as he got closer I was worried if he was too big to fit in it. Yet again, I was proved wrong and it seemed that Silver is a contortionist managing to slip in with these. He darted to the end of the tube that made me jump out my skin but thankfully he was now in. *Part one, done!*

I was holding the spatula tight against the opening but then realised I'd not thought this through! I was going to have to lift the tub out! That was all fine and well but I was not going to be sticking my hand in Mary's to lay it down or pick it up again. *SHIT! What the fuck am I going to do? Am I really stupid enough to chance it?*

I didn't think I was but what other choice I had? He was in the tube, the lid was off, I had the spatula over the end—I was too far into it to not do it. I felt sick and just want to put the lid back on but I doubted if he'd produce another sperm sack? Could I get it off him and give it to her myself?

Of course not! I couldn't find where to put it in a woman, never mind a bloody spider. That many eyes watching you fail too. Nope, I have to do it, I'll just have to be cautious.

Luckily, Mary was just sitting there as chilled as usual so I didn't have to worry as much about her. Well, only a little less. I lifted off Mary's lid and put the tube in so it was facing the lid and the small box that reached the bottom. I dropped the tub in hoping Silver didn't get hurt and slammed the cage lid back on.

Ok he's in there! The tube entrance had landed against the glass but at least he was in there. A minute later, I found the courage to open the lid again and using the spatula I pushed the tube flat. Done! He was in, he could get out the tub and I was unbitten.

I was not counting my chickens yet, though and had a lot more to do but for now I was happy, taking one tiny step at a time.

I waited. I had the lid open just enough for the spatula handle as I needed to keep this half in the cage, but now, all I could do was to sit and watch. I felt like I might get a heart attack but I convinced myself to relax and focus.

Forty minutes! Forty fucking minutes! I ended up having to let go of the spatula leaving it balance in there being held by the lid as my arm was about to fall off. Neither of them moved.

Mary hadn't gone over to investigate and Silver was staying put. Come on guys, I'm shattered and don't think I'll survive this much longer.

I decided when they would've finished doing the deed, I'd try to drop a tub over Mary while trying to get Silver back in the tub. Hopefully, it won't be long and I'd get them back safely locked away. I felt exhausted but the adrenaline kept me going. I was filled with relief as I saw some movement from Silver. "That's it son, the faster you come out, the faster you can get back in. Didn't think you would be scared, acting all macho every other day. Maybe this will teach you a lesson and make you appreciate me more from now on!"

He was all the way out now and he appeared to be actually shaking. His abdomen was vibrating so fast, I was worried he might get a heart attack too.

"It's ok wee man, you can do this, I believe in you."

I took out the cricket I had in the tub beside me and with the tongs, I dangled it in front of Mary. I couldn't let it go in the tank as knew how long she took to eat and didn't want Silver getting distracted and becoming dinner himself. They were both just standing facing each other, Silver shaking in his boots and his fear making me shake the cricket in front of Mary. "Come on Mary, take it. Come on!"

Snap! She took the cricket, and as soon as I had the tongs out Silver took the opportunity and advanced closer.

This is the moment of truth, she will either let him climb over her head or drop the cricket and grab him. I can't look! But, I must look! I need to get him out if it goes bad, although I doubt I'd have much luck untangling two aggressive spiders.

Thankfully, Mary lets him slowly climb closer and within a minute or two he was in position. I couldn't believe he was doing it, I thought the first time might be a flop but he was actually doing it. I felt like shouting, "go on my son" but caught myself in time. I thought he would be on and off again but he'd been sitting there for four minutes now.

"What are you doing, Mate? Drop and run, we've been through this. Don't sacrifice yourself for this mission. I feel for you if you can't find the hole either but you're running out of time, Mary's not going to hold that cricket for much longer."

I absolutely shit myself when he seemed to listen to me and darted over to the other side of the cage. I grabbed the spatula and quickly dropped in the empty individual dessert tub in, just missing Mary. Slowly, I nudged it on her without taking my eyes off Silver. As usual, Mary just sat there and let me do what I needed to. Then, I started nudging Silver back into the tub. He didn't hang about this time and seemed relieved when he saw the opening to the tube again and rushed in. It all happened so fast. I held the spatula over the opening as I place a small rock on top of the tub over Mary. It was not heavy enough to squash her but would have hopefully, stopped her from being able to flip the tube and get out while I tried to move Silver back to his cage.

While I was waiting for the magic to begin, I was smart enough to set Silver's cage back up so all I needed to do was to get him back in safe. I considered trying to slide him out by tipping the tube in but that was one of the stupid ideas that would get me killed.

Instead, I slowly loosened it in until it was touching the bottom and then lifted it back up so the tube was lying diagonally with its face downwards, and spatula still in place. I withdrew it back slowly and put the lid back firmly in place hurrying to get Mary's back on to. I used the tongs to tip the tub off Mary and slowly lifted it out of her cage, replacing the lid and screwing it back on tightly. I turned back to Silver. "Right! Final step, wee man and you will be home and dry."

It took him a few minutes to start venturing out the tube again but it was like he realised he was back home to didn't take long. Afterall, the tube was a clear plastic and these guys preferred to be in hiding. Once he was out I lifted out the tube, firmly fix the lid back on and kept both the cages back on top of the unit. DONE!

I felt like it took ages but also went really fast. Sitting on the bed, I tried processing it all. *I've done it. They've done it. It's done.*

I really wanted to shower as I felt like I'd just completed a marathon from how much sweat I'd produced but in no way, I was risking to wake Mum up. I glanced at my brick of a phone to find it was just after 5 a.m. *How the hell?* I considered giving them both a cricket but the sky was already getting lighter, so it would be bed soon for them. I decided I'd give them extra tomorrow and tried to catch a few hours of sleep for myself. The adrenaline might have kept me awake, but now I couldn't enjoy the excitement as I felt dizzy and sick. Sleep was very much welcomed.

Chapter Nine:

But will it hatch?

I was absolutely gutted! Seven weeks and nothing. I knew there was a chance it wouldn't work but Silver never produced another sperm sack so I couldn't try again. I stayed up until 3 or 4 every night and nothing! My initial plan didn't involve breeding them, so I didn't think I'd need to. I thought the venom would be enough so I didn't do a huge amount of research.

It was not exactly like I wanted my search history to show "how to breed a deadly weapon" as that wouldn't look suspicious at all. I couldn't believe I'd have to wait another whole year! Even a person with my amount of patience would be dented at the thought of another year! Why didn't he produce another sack? He was clearly ready and old enough otherwise he wouldn't have made the first one.

Maybe, I was just exhausted and needed a night's sleep to lift my spirits. Even Mum noticed. I had to made up the excuse that something happened in the tank so I was back down to having just two fish. I think she feels genuinely sorry for me which I also feel bad about. Lying here on my bed, I was feeling miserable for myself, again! Why the hell can nothing go right? Just proved, why I needed to do this.

I had to switch the T.V. off because it seemed to have decided to just kick me in the balls by only showing people who succeeded in life. *Fuck all those twats! Might take a year but it will be fucking worth it!*

I turned off the lights, chucked in a cricket and couple of worms to the guys. They were not up yet as it was quite early but I was feeling miserable so I went away to bed, ready for whatever disappointments tomorrow held.

Well, breakfast with Mum was a hoot!

She gave me three little boxes and proposed, "if this makes you feel better, we can bury the fish in the garden?"

"Do you think I've kept them upstairs while I prepare for a funeral?"

Her face lost its colour at once, and I realised I'd hurt her feelings. I felt awful, and I knew I needed to snap out of it as upsetting Mum wasn't fair. I suggested, "I'll get us a chippy tonight? We can have a few drinks together."

It cheered her up a little and she countered, "I think we should watch a funny movie while we eat. There must be some good ones on sky apparently."

"It's a date, then." I said and went away to have a shower.

I actually felt a bit better. No doubt, the movie was shite and not funny but it would pass the time and make Mum happy, so that was all that mattered. I was going to go out cycling after the shower, hoping that it would take my mind off it. I didn't want to face any locals during my outing, but I could use spending some time in the fields.

I was starting to feel a little resentment towards Mary and Silver after everything I did for them! I hadn't even filled their water bowls up yet, which was usually my first morning task. I decided I best did it before having a shower as I might forget and it was too dangerous a task to do when they are awake.

I felt a little shocked when I saw the cricket and both the worms still wandering about the tank. Maybe Silver was in a huff too and decided to stay in bed all night?

Nah! The guy is an eating champ! He could probably beat me in an eating challenge. I could see the side of his leg through the entrance to the hiding hole so I know he was there. I'd never disturbed him during the day before but something didn't seem right so I decided to lift up the wood for a wee peek.

I jumped a little as his leg shifted slightly from me moving the wood but it was reassuring. I lifted it a little more though it didn't feel like him as he didn't raise his legs when I poked his tank. He didn't move. I lifted it even higher but again, nothing. My heart sank. I quickly closed the cage and decided to check it again, in case, he'd just shed and he was hiding elsewhere. No, he didn't.

He was not anywhere else. I was turning the other wood and moving the moss but nothing. I took the lid off the tank and lifted the wood up completely when I became certain he was not anywhere else in the tank.

It should have definitely woken him up.

He still didn't move. I placed the wood to the side of the tank and gave him a nudge with the tongs but still, nothing. I gave him another harder nudge and he rolled onto his back, legs still bent inwards. I replaced the lid and darted over to the computer.

Do spiders play dead? Do they hibernate? What is he doing? Why is he just lying there?

I could feel the tears dropping down my checks, I heard my heart thumping and breath quickening.

Are you fucking serious, big man? First, the venom doesn't work, then no babies and now you've taken Silver! Why the fuck do you hate me so much? Why can't you let me have one thing? I've never sold my soul to the devil but I'm scared with how close I am!

I landed on the bed with a thump and screamed into my pillow. Silver was a wee prick but he was my wee prick and at least listened to me when I spoke. He lifted his legs wanting to bite me but, still he kept listening. Talking to Mary was like talking to a glass ornament! She hardly moved or did anything. Not that I loved her less, but with Silver, I had a "bro code".

I couldn't bring myself to go over to his tank again. I felt a familiar pain in my chest that I definitely couldn't let myself feel again. I went for my shower, just sitting in a crumpled heap letting the water gush over me. Mum says things come in three but that was a low blow!

I was racing everything round in my head. I could just about afford a new male but then I wouldn't have been able to afford the rest of my plan. But what was the point of having the money for the future if I didn't have the tools?

I didn't know what to do. If I thought I had felt deflated last night then, I was clearly wrong. Kick a man while he's down big man! You are probably pissing yourself laughing that you were going to watch me go through all that knowing you were just going to kill him off.

I felt so angry at myself for caring. I promised myself I'd never care for anything again other than Mum. One team, two people, that's it.

I pulled myself together, get dried and dressed. I realised I had brought the little boxes Mum had given me so I decided I'd pop him in one then put him in the bin.

Wait! I couldn't do that. What if someone found him? Could they still get a bite from touching the fangs?

I knew I would have to take him to the field and cremate him. It'd save me from him being found and would be like a wee ceremony for him. Mum caught me on the way out clocking the box. I was too occupied to even remember to hide it. I said, "I decided you had the right idea. I am going to have a wee ceremony, and pretend the fish are in there."

She hugs me tight. "Should I come too?

"No, I want to do it alone."

Backing off, sensing I needed some space Mum headed back towards the kitchen. "Don't rush back" she shouted as she entered the other room, "I'll wheel myself down to the shop and chippy."

Bless her, the image of her trying to balance her cider and all the food while wheeling herself home does make me smile for a second. "It's fine, I'll get it while I'm out," I shouted back.

Only catching her response of "if you're sure dear" as I race off on my bike.

I couldn't think about it too much or I wouldn't have been able to do it. I bought a little "one time use BBQ" from the shop and replaced the coals with wood. I walked round the whole shop with him in my hand not caring what anyone thought. *A last venture for you, wee man.*

I totally forgot what I went for and just found myself wandering about before I gathered some things and left. I looked in the bags to find out that I bought Hamburgers. I guess, it's just habit when you're buying a BBQ.

Death burger coming right up, if only I thought Mum could deal with that. The fire was crackling and cinders drifted on to my jeans, I snapped out of my thoughts too late and realised I now have lots of little holes in them, who cares. I promised Silver I'd take good care of Mary and eventually got the courage to place him in the fire. The noise was awful and I felt the tears again. There was no smell, not even the smell of wood. Nothing. Just the tears and the feeling of yet another thing being torn from me. "It's ok son, you just rest now. You had a bumpy start coming to me and you never did grow back that leg, just shows that if you push hard enough then nothing can stand in your way. I'll complete the mission, for me, for Mary and in your honour."

When I was sure there was not much but ash left, I dug a hole and emptied the contents of the BBQ in to it. While I was putting the dirt back over, I caught the site of a hopper from the corner of my eye. It was not time for them to be out but, I think it was a sign from Silver. He'll be here, with me, watching.

I grabbed the chippy on the way home, not feeling hungry at all but trying to put a good face on for Mum. She was so excited this morning when I had agreed to it. I opened the door and it was like she'd been waiting for me as she was right there within a second.

"How are you? How did it go?"

"All good Mum, it was just a silly wee thing but made it all better. You were right as always. Did you pick a movie yet as don't want this going cold." I handed her the food and she was chatting away about the movie but I'd zoned out and didn't even hear the name. I shouted back that I was just nipping upstairs to change my trousers as I got a little smokey and I'd be down in a second.

Sitting on the bed with my face in my hands, I tried to see how I was going to get through the evening. I felt tired but awake. Sad and angry. It felt like the pain was about to burst through my chest. The thought of having to pretend to laugh and eat was making me feel sick. I needed to do this for Mum but I just didn't see how I could. It wasn't helping that at the corner of my eye, all I could see was his tank just lying there.

They didn't do anything at this time of day anyway, but it still felt really eerie and still. I remembered I'd not given Mary water either. My heart sank again. What if she was dead too? I didn't think I could deal with that. I had to give her water though, so best suck it up.

I grabbed the syringe of water I had filled for Silver and approached her cage slowly. Eyes fixed on the entrance to her hiding spot. Oh! Shit I couldn't see anything, it was empty.

I closed my eyes and took a deep breath. As I got closer, I could see her sitting at the back of her tank. "It's a bit early for you to be up, Love."

Maybe she too could feel that Silver was gone? She raised her legs as I approached and for a second, I wondered from all the commotion, if I'd accidentally swapped them cages and it was Mary I'd just let go.

No, no. I would have noticed, they are very different in loads of ways.

I then saw it. It was Mary and she was being aggressive. I could reach in and kiss her. I was lost for words, "My amazing wee girl, you just flipped a horrible day on its head."

As she raised her feet again, I get another view and moved my head to the side of the cage. There it was, the wee fuzzy looking poached egg. *You did it my son, you really did.*

The anger and pain suddenly changed into huge pride. I was making fists to try to stop myself yelling out. YUS! Fuck you, big man! Can't keep this man down! You keep chucking curve balls at me and I keep batting them back! You might have my wee man but not before he gave me something even greater.

I remembered Silver and spoke out, "I knew you had it in you, son! Knew it."

The sack was so carefully wrapped up and much bigger than I had imagined it would be. I hoped she was not squashing them while being hunkered down on top. *No, of course not! It's strange to see Mary showing this aggression but so happy she is. She'll make a cracking mother!*

Inside that little parcel, were hundreds of little soldiers. I hoped they had Silver's spirit but Mary's calm side also. I was trying to imagine what a mix of the two had created.

Obviously, they'd look similar but with Mary and Silver being so different I wondered which type of genes would be stronger. I needed to start getting everything together for them. In about twenty days, I'd need to step up and take charge. It was a little scary being responsible for so many lives but I had to do it!

I'll do you proud Silver. With Mary at my side, I'm sure we'll reach our end goals.

I remembered what I came over for but Mary was having none of it. I kept trying to get the syringe close enough to fill up her water bowl but she was getting far too annoyed. I took the lid off with one of the plastic bottles on my floor and with the help of the tongs, I placed it at the other corner, filling that instead. I was so happy that I nearly forgot to close the tank properly. *Oh! Mary! You wee, beaut of a girl! I'm so proud of you too.*

"You coming, Rab?"

Shit! I didn't know how long I'd been standing there in my pants staring into Mary's cage. I didn't care, I could stand here forever.

"Coming," I yelled back.

Maybe it'd be a good evening after all! I could do with a celebration and drink. I threw on a pair of jeans I'd picked off the floor, grabbed a bottle of jack from the next room and raced down the stairs.

"Ready." I shouted, a little too over excited.

"My goodness! You really have cheered up."

"Well, no point crying over dead fish Mum. Come on, lets party like it's Friday night and not Wednesday."

She gave out a massive giggle and shouted, "Get off," while trying to push me away.

"You're not going to push me off while sitting in those wheels. Love!"

"Just wait," she replied, "just wait till I'm up on my feet again. You'll be sorry."

We both laughed hard and settled down with our food, Mum throwing a chip at me. She'd already let the trailers pass on the movie and paused it right before the beginning.

"Bridesmaids" I read. Yup! Exactly what I expected. It was probably going to be utter shite but I didn't care at all. I'd reached a milestone and just a tiny bit more was left to go. I would've watched anything, even paint drying on a wall. I was too happy to care.

I couldn't help sitting thinking about names. Obviously, I couldn't name them all but might name a couple. I didn't think I'd be keeping any as it was not like I could breed them together. I could picture it now! Loads of little tubs filled with lots of little personalities. Ready and waiting to complete their purpose.

I was snapped out of my thoughts by Mum laughing so hard. I decided to give the movie and go and I was soon in fits of laughter too. It was not so bad, the movie, and the Jack was slipping down nicely too. Silently, I made a toast to Silver. *Cheers! Here's to you, wee man.*

107

Chapter Ten:

That fucking screw!

It was day twenty! It felt like it had been twenty weeks and not days, but the day was finally here! I watched videos, got the little tubs ready and this morning the pinhead crickets arrived. Perfect timing! The tubs were only twenty-five by twenty-five centimetres, and I was worried that they were too small, but apparently it should do them until they get older.

I spent endless hours filling each with the moss that might provide enough humidity. Then, a layer of enriched cocoa soil. Then, a little bit moss. I then had to use a hot glue gun to glue an even smaller tub onto the side that could be used as a water bowl.

For anyone that thinks it's easy to use a glue gun, think again! Not only did I manage to burn nearly all of my fingers, but also, I was pretty sure, more glue ended up on everything other than the intended target area. I went through about thirty sticks and my carpet is rough to walk on in some places now. The glue just keeps coming out even when you have stop pressing the trigger. When you trying to put in a new stick, you have to try push the end of the previous one through first. It's a total nightmare but thankfully, I was finally done.

I put in a tiny little block of wood for them to play on and sleep under too. The lids had a little pop-up bit that would make it really easy to fill the water and pop in food. There were air holes on the lid and a couple on each side. The rim of the lid was slightly bigger and the sides slanted in a little so it'd be fine to have them sitting side by side, without limiting their air. I had cleared the two shelfs in my wardrobe hoping to fit most on there. It just meant I'd need to keep the door wide open during the day to give them some sunlight.

I'd put a long metal screw on the outside of the right-hand door and a tiny one on the inside of the left. That way I can tie a string round both, keeping the doors slightly open but not enough to make it creak back and forth. I felt quite proud of that little solution. It was cheap and easy, but worked a treat. I made up three hundred of the tubs so if there were more than that, the rest would have needed to all go in one tank together just now.

I laid out a white sheet on the bathroom floor, so I could see if I missed any. I took my floor lamp from my living room and using an extension lead, I kept it in the bathroom directly pointed at the sheet.

There were books holding down each corner of the sheet to stop it moving about. I had all the tubs in the bath ready to grab and fill and a tiny but sturdy paint brush to separate the eggs. I was going to do this in just my pants to stop any getting attached to my clothes.

I think I'm ready! Well as ready as I'll ever be. I think it's going to be a bit hard taking the sack off Mary but she isn't sitting on it all the time now and it would be a disaster if they hatched while still in her tank.

I grabbed the tongs and a cleared the takeaway tub that I'd lined with kitchen roll so not to damage the sack. I stripped into my pants and took a deep breath. "Right, Mary, it's time. Let's see what you have in there."

Luckily, Mary had settled back down to her calm chilled self, so when I lifted the lid of her tank, she didn't become aggressive anymore. It was day time and she was sleeping but instead of being in her hiding hole, she just chose to stay on the ground beside her sack. "Good girl. You've done your time so I'm going to take it and look after it now."

109

I gently grabbed the edge with the tongs and slowly pulled it off the side of the tank. Mary had taken one step back and was watching my move, but wasn't getting angry.

Maybe she had had enough of them and was looking forward to getting back to her own routine. I had to give it a few gentle tugs but finally it was detached and I laid it in the tub and resecured Mary's lid.

"There you go, honey."

I popped in a cricket, in case, she was hungry. I carried the little tub through to the bathroom, taking off some of the web attached and laid it on the sheet. Kneeling down, I suddenly felt a little nervous. *So much rested on me, I should not fuck this up.*

I had to be gentle and careful to separate the eggs without damaging them.

No pressure there then!

I checked around me to make sure I had everything I needed. I also had a big empty brown box that I was going to sit the tubs in once I filled so I didn't have to do hundreds of trips carrying them through to my room. I placed a hot water bottle inside and covered it with a towel. I slightly adjusted the light, took a few tubs out the bath and popped off their lids. "Ready!"

My hands were shaking but slowly, using the tongs and a fork, I managed to find a gap in the sack and prized it apart. Beautiful! It was packed with little eggs. It didn't even look like there would be enough room for this many. They were tiny, about the size of small raisins.

I took the brush and with utmost gentleness, I brushed the eggs apart trying to separate them. They had a yellowish colour with a pink tinge, like a beautiful little marble.

I saw a couple that were dark and sticky, and from my internet research I knew those were the dead eggs. I started putting one egg at a time into each tub and placed them in the cardboard box. I knew I needed to work fast so they didn't get too cold.

To pick each one up I was brushing them on to a teaspoon then very gently dropping them into the tubs. I was counting but I gave up and focused on getting them all safely rehomed. Like precious little chunks of gold, I wanted to make sure I got every last one.

The box filled up pretty fast and before I knew it there was no room left in it. Luckily there were only about fifteen eggs left so I scooped them up, popped them in their tubs and balanced them on the radiator to keep them warm.

At that point, I thought I was done. I took the sack which was now completely turned inside out and checked the full sheet on the floor. I couldn't risk even one getting away. I didn't think it would have hatched because of it getting cold and not being turned but I was not willing to take that risk. Satisfied, that I'd not missed any, I wrapped the egg sack in toilet paper and flushed it. I then removed the books off the corners and folded the sheet up, with corners inwards to make sure I caught anything I'd missed into the bundle.

Knowing the eggs were warm for a while now, I threw on some clothes and carried the sheet and some clothes I found on my floor down stairs, and put them straight in the machine.

As I turned it on Mum entered the kitchen. "Oh, so you do know how to turn that on?" Mum smugly asked me.

Usually, I bring my washing down and put it in the laundry basket and leave Mum to that task but I'm ready with for her comment with an excuse. "I dropped cola on my bed and with it being a white sheet I had to put it straight in so you didn't moan at me for ruining it!" I snapped quickly back. "Also, I don't even know if it's on the right setting but since the dial was already on that option, I just switched it on and pressed start. I even popped a tablet in and added some freshener. See I'm not just a pretty face after all!"

She smiled at me, hitting straight back with, "well, you better remember where the dial is since you'll be doing that more often."

See, that was the exact reason I didn't do things. You shoot yourself in the foot. You do something once and instead of being praised, you get punished. Fuck, sake!

I'd seen her trying to stand up a couple times but I didn't whip the chair from her and tell her that she could now stand on her own!

Whatever!

I headed back upstairs to finish sorting the eggs. I had a plug-in oil heater that I got for when the heating was broken and we had to wait over a week for a part of it to be fixed. Mum went nuts on the phone saying they were leaving a disabled woman with a son with no heating and no hot water to die from the cold. Failing to mention that she was only in a wheelchair and her son is in his thirties. Anyway, she must have made the poor woman feel awful as vouchers arrived in the post for us for buying two portable heaters. When Mum gets started there's no stopping her but, I was grateful she'd done it.

I placed the heater into the bottom on the wardrobe and put it on setting number two. I knew that the heat would damage the wardrobe but it was the cheapest way to incubate the eggs. Here came the pain staking job, filling the water bowls and putting them away.

The eggs might not hatch for a few more days but I needed the water in there to create some humidity. I thought I had done all the hard work but it dawned on me that I was going to have to refill all their water and turn the eggs every twenty-four hours. This was going to take a while!

I popped open the first tub and using the syringe, filled the little tub of water. I clicked the lid on and placed this one at the far back of the shelf, one down. It was such a long boring task but I knew it will be worth it. In a few months, when they are hatched and grown then they will all have to leave me so I might as well enjoy it while I could. Ten done, Twenty done, Forty, Ninety done. Three hours in and I'd finally hit 100. I knew there was not a huge amount left because there were loads of tubs left in the bath. 105,120, 132. I had to stop for a piss and to wake my legs back up! I was actually starting to feel really tired although I'd not really done very physical, think I needed to consider using those weights after all.

OW! For fuck's sake! It caught my toe again! I might have been a bit cocky about my door solution but now I'd been stabbed in the toe about ten times and had a hole in my sock. I was rethinking my joy for it. 150, 165, 200, 201 and done! I fall onto the bed exhausted, feeling like I did a full shift at a builder's yard. I felt a huge smile spread across my face though. 201 little babies. 201 little Silver-Mary mixes. 201 little soldiers.

That should be enough for my plan, it might not rid a huge number of arseholes from the planet but will make a small dent. Maybe I'd need to do it again next year but I needed to see how I could save the money to get another male.

I couldn't think about that just now. It was only 3 p.m. but I needed a nap and happily drifted off. I must have been a lot more tired than I thought I was as when I woke up, it was past ten o' clock.

I headed down stairs and found my dinner in the microwave.

"You ok, love?" I heard coming it from behind me, and turned to see Mum. "I shouted on you a few times but could hear you snoring from down here. Are you ill?"

"I don't think so although my throat is pretty sore and my nose is running, so maybe I'm getting a cold."

That would just be my fucking luck! All the work I need to do over the next few days and I seemed to have caught a bug.

"Meh! Hopefully it's not a bad one"

This just shows how fucked up my milky Scottish body is. Not one sniffle in the winter but nice weather and I'm choking up again, funny big man.

"Dinner is mince and tatties, so should go down easily." Mum said handing me the plate so I can take it back upstairs.

Mum handed me a box of paracetamols and a can of juice. "Try having a good night's rest." But then dropping in a sarcastic comment, "maybe filling the washing machine will kill you after all!"

Cheeky bitch! I think but we both then had a good chuckle.

.oOo.

Mary was still out and wandering about her tank. I felt really bad but I knew I had to do it to save the babies. A lot of Mums can turn on their egg sack and eat it. Not just that, but I think about how safe it would be trying to catch 200 babies from a tank that has a full-grown killing machine in it. *Nope! She will just need to accept that it had to be done.*

I dropped in two crickets and went straight to bed. I could definitely feel myself getting ill now, for real. I was feeling ok but my body was really sore and I was starting to feel a little hot. I took the paracetamols and curled up in bed. Maybe there'd be something good on the box.

For once Sky must have been taking pity on me and I found a show about animal venom. Snakes and spiders. *This will be interesting.*

They started by talking about the most dangerous snakes, about the survivors of the villages and the damage one bite could do. It was interesting but I was waiting for the spiders to be shown. The first was about the black widow. How small but powerful it is, where it likes to hide and the damage their bite can do. Then there was the trap door. I must admit, this one does actually scare me. I don't think it's the look or even the venom, it's the fact of how fucking fast it jumps out and grabs you! I didn't consider myself to be scared of much but could you imagine if you went to put your foot down and something like that popped out? I'd die right there with fright!

I remembered when I was coming home one winter's day and it was super dark. I lifted my foot to walk in the door and something hit the bottom of my shoe. It was quite a thump and I even heard it as it hit the bottom of my trainer. I dropped my bag and ran to the other side of the street. I was shouting on Mum to come check but she must not have heard me. I eventually had to brave going to have a look and found a big dirty toad on the doorstep. I hadn't noticed it because there were some leaves piled in the corner, but yet again, I jumped when it moved. I quickly opened the door and got inside, checking if the toad hadn't followed me. I definitely can't handle scary surprises.

The last spider they decided to describe was the Red Fang Wandering Spider. No way, how cool! They described how it's the most dangerous animal in all the world and is at the very top of the food chain. It has an ability that no other animal has, expansion. The host hands it over to another guy who has one as a pet, well, they say pet but they worship it and give it everything they have. He explained how he had become one with the species and no longer fears the danger. It was at that moment that his spider began to grow from behind him as he spoke. Larger and larger until you see the camera fall and a scream, as the camera crew tried to run off. From the sideways view of the camera, you could see the spider pick up its owner and start ripping chunks out of him like a T-rex.

The screaming continued and I woke up in a pile of sweat. I had fallen asleep but was shaking and sweating from the fear. I went over to double check Mary's tank was locked shut and went to the loo. It was 5 a.m. so I took more paracetamols and tried to get back to sleep. I still felt shaken up, even though I knew it was just a dream.

I must have been pretty ill though as it didn't stop me from falling straight to sleep again. Thankfully, this time I didn't remember dreaming at all.

Dreams are crazy, sometimes they are completely relevant to what you were doing or thinking about that day. Sometimes they make you believe the absolute impossible or some mornings you can't remember a thing. Very strange.

.oOo.

Oh shit! It was 1 p.m. before I was awake again and I felt like actual crap. I lied down thinking about how I was going to manage to sort all the eggs when I didn't feel like I could even get dressed.

Day one and already failing! I knew this was just another ploy from the big man trying to stop me completing my plan, but I wasn't going to let it happen.

I hauled myself up and slipped on some joggers and a t-shirt. I decided to nip downstairs first, to grab some food and something to stop my mouth feeling like a dessert. Then I had to start on my egg duties. Even though I didn't live in a castle or a mansion, climbing those few stairs felt like escalading down the Everest. The amount of effort it took to get down one step while holding myself up with the banister was enough to make me just go back and die of dehydration.

I finally reached the last step and Mum whirled into the hall. "Hey soldier," she said while looking at me sympathetically. "I've been to the shop and got you some of those cold tablets, a box of tissues, some Vicks and even made your favourite home-made soup. Potato and leek with a KitKat for after." She held out a plastic carrier bag with a big grin on her face. "There's a couple bottles of juice in there too and the soup is in the flask."

I couldn't decide my feelings right now. I mean I was happy Mum had done this for me but did she actually have to wait till I got to the last step? Not at least half way down, I could have reached for the bag. Also was she trying to keep me upstairs away from the risk of her catching it? I told myself to stop being grumpy and thanked Mum for all she did.

I turned and looked up at the mountain I now had to climb and considered just sitting on the step. What was the point in having all those supplies if I was going to be dead before I reach the top?

I heard Mum shout at me, "Don't let the man flu kill you." And she burst into laughter. If only she knew how unfunny that was. I needed to deal with little killing machines upstairs so falling asleep or dropping any might actually have caused me dead.

I could guarantee, it took me about twenty minutes to get back in the room and onto my bed.

I hoped the tablets made me feel better or I had no choice but to pick a couple eggs and leave the rest of them to try thrive on their own.

!3.49£What the hell! They better have me back to 100% or I 'll be going for a refund! Forty-nine pence was what we paid for paracetamols but Mum really went carte d'or on this one.

What? No fucking champagne for me to take them with? Bloody day light robbery!

I begrudgingly took two and poured out some soup into the cup lid. Mum made it a nice temperature to eat and not burn my face off, the good egg she was. Before I knew it I've had three cups of the soup and half the KitKat. I snuggled up on the bed, and I suddenly felt warm and exhausted. I allowed myself a nap hoping, I'll either wake up feeling much better or just don't wake up at all.

I was awake just one hour later feeling like I'd slept for a year. I couldn't decide if it was the tablets that should be dipped in gold or Mum's soup that has done the trick but I was feeling a lot better. The thumbing headache was gone and my body didn't feel like it was made of lead anymore, so I decided to sort the eggs before I ran out of energy again.

After two hours, I started to wonder why I didn't just put two in each tub. I knew there was a risk that only one would live but it would half the time it was taking me to sort them. I remind myself to shut up as it was just because I was ill that it felt harder and will get easier, eventually. Well, actually it won't as I'd need to be careful not to get bitten once they hatch, but it's all going to be worth the effort in the end.

Over the next four days, I continued to turn the eggs and fill any water that was evaporated and slowly recovered from the man flu. I couldn't lie; it was touch and go. Trying to keep up with all the needs of these wee soldiers while walking around in the state I was in. I kept waking up practically a zombie but we made it through.

.oOo.

Today when I opened a tub, I got my very first look at a tiny baby Mary. It was not exactly what I expected— it was like a little glass statue, not the nice dark colour like its parents. I couldn't see any red near the fangs either but maybe that will all come with age. There were only two hatched today but over the next three days, there were 146 little wrigglers.

Some of the other eggs went dark and sticky. I didn't know why as I'd treated them all the same but I was still happy with my lot. I needed to wait another few days to see if any the other hatched before I flush them.

I was actually surprised how the wee buggers could run so fast. They needed no time to learn how to use all those legs. A couple of times I'd nearly dropped the tub from fright but luckily, I caught it each time. They might be tiny and young, but they are already showing their own wee personalities. There was one I called Milver—I had no clue if it was a boy or a girl but at only two days old it raised its legs at me.

It reminded me so much of Silver. I know the name is not a great one but there was not much else I could make when trying to merge the two names, Mary and Silver. I'd put a wee sticker on that one's tub so that I remembered to be more cautious when dealing with it. I didn't get to see them much as they were always hiding when I popped in their food or refilled their water. However, whenever I did, it felt amazing just to watch them practising to hunt. It filled me with a feeling of pride but I was not making the same mistake I made with Silver. I was not allowing myself to become attached. I'd mark the ones I needed to be most careful with but no others would be receiving a name.

Time seemed to be moving very quickly. It had already been eight weeks and I still didn't have a concrete plan in place. I knew what I was going to do but still needed to work out the little details. It was only a few weeks until the dispatch date and all I had was a little brown box, lots of little spiderlings, no pair of socks without holes and feet that looked like a cat's toy. All thanks to that fucking screw!

Chapter Eleven:

The sweet smell of revenge

The time had come. The people selected, and the method was chosen. Although my plans had changed along the way and it took a while to get here, I felt confident that this time it was going to work. I just needed to work out the best type of package to mail them in. I settled on three different options and three little lab rats to test them. I had to be very careful on who I picked otherwise, I could be caught before I'd even properly begun.

I needed to choose people that lived close enough that I could hear of the outcome, but not close enough that it leads a trail back to me. Someone, whom people know enough to talk about, but not care enough for to dig too much into their death. One would think this would be a difficult task, but it actually was very easy and right away, I knew three people that fitted those roles.

My first lucky rat, and that was a great name to describe her, was Amanda. Stumpy, miserable, selfish, greedy bitch. Ms Amanda Morecombe. The woman that takes and takes but never gives. I didn't really know Amanda before the crash. I'd heard of her and knew she had done all the legal work for Mum and Dad's wedding but that was it.

She doesn't really socialise in town and never attends any of the organised events, not that I would have ever blamed her if I didn't have the pleasure of getting to know exactly what type of person she is. Living up in a lovely old farm house, heated with a large log fire, probably whipping her arse with five-pound notes! Not another house for good few miles and her field filled with all her fat lazy cats. She has a couple friends in the village that sometimes visited her but mostly she takes long weekends in London, Birmingham and Bridgeton living it up with her old mates she had left behind. I didn't get her though, if she liked that life so much then why did she gave it up to move somewhere like here?

Mum says it's because she could charge whatever she wanted being the only Solicitor for the villages and she was clearly not a very good one so, she might have not done too well in the main cities. I suppose, that makes a lot of sense.

The first time we met was in the hospital literally days after the accident. I couldn't understand why she was there at first, but then realised it was because she had to deal with Dad's will and Death Certificate. Mum just laid there and nodded, not giving two shits about the words coming out of her mouth.

At first, I felt this was quite rude of Mum but now I wished she had just punched the greedy cow in the face. *Talk about squeezing an orange for every last drop!*

She started coming to the hospital more and more pressuring Mum with her grand ideas. Literally, the woman is a vulture—one tiny spec of blood and she's all over it like a rash. She was talking about claiming on the car insurance, claiming Dad's life insurance, claiming on Mum's own life insurance and if that wasn't enough then she suggested we should also be suing the council for not monitoring the health of the trees. Apparently, it's their responsibility to check that none of the trees are weak and starting to break to prevent things like this happening.

Mum ended up giving in as she didn't have the fight to keep pushing back and before we knew what was happening Amanda was around every day.

At first, she acted like she was concerned and trying to help. She said things like, "You're going to need the money, hun. I can't rest knowing what a horrible thing you have been through and still have to worry about money."

It would make anyone think she really was genuine and kind but this didn't last very long.

Soon her sentences changed to— "You're going to need the money as there's no way you can go back to work in the state you're. Then, you will lose your house and put your child on the street."

This was when Mum ended up giving in and signing all of Amanda's documents. Mum was not in a fit state to sign a birthday card, never mind, all those contracts Amanda was handling her, but at least after that she started coming less and less until she had everything she needed and stopped showing up. It's fair to say she never did show her face again once the letters started coming in saying they classed this as an "Act of God", and will not be paying out. There was one good news though.

The car insurance was writing off the car so they were paying out the value for it. This was short lived though, as the very next day, Amanda's bill fell onto the mat. I remember Mum's face when I took the mail up to the hospital for her. It had only been about two months and here she was looking at a bill for thousands from someone who had pretended to care and was concerned about our finances. Like everything else, Mum didn't have the strength to fight. Well, what would she have done anyway? Go to the Solicitor. The only one around. The one who sent the bill.

I wondered if she'd have then billed us for checking out our complaint. So, the money came in for the car and went straight back out again.

Finally, Mum got home but she wasn't the same woman. She lost the love of her life, her mobility, her car and the bills were pilling up. I'm sure you will agree with my decision to bin the next letter that arrived, a card from Amanda saying "glad your home, get well soon". The actual cheek of her. It was a cheap tacky card that basically was advertising her firm while rubbing it in our faces. If we were going to end up on the street, we definitely knew who would be to blame.

It was her actions that made it not only easy for me to decide on Amanda but also on what to send her. Realising that she'd pretty much do anything for a buck or two, I gathered some items that I knew she'd be desperate to read right away.

I printed off some leaflets about a seminar that was happening the following year in Newcastle where they were going to invite lots of "claim victims" from lots of different situations to help them in finding a solicitor to take on their case. There was a free stay at a five-star hotel, dinner and champagne reception. I even added a complimentary chocolate, business card and name badge to make it seem more professional. It stated that they would be taking applications for another few months so that gave me plenty time before she'd have found out it was a fake. I placed an extra piece of cardboard in the bottom of the box that created a gap where the spider could hide and prevented it getting squashed. Everything was ready and I started to feel excited.

I didn't have to worry about posting this one as most people have their parcels sent to the post office and collect them from there, so I just had to try and slip it in without Lizzy or her mum seeing me. I put a stamp in the corner so it would look like it had been sent in and not hand delivered. There was no way they would be able to ever link this parcel back to me so this was the best route for my lab rats' deliveries.

First thing tomorrow morning, I'd pop in a spider and take it straight to the post office. I hoped Amanda was enjoying her last evening. I hadn't felt this excitement in ages and it made all my work of the last few months worth it. There had been a couple casualties along the way but I still had a strong army of 121. I hadn't quite got the feeding and humidity right at the start but of fear of leaving an internet search, I persevered and got there in the end.

Caring for all those little legs wasn't as easy as I thought but we were in a good routine now. Tomorrow would mark four months since hatching so they were of a good small size but still had powerful enough fangs to break human flesh. I was initially going to wait until six months but I became impatient and couldn't wait any longer.

.oOo.

When I arrived at the post office Lizzy was there but at first, I didn't even recognise her. She'd cut her hair really short and she was wearing a suit. To be fair, she looked really good, just a shame she didn't got the personality to match it. I saw her bag and a plastic bag on the shelf to the side and could see Amanda's name and address on the mail. *What the hell is going on here? Have I caught Lizzy stealing mail?*

She might not want to be doing that as she might get more than what she bargained for. She caught me looking at her. *SHIT!*

Before I even realised my mouth has opened, "Are you stealing the mail?".

Luckily, she laughed and explained, "I have a meeting with Amanda today I'll take it to her to save her coming in for it."

No! Fuck! What am I meant to do now? I couldn't put the box in now as she'd notice it since she'd been through the mail to collect all of Amanda's! What am I going to do now?

If I had a bloody ladder that reached you big man, you would be getting a punch in the face!

I was trying to think quick and looked around for anything I could do to get two seconds alone with the bag to pop the parcel in.

Think man, think!

"Fish food."

"What?"

Shit! I didn't realise I had said that out loud!

"Sorry. I mean, I'm here for fish food. Where do you keep it?"

Pointing me to the place, she said, "in that aisle," while continuing to button up her jacket.

I walked in the direction she pointed to in a panic. I'd missed the chance now. Why the hell did I say fish food? Fuck's sake man how was that going to help? As a desperate last-minute attempt to try one more time, I grabbed all the fish food off the shelf ramming them into my pockets. "Lizzy, that there's none here. Could you check in the back please?"

She came around the corner all ready to leave clutching the bag. "That's weird. I'm sure there was like five when I checked the shelf this morning. Sorry Rab. Here, hold these while I go have a look." She handed over her handbag and the bag containing the mail. I didn't even wait till she was completely out of sight before chucking the parcel in the bag, and then took the little tubs of fish food out my pockets and kicked them under the shelf.

My heart was beating so fast but I felt massively relieved. It was nearly all lost there, the parcel was so close to coming back home with me but I saved it just in time. I heard the stock room door open and I could hear Lizzy shouting back "thanks" to her mum. "I'm so sorry, Rab, there's none back there. I've asked mum to order more but it will take a couple days. Do you have enough to last you till then? If not, I can pop some round later."

"No, no, it's fine. I'll pop up to the bigger shop as sure they will have some there."

"Well, let me know if they don't and I'll drop some by later. I really have to go as I'm going to be late but I'll catch up with you soon." She took her bags back from me and rushed out the door, just having enough time to shout "bye".

I realised I was walking about with a huge smirk on my face but I didn't give a shit. I wondered why she was meeting with Amanda? I hoped it was an easy, quick job as Amanda wouldn't be around to complete anything long term. I imagined if I killed two birds with one stone—well, one spider, but what a jackpot that would be!

The day was just getting better and better. I found myself heading into the charity shop, no idea why, but I might as well have a nosey while I was there.

"Rab?" I heard the woman from the counter shout. "I was waiting for you to come in."

Eh? Why the hell would she be waiting for me to come here?

124

"The other day a guy dropped off this floor standing fish tank, like a proper lava lamp type shape. It's quite big but not that heavy. As soon as I'd seen it, I thought of you as Lizzy always talks about how interested you are in your fish. I've kept it in the back for you, just give me a minute and I'll bring it out."

This was exactly the type of thing that would usually piss me right off but not today. My two little fish could probably do with a change of space and since Mum was starting to get on her feet a bit more, I really needed to set a proper one up, in case, she ever came up the stairs.

Fuck it! I might even buy a couple more fish and make it look like a proper wee set up. Mum thinks I've been doing it over a year now so it will need to look at least a bit fuller. I was broken from my train of thoughts when I saw the woman trying to drag something out the back and I stopped her before she gave herself a hernia.

"Sorry, I didn't actually think it was that heavy as the young man lifted it in with no bother."

"It's fine." I took over lifting it from her. The thing was enormous! It was taller than her and I couldn't even get my arms around it.

"Quite big?" She asked.

I liked to know how she would describe a giant. It was more awkward than heavy but I had my bike and trailer with me parked outside the post office so it wouldn't have been a bother getting it home.

"Pretty neat," I said, "but how much is it?"

"Oh! Eh... I didn't think about that, just knew how much you would like it."

I emptied my pockets and had a total of £13.24. I offered her the money. "Will this do?"

"That would be perfect." she said taking it and putting it in the till.

"Why don't you just sit it down here and go get your bike so you don't have to try carrying it there."

Thanking her, I dashed out to get my bike.

I was actually really excited about setting this bad boy up. It was a lot bigger than any I would buy but I thought it would look cool next to the little sofa I had and it had tonnes of space for the fish.

I was back at the shop in no time.

"Oh, I forgot about the two plastic bags that he dropped off with it. It has all the wires for the light and heater etc so I've put them in the tank for you Rab".

"Fab!" I said. *Fab?* I'd never used that word before but again I was having a good day so I let it pass.

Getting it in the house and up the stairs wasn't an easy job but once it was in, it looked even bigger than before. Luckily, our houses had tall ceilings because I needed to be able to still access the top. I was worried the weight of it might crash through the floor once filled but surely the floors were made of stronger stuff. I opened the bags to see what was inside and found the manual.

Bloody hell! This thing must have cost a bomb!

There was a built-in heater, lights and even an automatic feeder. There was only one wire so it was not even like there would be wires everywhere. The bags were mainly filled with lots of tall fake reeds that were all bent from being in the bag but could be re-shaped. There were ornaments, water treatments and food. I felt bad now giving so little money but, I decided to give them my old tank to try even the barter.

It took me about an hour to carry the pots of water through from the toilet, planting the reeds and placing the ornaments. Moment of truth, I needed to now plug it in and if it wouldn't have worked, I knew I'd be super gutted. I filled it with warm water instead of cold to help it set up quicker. I couldn't wait to get the fish in it. I put in the water treatment and decided an hour should be enough for it to be ready for my fish. I clicked on the switch and *WOW*.

I didn't have any other words—it was just amazing. It might convert me to a fish fan after all. I started up the computer to looked at what other type of fish I would like while I waited and found myself googling about the tank. The manual said it's a Column Expedition Tank and with a quick search I nearly fall off my chair. £899!

I looked again, to check if it was a misprint but, on another website, it was a similar price.

To be fair, it looked worth it. I started looking at the fish but got bored and confused with trying to work out which fish could go with which so I turned to feeding and sorting my wee army instead. By the time I was done the tank had been running for nearly three hours. I popped my fish in. I thought they would dart everywhere enjoying the freedom and space but they both just hung about for a bit. Maybe they were in shock and thought that they had been dropped in the ocean.

If I was a fish, I think that was the tank I'd have wanted to live in. I sat on the sofa admiring the tank and felt my body drifting off.

.oOo.

Mum woke me by chapping on the door. *Why the hell is she not just coming in? Probably has her hands full again.* She was doing super well with her walking and sometimes she even walked to the toilet or walked to the kitchen to make a coffee instead of using her chair. I think she gets frustrated when she has to be in her chair always to go out but we never know when she'd need it so, I didn't want her getting stranded somewhere.

I ran down the steps and opened the door to find Lizzy.

"Oh! Hi," Lifting my hand to my hair I realise I must have bed head because she was staring at me funny. "Sorry, I've just had a nap." I must have sounded like a total dick to her! I felt the urge to explain myself further, "I don't usually need a nap but it's been a busy morning." Rubbing my hair into place and smiling awkwardly.

I jumped out my skin when Mum appeared at the living room door and spoke all of a sudden, "who is it?"

"Jesus Christ! Woman you'd make a good burglar!"

"Come in, Lizzy." Mum said and I stepped aside to let Lizzy pass.

"Go make some coffee Rab, while Lizzy and I catch up."

Fumbling around the kitchen I glanced at the clock. It's four o'clock! Must have really needed that sleep.

"I've come to speak with Rab." I heard Lizzy saying to mum.

Why the hell does she want to speak to me? I wondered.

Heading through to the living room with the coffee mugs I saw the Lizzy holding a tup of fish food. Fuck! I started to panic. They must have cameras! Well, of course, they do! How am I going to talk my way out of this one? How could I have been so stupid? Suddenly I felt all hot and couldn't seem to stand still.

I turned to see Lizzy speaking but I couldn't fully concentrate as I was trying to think of what I was going to say to her.

"Sorry what?" I had to ask her.

She seemed calm and friendly and not at all angry. "I said, I'm sorry about earlier. We did have fish food. I found it under the shelf." Lifting her hands up to reduce my confusion. "I've no idea how they got there but the only thing I can suggest is that maybe some yob hid them there. Actually, maybe I left them on the floor while counting them and they rolled under? I've brought you one in case you didn't manage to get any at the other shop."

"Thanks, you didn't have to come just to give me that. I actually found some upstairs. I had forgotten about."

"Well, I didn't just come for that." Her gaze fixed at the floor as if she was about to say something embarrassing.

My eye brows raised as I snapped back. "No? Well, why did you come?"

Fuck! That sounded really rude!

"I mean, what can I help you with?" I try to clarify in a gentler voice.

"There's a couple of things actually. I can't say too much just now."

I stood staring at her. Why would she come here to tell me something if she couldn't actually tell it to me?

Lizzy must have seen the confusion on my face. "I have a proposition for you but I just need to work out a couple things with my mum first."

Still realising I was clueless to what she meant she continued. "The meeting I had this morning with Amanda..."

I noticed Mum rolling her eyes from just hearing the name Amanda.

"Well, it was the completion for my purchase."

"Eh? What did you buy that you needed her?" Mum's voice sounded slight nasty.

"Mum, let her speak." I interrupted her and turned back to focus on Lizzy.

"As you know, my dad died and he left me quite a bit of money to help me through life. The empty shop in town went up for sale and I thought it was a sign."

"Hold on, you and your mum already own a shop. Why would you need another? Are you downsizing? As that shop in town isn't very big?" I realised I was firing all these questions at her but not actually giving her the chance to answer.

"No, Rab, just listen."

I was unintentionally pacing around the room so decided to sit on the floor to seem more relaxed.

Lizzy waited until I settle myself down then continues. "I decided to buy the shop so I can open my own fruit and veg place. I know our current shop sells some but we don't have much space to hold perishables and everything in my mind started falling into place." She took a sip of her coffee before continuing. "The farmers round here have some amazing fresh produce. Berries, potatoes, peppers and more. I think it will be great to bring some local produce to the town. The farmer said he can make a delivery every other day and any fruit that's starting to go bad he will buy back to feed to the pigs." Her face lighted up and I could see how passionate she was about this also by the way she was flaring her arms. "Then there's the fresh milk and cheese from the other farms. I know that's not fruit and veg but it's more about locally sourced fresh produce." She lifted her coffee mug back up and looked at both Mum and I waiting for us to speak.

"Ok. That all sounds good, but why are you telling me?"

Does she just want someone to brag to?

"So, here's the thing. I can't leave my mum to run the shop all on her own as that wouldn't be fair, so... I need a cashier."

It was like she could see the wee hamster in my head running even faster on its wheel but still not clicking on what she meant.

"It won't be anything difficult as our current paper boy is getting a little old now for his position. He's 19 so I've already hired him to do the morning stuff. He's used to early starts so he's going to take in the deliveries each morning, put the stock away and collect any produce starting to turn bad. It will all be done before opening at 9 a.m. All I need is someone to sit in the shop and put the sales through the till for the customers. I've ordered an amazing machine. When the customer picks an item, puts it in a brown bag, the machine weighs it for them. It then prints out a price label to be scanned. All I need is for someone to scan it then take their money. I know you haven't found a job yet so thought you might be interested? I don't need an answer right away and obviously you will be a full paid member of staff. I'm not looking for you to do it as a favour."

"Wow! Rab, how can you say no? That's not an offer that falls into someone's lap often!" I turned to see Mum speaking this to me with a large grin on her face.

I looked back at Lizzy. "Eh, I'm not sure what to say..." I try to voice out stumbling for the right words.

"Say yes!" Mum piped up again.

"It's ok." Lizzy said, noticing I was not feeling the same excitement as her and Mum. "I'll give you time to think it over then you can come let me know when you've made up your mind."

"Thanks, I don't mean to seem ungrateful. It's just a big surprise." I told Lizzy realising I was flattening her excitement a bit. "I'll definitely think about it."

We all sit quiet for a bit when Lizzy and Mum sip at their coffees smiling at each other.

The silence doesn't last long before Lizzy chimed in with another request. "There is one other favour I have come to ask you for."

"Ok, go on." I said feeling a little suspicious. *What else could she possibly want?*

"I know this is going to sound a bit cheeky but I heard you got that tank from the shop today."

"What tank?" Mum asked.

"Just a fish tank I got from the shop today while I was in town."

"Another one!" Mum said in surprise.

"Mum, I'll tell you all about it in a minute but let Lizzy finish first."

Lizzy smiled. "Pops is getting quite old and seems to have just gone downhill since Dad died. I've been going over and helping him look after the garden, plants and fish but with me starting this adventure I'm not going to keep doing it."

Wait! She better not be asking me to go do the codgers garden, I struggle to keep a plastic plant alive, never mind real ones.

"Lizzy, I'm not good with gardening, plants or even older people for that matter." Lizzy burst out laughing seeing the genuine concern in my face. "No, No, I don't need you to do any of that!"

She laughed again as I gave out a huge sigh of relief. "I have spoken with him and we've agreed that it's time for the fish to go. It's not an issue of just feeding them but the cleaning of the tanks and sorting the filters etc. He's not as able as he was and it's just starting to become a nuisance. So, I was thinking...would you be able to take them?"

"Yes, of course!" I said that a little too quickly and enthusiastically wich puts a huge smile on Lizzy's face.

"Thank you. It will mean a lot to him knowing they are in safe hands."

"It would be no problem at all!" I said excitedly.

131

"I'll give you free fish food anytime from the shop so you're not out of pocket. Have you had a chance to set it up yet.?"

"Yeah! I set it up right away. It's amazing. Do you want to see it?"

Did I actually just invite Lizzy upstairs to my private wee place? Why does it not feel weirder?

It felt normal and comfortable, surely that was not right. Must be the excitement of the tank that was making it ok.

"Yeah, I'd love to!" Lizzy agreed.

Even Mum seemed excited. "I'm not wanting to miss this big reveal of something that's put such a big smile on your face!" Mum said.

Mum hadn't been upstairs in years but because there was Lizzy to help we managed to help Mum up the stairs. Lizzy behind her and me at her side in case she falls.

"Oh Rab! That's incredible!" Mum plonked down on the sofa and stared at it like she'd never seen a tank before. I couldn't blame her—it really is beautiful. "Why didn't you put it in the living room downstairs? I could watch this for hours."

"Well, just means you will need to practice the stairs more and getting to watch it can be your reward."

She giggled and so did Lizzy.

Lizzy gushed, "It really is massive! When Dotty from the shop told me she had a tank for you that was big I didn't think she meant one this big."

I told her my shock when I saw her trying to bring it out and we both had a good laugh.

We sat admiring the tank for longer than we expected, before Lizzy announced, "I have to get going. Need to help mum at the shop before heading to Pops. I'll tell him they will be going to a very good home but I won't be able to collect them tonight. Could I bring them round in a few days?"

"Yeah, that's fine."

She retorted, "and maybe you'll have an answer for me by then?"

I threw her a raised eyebrow for her cheek. "We'll see!"

"Do you want help getting back down stairs before I go?" Lizzy asked Mum.

"I'll like to watch the tank a bit longer, if that's ok with you Rab?"

"Of course not." I gave her a serious look and then smiled at her. "I'll walk Lizzy to the door then get us a fresh brew so we can watch it for a bit together." *It's so good seeing Mum this happy.*

After returning back from seeing Lizzy out I sit beside Mum in a unawkward silence. It's feels really nice having mum up here.

"Thanks for coming up to see too, Mum." I smiled back at her.

"It's like being on holiday without having to travel." Mum replied, sending us both into fits of laughter.

We sit chatting for a while and then I helped Mum down stairs for her to start on dinner. I love that mum will be able to start coming up the stairs again but I better make sure I don't forget to lock my bedroom door.

.oOo.

We were just finishing up dinner when the phone rang. All I heard was Mum saying, "No, I can't guess, what is it?"

But that was enough to send me upstairs. Mum would be on that phone gossiping for ages and I was not in the mood to listen. I needed to go check on the babies and Mary so I waved to Mum and gestured that I was going upstairs.

She showed me a thumbs up so I cleared away our dishes and left her to it.

The wardrobe felt a little cold so I turned the heater up a little and glanced over the tubs making sure they were all properly closed and not knocked over.

OMG! Yet again the door had slowly closed and again that fucking screw was in my heel! I'd miss the wee guys when they go but I'd be so happy to remove the bloody screw. It had already ripped all my socks, cut my feet to bits and ripped some of the clothes I had in the bottom of the wardrobe. I was about to kick it but knew who will come off worst.

Mum started shouting for me and I panicked, worried she'd fallen over again and darted down the stairs rushing into the living room. I found her still sitting on the sofa where I left her and felt relieved but annoyed that she worried me like that. But she did look a little in shock.

"What is it, Mum? You, ok? What's wrong?"

"I'm fine," she said, "but that Amanda's not."

Amanda! How the hell did I forget? My mind was busy with the tank all day that I totally forgot about her.

"What do you mean Mum? What's wrong with her?"

"Well, one of the girls were meant to be going to her for dinner but they found her collapsed on the kitchen floor."

"Oh, No! Was she dead?" I tried saying it without smiling.

"No, but nearly. Suspected heart attack. They rushed her to hospital and have managed to stabilise her heart rate but they have had to put her in a coma and are keeping her in ICU."

"That's crazy!" I feign as much shock as I could on my face. "It must have been a bad heart attack."

"I know. I mean, I don't like the woman but I don't think she's very old. She's def not in a great shape and has a bit health weight on her but it's scary to think that can happen to someone so young."

"Scary indeed."

I reached over and laid my hand on Mum's shoulder to try comfort her a bit. I nipped to the kitchen and get Mum a cider. Trying to reassure her a little, I smirked, "your heart's already dead Mum, so you're fine."

She punched my arm laughing. Mum hadn't been drinking these days as she was concentrating on walking but she took the cider happily and stuck on the TV.

Making sure Mum was ok I left her to her TV program and headed back upstairs. I sat stunned on my bed. How did I forget? That was crazy that it did actually work, well nearly work. If she hadn't been found then it definitely would have killed her. It still might, I'd need to wait and see. Maybe they were still a little young, maybe their poison wasn't at its peak but then again, I didn't know how long ago she was bitten. I'd give them another few weeks before I send out number two.

Chapter Twelve:

Another perfect little Lab Rat

It took just over two weeks but she was finally awake. Amanda, the lucky cow. Hospital Doctors put it down to a heart attack, and told her to take it a bit easier. They even referred her to a dietician. She was sent off home with a monitor and told to ring 999 if the alarm sounded.

I was not that annoyed that it didn't work. Well, not as annoyed as I should be, because it wasn't a massive failure. Maybe the shock might make her a better person. *Seeing that no one really ran to your bed side to hoping you to wake up might do the trick?*

I wouldn't hold my breath though, as I'd probably end up being the one that dies.

I'd given it another four weeks, in case the spider wasn't big enough and I was just finishing off number two parcel.

The next unsuspecting victim was none other than that creepy, loose-fingered Martin. That's right the far too hands on "handy man" up the street. I realised that I didn't even know his name but found it on the town notice board offering his services. *Yeah! We all know what services you actually try to give but the world will be a much better place for everyone with you gone.*

He had not done anything directly annoying to me personally but I hated the way he leered at every female. The way he sometimes shifted his trousers around clearly trying to hide a stiffy. Dirty prick. I was doing this one for every woman in the world and every female ever to be born in his "would have been" life time.

Now Martin was not going to give a box of leaflets a second look unless there were naked woman all over them and there's no way I could get away with sending a free porn unknown, so I had to think of a different option. Most wood working types love wooden puzzles and I thought this would be a good choice if I put it from a new wood supplier showing off their product's quality. But the more I thought about it the less convinced I was.

He was not a full-on joiner buying lots of wood and I was pretty sure the guy wore slip on shoes as he couldn't even work out how to tie his shoelaces. *Nah! I think a puzzle would be less desirable for him.*

There had to be something he was interested in but I didn't dare ask any questions about him as that would look a bit funny if he was dead a couple days later. This one was going to take a little more thought. I decided to follow him when I could to see what he tended to do.

Two days later, he entered the charity shop while I was there dropping off my old tank and answering questions about how the new one was. I needed to do something I'd never done before and kept the conversation going a bit longer so I could watch what type of things he was looking at. This would've been quite hard for me but I realised if I just stood there, the woman just kept it going. She must be lonely and didn't even seem to care that anyone could be stealing anything as she was not paying one bit of attention.

"Christine!" A voice bellowed from Martin's direction and I looked over to realise it was him calling. *Really? You are the one that's going to break our conversation when it's you I needed to watch?*

"You checked all the bit are here for this, Love?" He was holding up a jigsaw.

"Of course, I did, Martin. I know how much you hate a jigsaw with missing pieces."

"And that my sex little lady is why I love you."

137

Oh! Come on! I nearly vomited. She was like at least twenty years older than him. *Would you really take anything you can get?*

I thanked Christine again and left. I knew what he likes now which was good as there was no way I could stand being in the same room as him for a second longer. I jumped on the computer as soon as I was home and started searching through jigsaws on eBay. I couldn't buy one here as then it will lead back to me and I needed to find one that I could relate back to a believable sender.

I found the perfect one. It was basically a half-naked lady but I needed to make sure it was something he wanted to do right away. But who the hell could I send this convincingly from? It was not like I could put from a new sex shop or men's bar as there was nothing like that round here and I didn't think the man had ever left the village.

There was another one that got a wooden boat on it but that was not going to be very exciting. I knew I needed to choose the nude lady one and would need to work out how to send it. I hit "buy" as I'd have a couple days to decide and go to the babies to pick my next little soldier.

I needed to pick them in advance because I didn't feed them for three days before I sent them. This helped make them hungry and more aggressive. I knew that was cruel, but there was not point sending a chilled-out roly-poly one as they'd until they can escape. I picked one that was on my semi-aggressive list and placed it on the other end of the shelf. "Right, Dude! You're up so start getting ready."

Since getting the fish tank I sat in the living room a lot more these days. I found it calming and a good place to think. Now I'd got about thirteen fish so it was lively and interesting to watch. One wee, sucker-type fish decided that the little ornamental house is his and doesn't like it if any other fish try to come in. It's funny to see that they have their own little personalities too. I let him have it as the others still have lots of other places to hide and play.

There's one that has a nibbled tail but it hasn't got any worse so I think he must have sorted the beef he had with the other one.

I sat back and tried to think of what the hell I was going to do with this jigsaw. I knew what I had to do with it, but where should I portray it to be parcelled from? But nothing came to mind. Mum yelled calling me down for dinner and I brushed it off my mind for now. I'd got time, there was no rush, and I was sure I'd work it out.

Three days later, the jigsaw arrived. Perfect timing! It was getting harder lying to Lizzy that it's tank stuff because she'd seen the tank and would probably look out for anything I say I've bought. So, I played the low card and told her it was a tool kit. I told her I didn't want to get Dad's tools out as it might upset Mum but there were a few things at home that needed a repair so I'd just ordered a wee screw driver set.

She knows not to pry on a subject like this one so I believe, she'd never mention it again. I actually felt a little bad lying to Lizzy as I didn't find her as resentful as before now that I'd got to know her a bit more.

She'd been round a couple times now as I accepted the job offer and we were trying to sort out a contract. It usually just turned into us sitting, laughing, and talking about everything other than work. She'd been a bit stressed the last few weeks as I was amazed that I was bothered by her stress. At first, I was annoyed at myself for not hating her anymore. But she's ok, still a nosey cow but she's harmless with it. There's one thing I learnt about her during this time. At least, she isn't a gossip. She asks questions to others, because she genuinely cares and doesn't go around spreading news of people's lives. I think, that's one reason why I didn't hate her anymore I wrapped the parcel in brown paper and put a note on it.

"To Martin, saw this and thought of you. Enjoy it."

I even added three kisses to increase the effect. I didn't write the note for the victim to decide where it came from because my hope was they'd be dead and not have a chance to check. It was so they didn't get suspicious right away. If I didn't put a note, they'd wonder if it was actually for them and might not even open it.

I knew they'd try work out who sent it but by then, it'd too late. I carefully opened the box and emptied all the pieces out, being careful not to lose any or make them dirty. I then did the same to the bottom of the box, so I could pop in the spider and it'd be safe during its journey. I put most of the pieces back in whilst keeping the little hole clear. I was worried about how I'd get the wee guy in but with the tweezers, I just hold them to the hole and they tend to run in by themselves. No problem at all. I still did it over the bath as I'd still got to be careful, in case, I dropped it or it runs. My plan was to do the same as last time and try to drop the parcel off at the post office but then I found it wouldn't even be necessary.

Martin sometimes had parcels delivered straight to his door, and when he was out, they just left them on the doorstep. If I chose my moment right, I should be able to save myself the trip to the post office.

Choosing that right moment was a mix of planning and good luck. I needed to wait until the delivery guy had left, so he doesn't take note that there's a parcel already. This wasn't like the big cities though. We didn't have different deliveries from different companies all day. It was just one so I knew he'd find it suspicious if there was a parcel already there. I also needed to wait till Mum went out because she'd be very suspicious if I left and be back within minutes, so I picked a Wednesday. On Wednesdays, she has her physio as the first thing.

The neighbour next to us was driving her there so I knew she'd be out too. The next house along was of a nurse's who worked night shift, so she should be in bed and out for the count. The very last house before we reached Martin's was a young woman with a child who dropped her child off in nursery. She then went to work in the pharmacy for a couple hours before returning with the wee girl.

If the delivery man came on time which was usually about 8:30 a.m., then everyone should have been away and I'd have the opportunity to drop off his little surprise. I couldn't predict any cars driving past so I'd have to be hidden in my jacket. I felt sorry for little number two, but I needed to basically frisbee it in from the road side. I was not risking being seen in his front garden.

I was hoping the jigsaw arrived a little earlier so I had more time to prepare the bottom and make it as unnoticeable but I think, it looked fine with just the few hours I had. The following day was Wednesday and the glue took ages to dry, so I packed everything the night before itself. I couldn't stop worrying that when the person that finds him dead might see that the bottom of the box had been changed, it might stick in their mind. To put my mind at ease, I decided to get a little more creative and have a cover plan for this.

I added to the note that there was a little surprise in the bottom of the box for him, but he could see it only once he had completed the jigsaw. I then popped in three pin-up girl postcards. They were quite respectful pictures of the women and were not sleazy like the girl on the jigsaw, but they would do fine. I also had these at home as Dad's artist friend used to send these to him. He knew my dad appreciated it but he never wrote on them, so they remained blank and looked like new.

At 8:15 a.m. the doorbell rang. It was the neighbour to collect Mum. Now, I knew the street would be empty.

I heard Martin leave in his van at just after 7 a.m. so he was definitely gone and although I didn't see the nurse coming back, I was sure that she was fast asleep by now. Her car wasn't there late last night, so she'd definitely been out to work.

The clock showed 8:43 a.m. and the delivery man was here. I was glad to see he had a couple parcels for Martin as they'd make mine look less suspicious.

Shit! I think he saw me watching him as he was heading right for my house and rang the bell. I finally opened it after composing myself. He handed me a parcel and walked off.

Oh! A parcel for me? That was strange as I was not waiting on anything and I got all my stuff sent to the post office. It was not very big but really heavy. What the hell could it be? Maybe someone was playing me at my own game?

Nah! Don't be stupid, no one would think of that.

I was delighted to find it was a book, an encyclopaedia of fish. There was a wee note with it too.

"Hope this helps you more in caring for Pops' fish."

Ah! It's from Lizzy.

She didn't have to do that but I was grateful. I minded myself to thank her when I see her on Monday. Monday was to be the first day at my new job.

I did not have the time to look at the book right then, as the guy had drove off and I wanted to get it done quickly. I couldn't risk as Martin sometimes popped back early for lunch so I shoved the parcel under my jacket and headed out the door.

Within seconds, I was at his gate and as gently as I could, I threw the parcel into the corner of the porch with the others. It was not cold today so number two should be fine hiding in the box, as long as he does not come out the hole and try to build the jigsaw himself.

I rushed back to the house relieved that not even a car drove by. There was no way I'd be caught. Another success! I just hoped he'd finished that other jigsaw he bought the other day so he was ready to start mine as soon as he opened it.

If he waited a few days, a dead spider wouldn't be able to do the job and I worry he might find it. He'd then start asking questions about how a spider could have gotten in there. I had to stop my mind racing into a panic so I dragged myself back upstairs to sort all the other little soldier before getting all my stuff ready for Monday.

Lizzy hadn't set a dress code because she wanted it to be friendly and casual but I still needed to be clean and smart. I picked a pair of dark blue jeans, a dark green T-shirt and a black hoodie, in case, I felt cold. I got black trainers so that should all be fine. I couldn't decide if I should take a shower on Sunday night and shave, or leave that until the Monday morning. I didn't think it will matter too much and it was just the nerves kicking in.

Mum arrived back from her physio session and I went down to make her a coffee. She was always super tired after these sessions so she liked to settle down on the sofa with a coffee and then take a nap. They must be working her too hard but I'd not been there with her in a while so I needed to attend soon to check they were not pushing her too hard.

I didn't want them breaking her before she even got really started. I hoped she'd told the Doctor that she managed to climb the stairs twice until now. I jumped out of my skin when I found her sitting in my living room, but she was just quietly watching the fish. She loves it even more now with there being lots more to watch. I'm happy that she likes it.

It seemed to give her peace and in a way it does for me too, so if she's happy to push herself to get to see it then it was a good thing. I proposed if a stair lift would help because with it, I wouldn't have to worry about her falling down the stairs. But she brushed it off by saying, "well, that's not going to help me to walk."

I was secretly glad I didn't push the idea when I looked them up online and saw the price. It's strange that the people who need these types of things don't always have such huge funds because they usually can't work, so how could the companies justify that kind of pricing?

Mum dozed off on the sofa and I decided to go for a walk leaving a note for her saying "I'd get us a chippy for dinner. I needed to go get stuff to take for my lunch on Monday. It will also give me the chance to go say thanks to Lizzy for the book."

I went into the fields and laid there for a bit enjoying the sun. Remembering when I was out hunting for Mary and Silver. It brought all the memories back of the day I had to say "bye" to the wee man but I was grateful he left me his babies to care for. I also found out on one of the Sky documentaries I watched a few weeks later, which informed that some male spiders just die after mating. At least, it reassured me that I hadn't hurt him in any way.

After a while, the wind started to get cold and I went in the direction of the shop to pick up some ham. Lizzy was not here today. She was apparently at the new shop with the paper boy finishing stocking the shelves for its big launch tomorrow.

I turned the corner onto my street and saw a huge commotion. There was an ambulance blocking the road. *No, Mum! Is Mum hurt? Has she fallen?*

I ran towards home but then stopped when I saw the paramedics coming out of Martin's house. Martin was lying there on a stretcher. He'd got a mask on so he must have been breathing but he was as white as a ghost and didn't look very responsive.

I was about to crack a massive grin when I saw Mum at the window signalling me to get inside.

"What's going on out there, Rab? What's happened to Martin?"

"I don't know Mum. I just walked onto the street."

The ambulance raced off with sirens blazing and mum headed out to gossip with the neighbours. I noticed she hadn't taken her chair so I followed her out with it so she could sit down. It was at that moment she realised her legs were sore and looked very grateful for me bringing it.

I came back inside and let them chat as I didn't think I'd be able to hide my excitement. I popped Mum's fish supper into the microwave and sat down to enjoy my battered hamburgers. I was not heading upstairs as I wanted to know all the gossip when Mum would have got back in. I was not missing this for anything.

Mum came back in looking disappointed. "No one really knows anything. They all just saw the ambulance turn up and head straight in so he must have called for one himself but he didn't look in any fit state to use a phone! They are going to lock the house up for him then head up to the hospital to find out more. They said they will phone me when they have any news. Poor woman, should just get a job at that hospital! Being there with me all morning and now having to head with for Martin. I can't tell if she's helpful or just super nosey. Probably a bit of both, eh?" She babbled around while I gave appropriate nods hiding my glee.

I got her dinner back out and she switched on the TV, as we knew it was going to be at least a couple hours before we heard anything. She hated sitting in her chair now, but I could see she was struggling to get on the sofa.

I helped her on it and placed the phone by her side. "Remember Mum, it's a marathon, not a race. You're doing amazing but don't push yourself too much. I've got to do a water change on the tank so call me if you need me."

I needed to get this water change done but I couldn't concentrate. I was too excited. I felt like I was finally going to hear the news I'd been waiting on for so long. I started taking out some water trying to get my mind off Martin because I didn't want to get my hopes raised again for nothing. It seemed that I had a snail problem in the tank as there were at least three times more than there were on last week's water change.

I grabbed the book to see if it had any information, but for holding every bit of information on each type of fish, there was nothing about snail infestation. I didn't mind the wee buggers but the tank was starting to look a little over run by them. I finished the water change then click on the computer to see if I could find out some more.

I couldn't sit picking them all out but surely anything the tank had affected the fish too and I didn't want that. I saw online a couple different bottles and remembered seeing a similar bottle in one of the bags. *Perfect! This will do the trick.*

It took me a little time to work out how much I needed to put in with the tank size but I was happy that I could do something of it before the problem becomes worse. I also read online that you could use a blanched lettuce leaf but there was no way if I dropped a lettuce in there, I'd be able to get the bloody thing back out.

I heard the phone ringing and ran downstairs to see what the news was. I had to wait a few minutes until Mum could speak and tried not showing how impatient I felt. *Come on woman, is he dead or not?*

I could work out by Mum's face that something big had definitely happened, but her face wasn't giving anymore away. It felt like a lifetime until I heard her say, "Ok hun, just let me know if you get any more updates."

"Well, what happened? Is he ok?"

She tried to put her words in the right order and said, "I think so. I mean, she didn't say he was dead but they are still working on him trying to save him. It looks like he's had a wee cut on his hand that's got infected or could be sepsis. They have been trying to stop the infection spreading but it must be a bad bacterial one because it's moving rapidly. They have rushed him into theatre to take the arm off to try and stop it getting to his heart. They haven't said much else as she'll need to talk to the doctor or surgeon after to see how the operation has gone."

Suddenly I felt a bit worried. "And how would that have happened?" I asked Mum.

"I'm not sure but you know what work men are like. They get a cut and just put duct tape over it. Not exactly the cleanest of people. He's prob cut himself with a dirty tool and left it till it was really bad, but then once it's in the blood stream then it's not as easy to fix."

Over the next three hours the phone rang another two times, and we found that his arm had been removed and he's had two blood transfusions so they were finally starting to stabilise him. They agreed it's been an infection that has got into his blood stream and just started spreading rapidly. They were worried though about his brain because it was starved for oxygen for more than three minutes and not just one. They won't know more on that one until he was awake but for now, they were just hoping he makes it through the night.

Ok! So, it's not a win yet but it's looking more likely.

I told Mum that he was not going to be much of a "handy" man now and she darted me a stare, but I saw her trying not to laugh. It was getting late and the neighbour was on her way home, so she won't be back at the hospital until tomorrow. We won't find anything more out tonight. Apparently, Martin didn't have any family here so they agreed to call the neighbour if anything changed through the night.

I said good night to Mum and headed up to give Mary her dinner. Mary didn't seem to care that I took the babies away. She went straight back to her routine and was back being relaxed and not fussed about much. I sometimes worried that she may get bored in her wee tank but then, it was not like I could let her out for a walk.

Chapter Thirteen:

A plan coming together

Monday was finally here and I'd only been at this new gig for an hour and was already bored out my skull. Lizzy was showing me how to sign in and out the till, how to scan the codes and how to take different kinds of payment. I thought I'd be coming into an open shop but she delayed the launch till ten so I had a chance to learn the basics.

It was her fault though. I was meant to be coming in yesterday to be shown all this but she had problems connecting to the main system, whatever that meant. She was only able to phone through and get it sorted this morning. I was grateful she'd given me this job but I couldn't stop thinking about Martin. They managed to get him stabilized onto some machines but he was off them since yesterday. Other than the neighbour, no one else had been to visit him and there were not many people asking after him so I didn't think they cared much. I knew the hospital always had to try and be seen as giving hope but I wished they would just say if they think he'd wake up or not. It would at least save the neighbour phoning in constantly.

I played Lizzy's little game of pretending she was a customer and scanned her shopping through. She seemed happy enough with my work, well it was not like she had another choice as it was five to ten and there were a couple people waiting outside. I hoped it was successful but I also didn't want to be busy all the time.

Lizzy opened the door but it seemed like most of the people had come for a chat instead of buying anything. If you just wanted to chat with Lizzy, you could have caught her at the other shop anytime. But, since the village was filled with nosey bastards, they couldn't miss the sight of a new store being opened. I saw Mum being helped in the door. *Oh, for God's sake! Not you too.*

Mum gave me a wave and went over to congratulate Lizzy, "looks like a success."

Even though we'd only been open twenty minutes and not one sale yet, Mum already thought it was a success. She turned to me, "You don't look too bad behind that desk, son. People wouldn't even know this was your first proper job."

"Thanks, Mum."

She handed over a bunch of rhubarb, "I'll make a pie after dinner."

I ended up giving up trying to explain to her that she had to use the machine first to weigh and get a label and called Lizzy over. "Could you please show her how to get a label for these? I can't just scan the fruit."

Lizzy took over the situation and spent a good ten minutes showing not just her, but other people too how the machine worked. She'd got patience of a saint, that woman.

By day three, the place had settled down and I was actually starting to enjoy it. Lizzy gave me an iPad that we used to do our stock counts and orders, but during the day it was not needed so I got to play on it. I could play games, watch movie, go on the internet or just even listen to music. It was annoying if a customer came in when I was at the best part of a movie, but I couldn't really complain when I was getting paid mainly to sit here playing.

When I finished for the day Mum was waiting on me to get in the house.

"Martin woke up! Well kind of." She shouted at me as I was closing the front door.

"Eh...What? What do you mean?" I shouted back trying to hide my annoyance.

Mum was all giddy and excited. "He has opened his eyes and is breathing on his own! But he can't speak or move. They can't find anything wrong with his limbs so it must be his brain."

I took off my shoes in a hurry and didn't even put them away. Sitting closer to Mum, so I knew I was hearing things right, I ask, "so, does that mean the dude's now a vegetable?"

"Rab!" Mum yelled at me, clearly enraged by my question. She was not playing around, she was serious! "That's not what it's called and you shouldn't be saying that."

"Sorry, Mum. I just don't actually know what it is called. Brain dead?"

"It's clear he's suffered bad brain damage which was what the surgeon was expecting." Mum continued.

"Wait," I said, "so, if they knew he was going to be like that then why did they save him?"

Again, Mum looked at me angrily but didn't shout. "They are not there to make those choices! Their job is to save lives regardless the outcome. There is a chance he could recover, a bit anyway, but they said from the brain scan this morning its looking unlikely. The neighbour is trying to find a way to contact his family in Sweden to organize what's going to happen next."

"I didn't know he was Swedish!"

"He's not. His family moved over there but, he chose to stay."

"Gee! The guy really doesn't like to travel."

"This is no time for jokes, Rab!" Mum snapped back.

I knew the guy was not actually dead but again, I was so much closer. I felt confident that if I sent out all the little troops today, then at least some people would die. I had one more person I wanted to try it on first as I had a fantastic idea.

It all rested on Lizzy but I think, she'd be easy enough to sway to my idea, after all, it'd help her business. If my plan was to go ahead, I was going to need one last large investment to complete it. It was going to hurt but I knew I needed to do it. After all, it was just stuff and I still had my memories. I took a deep breath and started getting on with the job in hand.

Dad's watch, record collection, his suits and jackets, and most of his large tools. Mum never went in the shed, even now, she couldn't get out the back door. She was not interested. She said I could have the tools many times before but I always had to see the pain on her face when I used them so I just left them alone. I didn't think Mum would have cared if she found out I'd sold them but, in case she does, I needed to have a reason for the money.

I listed them all online. Even if some of it didn't sell or sell for less price, I should just have enough for my plan.

This work malarkey was kind of getting in the way of my plans. Not because I was there but I needed to find a time to pack up all the items I had online and box them to go, in case, they sold. But mum was always about when I got home. I might need to find out when her next bingo night was.

I was waiting for Lizzy's arrival to go through my idea with her so she said she'd come on her lunch break. I didn't know how she did it all. Two shops, her pops, helping her mum, still helping at the farm and always finding time for anyone who asks for it.

Lizzy had come along a few times on her break, bringing my lunch with her. Bacon rolls, sandwiches and even a chippy once. She said she knew I was alone all day in the shop and kept saying she will hire someone else soon so I have company. She didn't seem to believe me when I said I liked it that way. I've been honest with her and told her. I sat watching movies and play games on my phone and preferred to do this without someone else there as they will want to natter instead and annoy me. She laughed at how antisocial I sounded, considering I was now in a customer facing role. I reminded her that I didn't actually apply for this job and really if she thinks about it, I was doing her a favour! We both laughed.

I was serving someone when Lizzy turned up and she started making faces at me trying to put me off from counting. *And this woman calls me childish.*

I could smell she'd brought bacon rolls and I realised how hungry I actually was.

151

Bacon and sausage this time. Plenty tomato sauce on it too. Perfect!

"Thanks, Lizzy! But I thought we had agreed it was my turn to pay for lunch?" I said taking a massive bite of the roll.

Lizzy hopped up to sit on the counter, nearly sitting on a block of cheese I had just recovered from the fridge after finding it was out of date.

"Well, did you go out and get lunch?" She sneered at me being all cocky.

"No, I've been here." I pointed to the floor. "Customers don't serve themselves, you know." I imitated pushing her as if I was going to push her off the counter.

Lizzy grabbed my arm. "Stop. You're going to make me drop my lunch!"

"Well, maybe you don't deserve lunch after all your bloody cheek!"

She swinged her leg to playfully kick me but nearly slid off the counter.

Composing ourselves after all the laughter she turned slightly more serious. "You know you can lock the door and nip out for five minutes, I'm not holding you hostage."

"You are kind of holding me hostage when you forget to leave the shop keys for me to actually lock the door." I laugh back.

"Oh, God! Sorry Rab! I keep forgetting!"

"It's ok the roll can be my payment for your forgetfulness."

"Eh... Well... I've already deducted the roll from your wage." We stared at each other and burst out laughing. Even though I enjoyed my alone time in the shop I did like whenever she came for lunch.

"This idea of yours," she begun, "do you have a business model and typed business plan for me to read?"

"A what?"

She laughed again, "Oh Rab! You're so gullible, let's hear it then."

"Well, funny you should laugh because I've actually made a, I can't remember what they call it!" *Shit! I had looked the term up online to impress her but now I looked like a fool.*

"A what?" She was waiting for me to speak.

"A... Eh... ready made one of my idea."

"Do you mean like a prototype?"

The Fucking smart ass!

She laughs.

"Yes, a prototype."

I handed her a small cardboard box that was A3 in size and about twenty centimetre deep.

I could see she was surprised at the weight but she was also holding back laughter.

"Ok, what's so funny?" I asked.

"Nothing, nothing at all." I saw her eyeing up the sticker I'd hand-drawn and placed on the top.

"Ok, I know that looks bad but obviously the stickers would be professionally printed. I had to draw one to show you what I meant."

I tried to draw her L-Fresh logo but failed miserably. She pulled the jute twine to untie the parcel and looked really surprised when she opened it.

"See, you're not just a pretty face after all Rab," she laughed.

"Who told you I had a pretty face?" She blushed from my question.

Inside the box, I placed a tissue paper and a small selection of our fruit and cheese. I also wrote a little leaflet inside.

"Welcome to L Fresh. I hope you enjoy this sample box and discover what fantastic produce we have here in Inverie. Please find the enclosed price list of everything we offer. I'm sure you will find it very competitive."

I had signed it off with "Lizzy".

"That can be changed if you want?" I begun to talk and she sat silent for what felt like an hour. *Oh, no, she hates it! I need her to be onboard, I need this to work!*

"Rab", she finally spoke, "it's beautiful." I stared at her in surprise.

"Really? I was worried you wouldn't."

She looked me at in a strange way. Like how Mum sometimes looked at me when I did something she asked or when I was the star in the nursery play. Like an adoring way.

I explain that with the cost of the box, produce, rope, tissue, printed leaflet and stickers it would only cost £3.20 to make a box. Then I explained that I'd looked into delivery companies and with the size and weight of the boxes we could send it Express for £3.50 a box. Not realising I was walking back and forward with my hand on my head as I spoke.

I finally round up the conversation. "So that's a total of £6.70 and if we sell it for £15 then it could make us a huge profit while getting more customers." I finally gave her a chance to speak.

"Wait, why are you talking about couriers?"

"I decided we should 'go big or go home'."

"Rab I've never seen you ever 'go big'. I felt my face go red and Lizzy nearly fell off her chair from laughing.

"You know what I mean Lizzy." I managed to squeak out trying not to show my embarrassment. "We could sell the boxes in here too but without the welcome leaflet. We could make a selection of fruit ones, veg ones and dairy ones too."

A huge smile appeared on Lizzy's face. "Know what, I'm in! You're basically the one that runs this place as I'm not here very much. I actually think you might be on to something! I'm happy to pass you the reins and fund your idea but I can't promise I can help much with it. I'll give you all the time I have but..."

"No, its fine," I jumped in. "I can deal with this all on my own. You have enough on your plate."

She laid her hand gently on my arm, showing she was grateful for my comment. "Well, why don't you order the stickers and set up a couple different options of boxes in the shop. We can see how we get on for a week or two before hitting the whole of the UK?

Or, taking over the world." She said in a deep evil character like voice making us both laugh.

"That will then give me time to do the numbers and get the money together that you will need."

"Perfect!" I say in too high a pitch. She smiles at my enthusiasm, oblivious as to why I was this excited.

I opened the iPad to give Lizzy a better idea of costs. "For 100 boxes, as my costs are based on wholesale to make it cheaper, and 100 stickers it would be £32. If you're happy to give me £35 then I can get the tissue and rope too."

"Ok!" She handed me her card.

"Why don't we order 200 stickers as they could be used for sealing shut the brown bags in the shop too?"

"Excellent idea! See, that's why you're the Boss." I turned as Lizzy jumped off the counter and we were face to face. So close, that I could feel her breath.

"Sorry." I said as I took a step backwards.

"No problem at all." She said blushing. "I better head off and get back to let my Mum go for a break. Just let me know if there's anything you have forgotten to tell me."

She left the store and for a minute I stood there smelling the remains of her perfume in the air. I couldn't describe the strange feeling I had but it was a nice warm one.

Snapping back into reality, my composure changed as a customer entered the shop.

.oOo.

The cost I quoted Lizzy was already for 200 leaflets, 200 stickers and 200 boxes. I felt a bit bad lying to her but I needed extra to make the ones for the boxes I'm going to actually use.

I was literally stealing from Lizzy and it wasn't like I didn't have the money but if the leaflets were traceable, I couldn't have my address all over it. If it linked back to a business address, then it could have been anyone really. Unlikely but not impossible. The shop phone rang and I was surprised to hear Lizzy's voice from the other end.

"What have you left?" I said making it clear I noticed how forgetful she could be.

"I've not left anything but I did want to ask you something."

"Ok?"

"Since, its Friday night would you like to come to the cinema with me? Not like a date or that." She stumbled out when I didn't answer right away. "It's just the next Saw horror movie has come out and no one I know will ever come with me so I end up sitting alone hiding behind my bag. I don't even know if you like horror, sorry, you probably hate them."

I interrupted her, "Lizzy, that sounds good to me."

"Great! Pick you up say seven tonight?"

"Yup, you know my address."

She laughed, "thanks, oh wait sorry for that."

"Bye Lizzy." I hung up the phone.

It was fine that she confirmed it was not a date as I really wanted to see the new Saw movie too. It would've made a change for me from waiting for it to come out and watching it alone in my room. I was getting what I wanted. I'd pay for the tickets to make up for using her card too.

I had the logo for the shop on the iPad so it didn't take me long to make up the templates for the promotional boxes. I just needed to sort what to write on the ones I'd be sending out. I should've planned all this out, but I was so busy preparing the plan for Lizzy that I didn't have much time to think about it. I kept the leaflet pretty much the same. I just needed to change the shop's name and the sign off from Lizzy. I decided to go with something generic so it could be anywhere. "Farm Fresh," that'd do and just put "from us to you" on the bottom.

I changed the sticker to the same name and picked an outline of a cow from the internet and it was actually was looking quite classy. With everything ordered, I paid with Lizzy's card but addressed the delivery to my name and the shop instead of the post office. This meant it'd take them an extra day to come once they'd found the place, but there was more of a chance of getting them before Lizzy did.

I fired her a wee message from the iPad showing the receipt and asked her to please not open them without me as I wanted to see they were good before showing her. I didn't want her opening them and finding out my hidden agenda.

For the rest of the day, I came up with different ideas for the boxes as I really needed to make this a success. If I was going to be taking the fruit for a hundred "online" orders, I needed to think out hard. I decided on three. A fruit one with the normal apple, banana, berries, and cherries. A vegetable one with a leek, half a cauliflower since the whole one didn't fit, two potatoes, some peppers, baby sweetcorn and a bunch of pea pods. The last one I chose was the "Cheese platter" box but then I realised that this was near £25 as it costed nearly double in produce. I might need to run that one past Lizzy. I added a nice packet of the oatcakes too.

I was so busy with my planning that I lost all track of time.

"Opening late, son," the woman said as she entered the store. "Don't worry, I won't keep you for long. I just need to grab a couple cooking apples for my crumble."

Shit! It was quarter to six. I was meant to close up at five. The woman must have changed her mind since after just telling me she didn't intend to keep me for long, she decided a fifteen minutes chat was in order.

I tried to politely hurry her along by starting to turn off the lights and jangling the keys. Ok, maybe not very politely. She took the hint and finally buggered off. I made sure everything was off and locked the shop door, running all the way home. Great! First time I didn't bring my bike and I was running late.

My dinner was ready when I got in and I started throwing it down my throat.

"Easy, son. Work couldn't have been that busy."

I apologized, accidentally spitting a little mince out my mouth. "I'm running late as Lizzy is picking me up at seven to go to the cinema."

A massive grin appeared on Mum's face but before she had a chance to speak, I jumped in, "No Mum, it's not a date!"

She brushed it off showing she didn't believe me but I didn't had time to fight with her as I needed to jump in the shower. Even though I took a shower in the morning I stilled stank of crushed red peppers from having to clean up the one I stood and slipped on.

Never mind using banana skins to make people slip! Bell peppers might feel firm but once those wee bastards are stood on, they ain't half slippery little fuckers!

I managed to have a shower but I was still rushing about when Lizzy arrived. Shit! Mum let her in and I shouted downstairs, "I will be right there in a few minutes."

I hear Lizzy shout back "Its ok. I've read the tickets wrong and the movie isn't starting until eight."

I was trying to finish sorting all the spiders without being too complacent and killing myself. Finally, I fed them and filled the water bowl of the last one and ran down stairs. Maybe I should have left the shower until after I had sorted them, realising I was back to being a sweety mess. "Sorry for loosing track of time. It's because I ended up closing the shop late.

She turned to Mum jokingly saying, "Sorry I think I have brought out the dark side of your son! Maybe he's now a workaholic?"

"Very funny" I sneered back at Lizzy.

"I've told your mum all about your ideas and I think she's super impressed."

Mum nodded approvingly.

Lizzy interrupted, "Well, we can chat about it when I get back as its already late and we don't want to miss the start."

Mum smiled back at me. "Don't keep him out too late Lizzy. He's got a bed time you know!" She smirked while winking at her.

"Very funny, Mum!" I yelled closing the front door quickly so she couldn't respond.

During the movie we kept screaming with fright and grabbing each other, but then it sent us into fits of laughter. So much so, that the usher had to ask us a couple of times to quieten down and scolded us for acting like a pair of teenagers. We didn't really care as it was the first time in ages, I was enjoying being out. We were surprised to see the ice-cream counter still open in the main lobby when we got out so with a look at each other's face, we decided, "why not?".

Both of us chose massive cones but then nearly dropped dead when the guy asked for a twenty. I felt like spitting it out and giving it back to him. Lizzy set us off again by laughing at the face I must have been making and asked me not to worry as it was on her.

"How the fuck can they charge so much so for a bit of cream and a cone?" I blurted out.

"Easy businessman! With all your plans you will soon have that as pocket change." Lizzy said trying not to laugh.

"Well, thanks for taking the piss out my dreams Lizzy." I said and we were off laughing again.

The sky started to get dark. "I better get you home before your mummy starts looking for you, worried I've kidnapped you." She voiced still laughing. I knocked at her arm that was holding the ice-cream so her nose got covered. She looked a picture! I ended up getting a stitch in my side and realised my ribs were quite sore from laughing so much.

"It's ok old man. The car is open, jump in." Lizzy said acting like my ribs were sore from old age.

.oOo.

When I reached back home, I was talking to Mum about my boxes idea but she was more interested in knowing about how it went with Lizzy tonight. "Looks like you guys had a great time with the number of smiles I'd seen as she drove up the street."

I forgot now that mum was out the chair a lot, she had found a new hobby of being a nosey neighbour. We didn't have the right kind of window covering for it so everyone could see her so she was going to make a name for herself.

"Mum, you need to get a net curtain before you get arrested for stalking people." I said making her laugh.

I couldn't laugh any more as my ribs honestly felt like Mike Tyson had a used them instead of his punch bag.

Mum finally changed the subject "I've had an update from the neighbour tonight."

"What's the update?"

"The family has been in contact and are sorting arrangement for him to be transferred to a special home for people of his...condition." Mum tried hard to keep the awkwardness out of the last bit as we still didn't know how one's meant to say vegetable politely.

"Gee! That must be costing them quite a bit of money to transfer him over to Sweden."

"Nah, they are sending him to one here to try and get the government to pay for it. Apparently, there's no point sending him over there as it's not like he'll notice them not visiting or have any idea of his surroundings." Sh sounded disapproving.

"They probably have their reasons. We don't know the kind of relationship they have had since they left." I surprised myself for not being judgemental, for a change.

"The neighbour felt that this was a little harsh and made that known. Apparently, the family put her back in her place saying he was lucky they were sorting anything for him at all. So maybe you're right." Mum thought for a minute before speaking again and I knew she had something juicy to share. "He didn't choose not to go to Sweden. Well, it's not really a choice to move abroad if you're in prison for the rape of three woman..."

My jaw nearly hit the floor, I knew he was sleezy, but I didn't think he was that bad. "How the hell did he get to move here with no one being told?" I said angrily.

"Well, apparently the police put him here with a new name as he was being threatened by one of the girl's dad and he wasn't backing off with any warnings."

"Good on that guy! Maybe someone should tell him where he is now and then the family won't need to worry about paying for a care home."

We talked long into the night with me having to curve the conversation off Lizzy many times. Mum started finding it funny and called me "defensive".

"How can I be defensive when there's nothing to tell?" I asked Mum. "No one else she knows like horror and she doesn't like going alone. So really, she guilt-tripped me into it." I said leaving out the parts about me paying and us getting ice cream after, which would just have encouraged her.

Mum had a few cans. "I'm getting quite tired so I'm going to call it a night. Can you help me get up the stairs so I can sleep in front of the fish tank?

"Really? I might be young but my back can't hatch pushing you upstairs   tonight."
She headed to the bedroom laughing and I realise she was just taking the piss to see what I would say.

I followed her with her chair and the can that she'd left half finished. She could get herself to bed with no problem but she still found it hard carrying anything while walking. I preferred to do it anyway in case she lost her footing. After a quick chat about our plans for tomorrow, I found out that she'd got the bingo!

YUS!

We say our good nights and I headed upstairs to feed Mary. It'd been a great day today but regardless of anything I needed to push forward with my plan and not let anything stand in a way.

Chapter Fourteen:

Third time lucky, but best of all.

I must admit, I was the most excited about this one. I knew I had a lot of hatred in me for many people but the feelings I had for this "sorry excuse for a human" went beyond that.

Even if I was caught after this one, it would still be completely worth it. I would be more than happy to rot in jail for the rest of my life as long as that piece of shit had got what had been coming to him for years. As mum always says "what's for you, won't pass you" and I was definitely not planning on missing it.

The worst thing about work was that I couldn't choose who gets to come into the shop so I have to just bear it.

Every time it took me so much not to fly across the counter and kill them with my bare hands. I didn't know why I didn't though as I doubted if anyone would jump in to help them. People around here might be too polite to ignore people or admit their true feelings, but they are a good judge of character. People often told my dad to stop hanging about with the low life but for some reason my dad saw something in him. Shame, that no one else had found it.

He made it clear on what an actual piece of shit he was after the accident, how he just abandoned us and then pestering Mum. Many times, I would walk in the room and find Mum pushing him off, trying to pretend everything was ok for my benefit. That was even before Dad died. The way she'd tolerate his comments and put on a fake smile so she didn't punch him in the face in front of me. He was there for every single of my birthdays, Christmas, even for my first day at school. He just never seemed to leave. Mum finally told him off and then one day poof, he was gone.

I was glad when he left. It felt like he was always trying to be a second dad to me, and that really bothered me. It didn't matter what pointless shit I was doing at school that week or how easy the homework was, he insisted to be there to help. I didn't understand why Dad put up with him.

I walked into the kitchen one day to find my parents arguing— they didn't fight often but everyone needs a shouting match sometimes. I heard Dad saying, "just because I can't have kids. . . "

Obviously, he meant after me. I didn't know why he said that, but something must have got broken. He continued, "you let him always take my place. I thought we always agreed I would be the. . ."

I'd had enough and walked in. Anytime I entered the room, it made them stop arguing. Sometimes, I would leave them to it so I could get more TV time or could finish the packet of sweets I was only meant to have a few.

Mum usually took me to school but Dad must have been worried I was upset from seeing them argue so he decided to take me instead.

I didn't know why Mum told him, "don't you dare." She could be a bit selfish like that. It was just one day when she was missing out, so I told her it was fine. I promised Mummy she could take me tomorrow and skipped out the door with Daddy who was standing at the door, ready to leave.

It was a sad day though as Dad told me he had to go to London for a big job so, he'd be away for a while. I tried to put in the pieces of the puzzle and thought that's why they must have been arguing as Mummy would have been upset that he wasn't going to be here.

He told me he would be gone before I got back from school but he would phone me lots and I could call him whenever I wanted, even on the times he was working because he would never be too busy for me. I couldn't actually remember how long he was away for but it felt like months and Mummy was so happy when he finally came back. Looking back, I wished he'd taken that leech because he ended up coming round every day.

This morning I grabbed the two little tubs I put aside a few days ago and carefully packed them in a box so they could breathe but not escape. It was their big day today so I hadn't fed them for four days to make sure they were extra feisty. One of which was Milver, I kept her especially for this job as she didn't need any encouragement when it came to her wanting to bite a hand.

I made my usual changes to one of the veg boxes but this time I added two sides instead of a bottom. The wings of the box still slid in and it actually made it look like it was just a much higher quality of box. It was my best work so far. Since I was putting two in this one, I didn't want them to meet and start fighting. Putting them in either ends and placing stuff in the middle, should solve the issue. I put everything in my back pack and headed off to work. I knew it was going to happen today because he always came in on a Thursday after doing his usual rounds of collecting his mail, having lunch at the cafe and then popping in to put that one or two checky bets on at the bookies. I was probably doing a favour for him anyway. What a stupid mundane life when you do the same things on each day each week. I knew he won't part with his money as he usually only bought one bit like an apple or banana but I had it covered too. I made sure I'd thought of everything this time as didn't want anything to go wrong.

He always showed up between three and half past three so I knew I had plenty of time to get everything ready and I didn't want to put my plan at risk by preparing it too early. At two o'clock I started putting it together. I took the modified box and started filling it with the selection of Cheese we had, knowing I couldn't risk putting the spiders in the fridge but the cheese should be fine only being out for a couple hours.

I took the box to the back of the counter and got out the tongs. This was a risk if anyone came in but it should be fine as no one came back here except Lizzy and she just left an hour ago after having lunch. I managed to get the little spiders in each end being careful to watch the hole from the first one while placing in the second, in case, it runs out. I said to Milver, "I know you won't let me down." And I get her safely in the hole. I quickly closed the lid making sure there was no gaps and tightened it up with the rope. I placed it on one of the stickers and slipped it under the counter ready for his arrival.

When Lizzy was here earlier, I told her that I was going to give away one of our "cheese board" boxes as a prize to our 1000th sale customer to promote them as they have just been added to the shop. She agreed and asked me how close we were to that number.

"I'm not telling you. You greedy bitch because you'll start buying single items to get it!"

She punched me in the arm for my cheek

"It's super close so will definitely be today."

I chose the cheese box as I knew he couldn't resist it. To be fair, he'd take anything that was free. I could have told him I had filled the box with dog shit but if it was free, he would have still taken it. *Oh! I should have thought of that before!*

I could have put wee chucks of shit in the cheese and told him it was a new recipe. Well, I was not bloody going to open it again now, those wee buggers could be hiding anywhere by now.

At three o'clock the bell on the door rang, but it was not him. I'd been keeping an eye on the till receipt numbers being ready to put through two random orders for it to be sitting on 999 when he came. The woman picked a bunch of grapes from the red and the green pile and headed to the machine to print her ticket. She stood there for a couple minutes all confused, before finally calling me over. She had placed both bunches in the same bag so didn't know if she had to pick green grapes or red.

I explained that it didn't matter, and they were both the same price by weight. That was only there so we could work out how to make it one option for grapes. The machine had its own pre-set options and there didn't appear to be one for "Grapes". I printed off her label and I was taking her over to the till, when I saw him walk in. Looking as cocky as usual and wandering about the shop, waiting to start up a conversation when I was finished with this lady.

I double checked the woman's receipt and saw 998. Perfect! I'd just need to ring through one thing. I was prepared for this too and had printed a label for an orange earlier that I had sitting by the till. I quickly scanned it through and hit cash. I'd put the money in once he was gone.

"Hey pal, you're looking particularly well today, must be hanging about with all this fruit and veg". Billy said all cheery.

"Eh, yeah". I replied trying to push out a laugh.

"How's things going? How your mum?" He continued but I zoned out as I was not interested in talking to him and would rather he would just pick his measly piece of fruit and go away. "Would you recommend anything for me today? Anything that's at its best or new in?" He asked this every week!

"Nope, just the same. We do have the new selection boxes, but they have more than one item in them so probably not for you." I felt the sharpness in my tongue and saw he looked hurt.

I didn't care. Soon I won't ever have to even see his face again, so he could sulk all he wanted.

In that very moment, a lady entered the shop hurriedly and ran to pick up a melon. "I've left my sleeping baby in the car," she said to him, "I need to be superfast. Do you mind if I go first?"

"No, go right ahead."

Oh fuck! I should have waited to put that orange through. She was now going to be the winner and it was not like I could just not give her it. I had popped the sign on the counter when the last woman left and he was already saying to her, "Oh! Look. You're the lucky customer, you'll win that cheese pack."

166

I took the melon from her not being able to do anything else and went to scan the sticker. "Wait," she said rumbling about in her bag, "shit! Sorry, I must have left my purse in the car."

She looked around waiting to see if either of us would offer but he was a broke prick and I couldn't be seen giving produce away.

She said she'd just need to come back for it another day as she didn't want to wake her baby just for a melon. *Well, why didn't she just go, get her purse, and leave the baby again to come back?* But she was looking quite pissed off so I didn't dare say that to her.

He tried making small talk with me again. "Have you changed your mind about joining me for fishing yet."

Nope still a big fat no looser! "No!" I said back quite harshly.

He handed over the banana that he's being shuffling about in his hands the whole time we'd been talking. "I'll take this, thanks".

He'd probably made it all bruised by now. I ring it through the till and like Lizzy said it made a wee tune.

He looked at me confused. "I've never heard it make that noise before Pal. Think you've maybe broke it." He smiled trying to have a joke with me.

"No, it means you've won the cheese box." I corrected him handing it over tying to act like I was doing it grudgingly.

"Nice, I'll have that as a lovely wee snack when I get home, unless you fancy cracking it open here and sharing it?"

"No, thanks. I can eat the cheese whenever I want and if you haven't noticed I'm actually working."

He felt the coldness in my voice and took the hint to leave with his surprise box. How could he honestly try being friendly to me after everything he'd done? Or more so, he didn't do what he should have done?

He called himself a friend, maybe, he got his dictionary from a parallel universe. See you never, you absolute, sad, sack. Hope you enjoy your cheese with an added bit of venom, prick.

I felt relieved and happy inside that I'd finally seen him for the last time. There was no need to be trying to cheer Mum up or reassuring her when this death will come out. Maybe we'd have a party and she could literally dance on his grave, probably not for too long, but I'd take her chair so she doesn't use her energy walking there. I closed the shop with a skip in my step and even bought a cheese box for Mum. She didn't come in the shop much as she was not one for fruit and veg but she did love a good bit cheese. That was not the only gift I'd prepared for her today, but I'd never be able to admit the first one.

.oOo.

I knew something was not right when I walked in the door and saw Mum's face.

"What's wrong?" I asked.

"Sit down, son." I did as I was told.

She inhaled a deep breath, "They have just found Billy dead in his car next to the lake."

I tried not to jump of joy but I couldn't even muster up a pretence that strong. I just asked, trying to hide the resentment, "so what?"

Mum snapped her head fast around to look at me. "What do you mean by so what?"

"Well, why are you looking upset?" I tried controlling my victorious grin and spoke effortlessly, "The guy was a complete waste of space. He could have helped this family but he chose to be a coward. I'd be more interested if you told me you went for a shite."

"Rab, don't talk like that!" Mum's eyes went red with fury. "I didn't bring you up to be so cold hearted, he's still a person and he was..." She paused for a bit before continuing, "he was Dad's friend and there were lots of happy times."

"Right, fine maybe that was a little mean of me but I still don't care. What did he do? Eat himself to death, the greedy pig."

She looked at me quizzingly and I realised I might have slipped up there. I covered up, "I mean, only a couple hours ago, he won the cheese box at the shop. I was just meaning did he just ram it all down his fat neck before he got home?"

There was silence for a bit before Mum seemed to shake off her thoughts and move on. "The police said they found a suicide note and a gun in the driver's door, although he didn't have any bullet wounds so must have just had that as back up. They have taken him to the morgue and have asked if we want to help organize his funeral."

The fucking cheek of the man! Why would the police come here to tell us? Why would they think we would want to help? Most people knew how close we used to be but they would have also remembered him bailing out on us and losing that place in our family. Where the hell was the rest of his family? I knew he moved here when my dad offered him a job but why didn't he return when everything went sour? What had he got here to hang around for? I knew he had a family because he used to bloody tell me all the time about them. He'd give me updates on how his nieces and nephews were doing and even set up a Skype call with them once but the image was so jittery that we couldn't see anyone and gave up in the end.

I met a few of them as he insisted. I went over for a bit when they were there for a visit. Poor family! Not because he's dead, but I actually didn't mind them and they had him as a son, brother, or uncle. Well, they didn't need to worry about him anymore. His mum was dead nice. She often told me to call her Granny a couple times but she was old and must've been losing her marbles. She was good at making me feel better though. Whenever I fell or got hurt, she used to bring me sweets and toys from home. Not sure where his home was, I think it was either Aberdeen or Dundee. Well, it was sad that I won't ever see his family again because even though I hated Billy I didn't mind chatting with them whenever I bumped into them.

I went upstairs because Mum seemed to be in a huff with me and I couldn't bother trying to work out why. I heard the door opening and Mum letting someone in. It sounded like Lizzy's mum and I heard them heading into the kitchen, shutting the door behind them.

I realised I'd left my back pack down stairs so I ran down to get it. They both fell silent when I entered. "Don't worry you don't need to stop talking about him when I walk in, I hated him too."

Mum looked at her with a look I'd never seen before. What the hell was wrong with them? Why were they upset? Dad always said to never try to understand a woman as it's too hard and, in that moment, I thought it was best to take his advice.

Mum piped up when I turned to leave. "We will be going to the funeral, Rab." She said it like an order and not a request.

Did she never notice that I was an adult and could make my own decision? I tried controlling my outburst, "No, I fucking will not. Why the hell would I go? Why would you go either?"

"We will go out of respect."

"I don't have any fucking respect for a twat like him."

I was about to lose my shit but Mum interrupted me. "I don't want you not going, in case, you regret it one day."

"Mum! Do you hear yourself? Why would I regret it? I'm not standing here pretending to be a big man and secretly dying inside. I know he was around lots when I was wee but I don't care about that now. I don't care about that time! Well, I do because Dad was there but not about Billy." I felt my words becoming angry.

"Look Rab, you're going because one day when you get older and maybe even have kids of your own. You might realise what you had and wished you had went!"

"Bull shit!" I shouted and slammed the door behind me.

I threw my bag on the bed and paced in the room. *What an ungrateful bitch!* I immediately regretted thinking that about Mum.

I knew she didn't know but I did this for her and now she was pretending that she had lost some one she actually cared about. I tried calming myself down.

Maybe Dad was right. Maybe, I'd never understand why they were acting like that. I supposed I was only young but they two down there had been best friends since school so they would have had many more years with them. Maybe that was why they were sad. Maybe his death made them forget about what a shit head he actually was.

Either way, I was not going. I never pretended that I even had one ounce of care for the guy and I was not about to start now. I felt angry that Mum even asked me to go. Maybe it was an age thing. Maybe they were taught that they had to show respect to the death even if it was the Devil himself, so that he doesn't curse them and come for them next.

Maybe that's why we always hear about the wee old buddies attending everyone's funeral. Maybe it was not because there was usually free grub and drinks after. Maybe they were trying to keep their clock ticking a little longer.

I somehow managed to make myself giggle thinking that it might actually be like shopping for their own. Seeing what other people do. What they like about it and what they don't. I never understood why people talked about their funeral. It wasn't like they were going to be around to see it!

Waste of money! Set a bonfire in the garden and chuck them on that, people can still be there.

Chapter Fifteen:

Choosing the wasters

It had been three days since Billy was found and I'd hardly spoken to mum. She was actually been busy sorting that prick's funeral! She asked me again about going and even Lizzy tried convincing me. Lizzy said that Mum was clearly asking me as Mum wanted me there to support her. I finally give into the pleadings of both the women.

I did however make it very clear to not to expect me pretending being sad and if anyone asked, I was not going to lie about my feelings. She didn't agree but we left it at that. I really didn't know why she needed me there as she had Lizzy's mum and it was not like there were going to be lots of people there to even notice if she went or not. It was probably ending up with his and my family.

Well, I'd be glad when it'd all be over. Lizzy was managing the shop from twelve that day so I could go. She wanted to close it but I wasn't having him affecting her business too. The post office was already shut for a day, because Lizzy's mum would be with my mum.

I was home by half past twelve like I promised and ran upstairs to get changed. I threw on black jeans and a black t-shirt. It was not the proper dress for a funeral but that was the best he was getting. He was lucky that he was even getting that.

Lizzy's mum drove us to the church and I couldn't believe my fucking eyes. It was like the whole village was there. Unless they were there to spit on his grave I couldn't understand why. Maybe I'd been wrong about these people. Maybe they were all two-faced arseholes.

I shuffled into the back of the church ready to dive out the minute it was over. I made it clear to Mum that I was not going to the wake and I think, she heard the sincerity in my voice as she didn't mention it again. People were looking at Mum funny and one person even said to me "I'm sorry for your loss".

Was I the one that was actually dying there because those absolute fannies had lost their mind? I bit my lip so hard to refrain myself from standing up and proclaiming how much I hated the guy and hated all them for pretending they didn't. Thankfully, the service started and no one else spoke to me. Lizzy's mum was holding Mum's hand and I could see Mum was holding back her tears.

I love Mum, but I was actually feeling angry towards her. Hopefully, it was just an act or it was this respect thing she kept saying about and after today we wouldn't even talk about him ever again. My first actual victim and she was ruining the enjoyment for me because she'd suddenly decided he wasn't that bad.

As soon as the doors re-opened, I was out. Lizzy's mum started shouting after me trying to tell me the car was locked but I told her that I was walking home.

It was about an hour away but I didn't care, even that wouldn't have been long enough to calm me down. I couldn't stop trying to work out why there were so many people and why they were so upset. I didn't think that I'd ever know the reason and just started calling them names in my head. I must have been walking quite fast as I was already at my front door and didn't remember passing any of the usual scenes.

It didn't matter as I'd gotten things to do. I'd people to choose. Wish I could just release them all on those fuckers in the church but there was no way I could get away with that. As much as I hated them all, jail wasn't the place for me. I knew to make my plan work, I'd need two spiders in each box. That meant I could

173

send out fifty-eight and then one flying solo. It was not what I hoped for but I knew it had to suffice for now. I switched the computer on and knew it was risky, but I needed to start searching for the lucky people's names. I was not going to search a name directly because obviously I didn't know them but I was going to look up big companies and then randomly select one or two for each.

I began by selecting some law firms, and then some police head offices. I really wanted to send some to the fucking high up doctors but that was risky as someone might recognise the signs and save them. The teachers, owners of large building firms, dentists and a couple from the gaming industry who thought it was a good idea to make stupid games for kids like grand theft auto. I held back on my wish to send one to the old Prime Minister as that would be a stupid move. There was no point trying to target high up people if you knew it was just their receptionists that'd open the parcel. I needed to try and hit people at work so no home addresses were on my computer, while making sure that they were not too important that they wouldn't actually open it themselves. There was just so many to pick from!

The front door closing startled me and I was surprised to see from the window that it was dark outside. The last couple hours had just zoomed past and I had fifty-one people selected from about twenty different companies. I had them written in pen on a note pad. I'd done it this way so I could just chuck the list in a fire when done. I had thought about putting them on the computer's notepad but I had no idea how I would be able to completely remove it and didn't want to have to chuck my computer in the fire. I was trying to concentrate on the last ones but could hear Mum sobbing and Lizzy's mum trying to console her.

The anger in me raised to a significant level, but I tried to ignore it. I'd already said my piece and it wouldn't have helped going down to have another argument. She could do whatever the fuck she wanted today but I would never understand it. I didn't want to understand it, and I didn't care!

I'd wasted enough time on that arsehole and now he was finally gone. There was no way he was getting any more time from me. I put my headphones on and tried to concentrate on picking the last couple of companies. I decided to send the last baskets to employees at three different chocolate and sweet companies. They charged way too much for sweets these days that poorer kids couldn't afford them often so that was a good reason in itself.

I finished writing the last of the names and addresses in my notebook and hid it in my underwear drawer. I was content with my choices although it would have been nice to try to get more people but from my previous experience, I knew it wasn't a good chance to send just one spider.

I couldn't wait to get rid of the little guys as feeding, changing water and just keeping them alive was a huge amount of work however, I'd grown fond of them. I think, I was going to miss them once they'd be gone. They did good. Nice and strong. And there were no fatalities yet, which I was surprised at but really as long as the temperature is right, they have food and water then, not much could go wrong. Mary on the other hand didn't seem to have a care in the world.

I wished I could bounce back like she did. Losing the only mate she knew, and then having all her babies taken, she still just plodded about and enjoyed teasing her prey. I wished I could know what she was thinking.

By the time I sorted all my wee soldiers it was well into the evening and I realized how hungry I felt. Mum hadn't dropped any food at my door or tried to call me down. She seemed mad at me or maybe disappointed, to which I had no idea. I didn't do anything wrong and even went to the goddamn funeral! There were more reasons for me to be angry at her than the other way around.

However, I couldn't stay mad at Mum for long. Even if it did hurt me the way she was acting today but I was hell trying to get her to forgive me, when I'd already bent myself backwards for her, completely swallowing my pride. I'd rather sit up here and starve. I heard Lizzy's mum leaving a while ago and Mum's bedroom door closing so she was probably away to bed but I was still not risking going down there.

I sat watching Mary for a while and then got into bed and checked the box for anything good to watch. As usual there was nothing great on it, but I found Spiderman running on a channel and I decided to watch it.

With the TV on I just laid there silently, trying to keep my mind from thinking how hurt I was by Mum and the rest of the village. I thought there'd be a massive cheer and party that the fucker was now dead but everyone actually seemed sad. It just didn't make any sense. Maybe they just felt sorry for the sad sack. I didn't want to seem rude by being so cheery. *Fake, weak, two-faced arse scratchers are who they are!*

To be fair, I didn't think much else of them before so I didn't know why it surprised me so much. At least, Lizzy didn't seem like she cared or even suggested she was interested in going to the twat's funeral. Glad one person saw sense.

I suddenly felt a little guilty that I was using Lizzy to complete my mission but then remembered the end result was more important than upsetting one person, especially if that one person was someone I'd hated my whole life. Maybe hate was a strong word. Now that I'd got to know her a bit more, I wouldn't say I hated her. But I still wouldn't say she's amazing.

I recalled that I never turned my phone back on since the funeral and found four missed calls from Lizzy. I sent her a text back saying I was fine and would see her on Monday at work.

I hoped she got the hint that I didn't want her coming to visit me before then. She had been visiting often these days, not because I wanted her to, but because it was easier talking business in my living room. When we were both at different shops, we could only catch each other for our hour lunch. The hour lunch had become a tradition. Lizzy brings me food from the shop. She said that it was included in my wage and she wanted to make sure I had something proper to eat but I knew it is her way of checking that I'd not just left or set the place on fire.

The shops were actually pretty busy and there were lots of regulars that came on set days and times. There's one wee girl Sophie who asked me every week if I've got anything different coming in. She is eight years old, I think. Once I bought in a dragon fruit and the other time a papaya. It was funny watching how much it blew her tiny mind. I didn't know any other exciting fruits but I'd need to look for another one as she wouldn't stop asking.

I finally found a fruit called lychees that I was able to order through the supplier and it took my mind off the dramas of the day.

I learnt where they come from, how they got their name and one little fun fact about them. I actually felt a little excited to show it to Sophie on her next visit. She always made me try them with her. Her Mum insists on paying for fruit she hadn't asked me to order and I'm usually sitting eating it too.

Sophie liked to ask questions about the new fruit to expand her knowledge. So, I tried to pick her up a new thing each week. Lizzy laughed at my "little bestie"! I think she is just jealous.

Lizzy says, "long as your careful not to order something with a big stone in it that might choke her, then all's good,"

We laughed when I suggested I'll buy that fruit for Lizzy, instead.

I smiled thinking about Sophie and Lizzy. I hadn't watch any of the movie and I realized I was actually exhausted so I turned the box off and settled down to sleep.

I had marked three weeks from now on the calendar, which was a Thursday. It was the only day of the week that it would work.

With the feeling of disgust and anger at people due to the funeral, I saw myself becoming a bit weak and needed to make sure I wreaked my revenge on this world. Mum was back on her feet again but that didn't change the fact that Dad wasn't here. I had to get my head strong and get on with it. I knew I'd feel better once the deed was done.

Chapter Sixteen:

Promotional Plan

The printer I ordered from Amazon arrived a couple days ago and was still sitting boxed, ready to be set up. I'd never set up a printer but it had instructions and it apparently was "easy". I'd bought extra black ink too so I should be able to get the address labels printed without having to order anymore. I had all the leaflets for the fake company under my bed but I couldn't find a template for address labels so I figured I'd make one myself. *It can't be that hard, right?*

 I didn't want to risk showing my hand-writing which could be used to track me down later, by writing it by hand.

I'd got all the boxes I needed at the shop so I just needed to work out the fruit order. I'd been busy over the last couple weeks showing Lizzy orders that have been coming in from our "online site" which was essentially me adding the pretend order information and saying the money had come into my account so I'd transfer it over. I couldn't actually attach the shop bank details to a fake site so I told her I couldn't work out how to do it, as it automatically added mine. It was all good though because in reality there were no bank details.

I was making up the orders on a "Demo type thing" and would be sending the money straight from me. Nothing that could lead them back to us as I'd create a proper site similar after the deed was done.

It broke my heart selling those records but I got £1500 which meant I could fund the last part of my plan.

I managed to slip in thirty-eight "online orders" and told her seventeen people have phoned into the shop to order one so I only needed to add another four fake orders and then I'd be good to go. It would bring them to fifty-nine boxes at £15 each so I transferred £885 into the business account.

I told Lizzy that because it was a promotion then there'd be a closing date which just so happened to be today. I had to make it on a Friday to give me time to get the fruit ordered for the following week and get the boxes made up. I texted Lizzy the final order numbers and put the fruit order through to arrive on Wednesday next week.

Lizzy wanted to post them all from her other shop but I told her it would be cheaper through the courier I have found, just for this bulk delivery. We could use the post office as further orders came in.

I had to make up a fake courier service too. It was hard to keep up with all the lies but had to be done.

In reality, I'd be taking them to another post office but it was going to be risky. I had a plan but this was where it could all go wrong however, it was the one last risk I need to take.

I had a delivery coming today of two large bags of shredded paper to go under the fruit. I hoped it was enough as I needed the little guys to be able to hide down in there so they were not squashed by any moving fruit. Each box could fit a blood orange, banana, little bundle of green and red grapes, a red and green apple and some nuts that we had just started supplying. I worked out an arrangement that should stop the fruit moving too much but needed the shredded paper just in case.

The delivery was scheduled on Thursday. It had to be this Thursday otherwise the whole plan would be ruined. I wouldn't be able to try again as the fruit will rot.

I was going to be breaking a few laws but the most worrying thing was that I didn't have a driver's license. If I was pulled over not only, would I be facing jail, but also, be driving a stolen vehicle, probably speeding and with loads of deadly parcels. There is no CCTV in these little places so I didn't need to worry about being disguised and I made sure I chose a place where I knew nobody knows me. There's no way I can jump the ferry as they knew me so I had to try and choose somewhere not too far to drive to but far enough away that I shouldn't be seen by anyone.

I had the plan in my mind. Derek, the mechanic has a small van that he kept outside his garage and the keys for it inside. He used it just for work so it will definitely be there. It will be Thursday morning so his Mrs will have been to the Bingo the night before with Mum so they will both be having a long and Derek was in Isle of mull for stag do so the garage will be empty.

The place I chose to send the parcels from was Sour lies. I knew you couldn't make this shit up! SOUR-LIES! What a great name for my devious plan to start the last leg of its journey! I found that it should take about an hour to get there and an hour back but I needed to give it about another hour at the post office, as it was going to take time to process them all. I had driven lots of times before because there were lots of little private grounds that you could practice on and the villagers didn't care if you had a license when they were drunk and wanted to get back home with their car.

If I left at 5 a.m., I should be there for the post office opening at 6 a.m. and would be back by 8 a.m. No one would notice and I could still be ready to start work at 9 a.m. I would take cash so there wouldn't be any bank details to be traced and would use a mixture of older notes instead of new ones from the machine.

Derek had a broken window latch at his garage and I'd been to check that I could open it from the outside. It was a little bit of body bending but I could fit in to get the keys and get back out. There was also no alarm as the box on the front was just a fake, deterrent. I was not sure who the hell it was meant to deter as he had told everyone in the village that it was fake!

By the end of Saturday, I printed off all the labels with the different names and address. It was easier than I thought it but after that, I had to become a technical genius and master a degree to get the bloody printer set in! I realised I couldn't just put the address on the box as I was going to have to put some paper round each package as I was worried the wee guys might get out the gaps in the side if the box was to be slightly squeezed at any point.

Also, I didn't want them looking unusual or anyone remembering delivering lots of white boxes so brown paper made them look less noticeable. I also printed off the extra labels to go on the top of the ones that were being packaged together but just randomly picked one of the colleagues' names in that company. I printed off return labels to a made-up company in the USA so that if in the very rare event that some box couldn't be delivered, I knew it will still be in a warehouse for ages somewhere and then probably binned. I knew that meant those wee guys won't make it but again sacrifices had to be made.

I really struggled to sleep and settle the next couple nights but finally Wednesday arrived and I knew I had got to move fast.

I told Lizzy that I needed to take the fruit delivery home with me after my shift so I could build the boxes at home because the courier company was collecting them from my house early the next day. Lizzy will meet me after work and bring the delivery up to mine in the car as is not all going to fit on my trailer.

The workday dragged and it felt like it was never going to be the time for closing. I knew how much work I had ahead of me and that I needed to be completely ready to leave and be at the garage by 5 a.m. I would use my bike to get to the garage and then use the van. I thought I would get them all on my trailer but started to worry if some might fall off and get damaged or the little ones might get too cold. The trailer was also a bit squeaky so I might wake someone with me trying to get it ready. I just needed to keep faith that Mum wouldn't wake up. There was a risk of some neighbour seeing me, but I had my excuses at the ready.

After what felt like a whole week, the clock struck 5 p.m. and I heard Lizzy parking up. "Wow, look at you Mr Organised!" Lizzy said entering the shop.

I already had the delivery at the front door ready to put it in her car. "Wouldn't want to be late for the collection tomorrow. Oh, did you remember to bring rolls of thick brown parcel paper Lizzy?"

"Yeah, they are in the car."

It doesn't take long to pack the car and in no time, we were parking up in front of my house. "Thanks Lizzy. I'll get everything out quickly so you can head home." I spoke leaving the car to start unloading but Lizzy jumped out the car too. *Shit!*

"Come on let's get this done, after all it's our adventure so can't leave you to do all the work." Lizzy said with a massive smile on her face. I was not fast enough to make an excuse before Mum opened the door and she started carrying the apples in.

How the fuck am I going to get rid of her? I couldn't have her helping me make up fake boxes! I could feel myself starting to sweat and Lizzy tried to comfort me with words I couldn't even hear due to my heart pounding so loud. Next thing I knew Mum was sticking her neb in too.

"I've never seen you this stressed before Rab. Clearly this means a lot to you!"

If only she knew how right she was.

We got everything upstairs into my living room and I went to retrieve the boxes and shredded paper. Luckily, I didn't put the labels on them yet or the leaflets inside. All three of us were all hands-on deck and the boxes began to fill.

I showed them how to fill the box so the fruit stayed put and before long half the boxes were already done. I was still trying to think of a plan to get rid of them. I could feel the sickness and dizziness taking over me. I couldn't get my head straight to think but then I heard the dreaded words.

"All done. Rab, can you go get the leaflets and labels?"

I looked up to see them high-fiving at their good work and I suddenly came up with a plan that could give me a couple more minutes to think.

"I've not printed them yet. I mean, I've typed them all up but just not physically printed them yet." I paused for a while before continuing, "It will take some time to print them. You both just continue with your evening plans and I'll finish them myself."

Lizzy, as helpful as ever, chipped in, "I've got the leaflets printed and delivered already. We can do them while you print the labels."

I nodded while staying silent and stood up heading towards my room.

"Shit!" I heard Mum say as I left the room.

"What is it?" Lizzy responded with concern in her voice.

"I've been having so much fun that I didn't realise the time! I'm meant to be at the Bingo in ten minutes and I'm not even changed!"

"Rab" I heard Lizzy shout, so I headed back through.

"I'm sorry, Rab, but do you mind if I abandon you to take your mum to the bingo?"

"Not at all." I said trying to act all cool and not show the joy and relief I feel. "Then you can just head off home as I can get the leaflets in while the labels print, then all done."

"Thanks, son!"

They both smiled at me and Mum darted off to get changed.

I looked around the room and noticed there was still a sealed box. I chimed pointing towards the box, "Lizzy, if all the boxes are made up then what it's for?"

"Oh, sorry. I forgot about that. It's a little tank that I was going to set up for my mum as she's missing Pops' fish but wonder if I can leave it here until I can get everything else for it so my mum doesn't see it and ruin the surprise. I should have asked before bringing it in, would you mind?"

"Yeah, no problem. It will be fine in the living room."

"Thank you!" She stepped forward and gave me a little hug. I just froze, not sure how to respond. Lizzy sensed my discomfort and pulled back. "Sorry."

"Don't be. I'm sorry. Just not used to hugging someone."

"I best get going or your mum's going to miss the Bingo. I am super grateful for all the hard work you're putting into the shop, might need to make you my partner after doing all this." I blushed.

"Business partner, I mean." Lizzy giggled, then started heading down the stairs.

She shouted out to Mum "I'll go heat up the car and meet you out there" and just like that they were both gone. Mum to the rescue again!

I couldn't bring myself to get the fake leaflets out until I heard the car leave just in case one comes up stairs and catches me. I heard the car pulling out its space so I waited a couple seconds before running downstairs locking the front door then diving back upstairs. *Ah! Time to finish this!*

I grabbed three boxes and took them through to my room. I knew I'd locked the front door but wanted to do it with my bedroom door lock on too as I couldn't have any surprises when handling the poisonous little biters.

I got out six little guys and put the labels on the boxes, setting aside the label for the outside of the box. I needed to be quick but also really careful. I couldn't just empty the tub into the box because it would then be full of dirt and water so I decided to place the little tub in the corner and with a chopstick, I nudged the wee guy out. I needed to try and do it with the second tub while watching the first guy and I suddenly realized how dangerous it was.

I can do it, I have to! No going back now!

I got the first two in the box with the leaflet and quickly closed it all up. I raced to get the next two boxes complete as didn't want any of them trying to escape through the gaps. But before long all the three were wrapped in brown paper and tied lightly with string to stop the boxes from slipping off each other. Now, I just had to get all the others done in the same way without killing myself and it'd be all done.

I sat at the edge of the bed panting but finally all was done. The journey shouldn't be too long so they should have enough air to keep them alive. I hadn't fed them for two weeks either so they should be nice and desperate for a bite. I was not sure where I was going to put them tonight? I didn't fancy sleeping in a room full of killing machines that might get out but also couldn't put them near the front door in case Mum falls into them.

My living room was the place I decided to keep them for now. Then, in the morning, I'd have taken them down to the garage. I knew I had only limited time to rest, so with the time being at 11:40, I didn't waste any time in heading to bed. Surprisingly, sleep claimed me within moments.

Chapter Seventeen:

Mailing Day

I was startled awake by a loud bang and the sound of Mum roaring with laughter. I could hear that poor bugger Nigel trying to get Mum to stand and literally having to carry her through to her room. I didn't even feel bad not going down to help as he knew he didn't have to give her a lift home. It was not his job until she was in the care home with the other oxygen wasters. I looked at my phone and saw it was just five minutes past one. Double checking that I'd set an alarm for half past four, I settled down to get more sleep. I heard the front door closing, locking and the keys being posted back through the letterbox. *Good man that Nigel, really.*

I could hear a phone ringing in my dream but couldn't reach it. I was stretching and stretching until I fall and hit the floor. I sat up awake to find out that I'd actually fallen out of my bed and indeed, my phone was ringing. I turned it over to see three missed calls from Lizzy. It was fucking 2 a.m., what the hell could she want? Was she ok? Did she find out my plan? Was it her mum?

My hands were shaking but I managed to hit the dial button on her contact. "Lizzy what's wrong?" I spoke the minute she answered.

"I'm ok Rab. It's the farmer."

"EH?"

"I'm actually nearly already at your house. One of the heifers is struggling to calf and he really needs more pairs of hands, can you come help?"

"Of course, I'll be out in two."

I threw on some jeans and a hoodie from the floor and raced downstairs. I could hear mum snoring her head off.

Lizzy arrived as I was locking the door and I jumped in the back of her car telling her to just go. I'd never delivered a calf before but after loads of lambs, I was sure it couldnt be much different.

"I help out with calving patterns every year." Lizzy said racing towards the farm. She must have caught my confused look in the rear-view mirror. "Calving patterns. It's what they call it for cows, just like lambing is for sheep."

"I didn't know that." I was referring to not knowing that Lizzy helped with the calves not that it was called calving patterns... Well, actually, I didn't know either.

She continued, "usually, all the calves are born by now so they were worried there was something wrong with this cow's pregnancy already. The vet thought she had maybe just been caught late by the bull but the farmer knows his stuff and knew he had removed the bull at the right time." Glancing in the mirror to check I was still listening, she huffed, "looks like the calf is really big so she's struggling to push it out so that's why he needs more hands."

"Eh, hold on." Felling a little rude for interrupting her, as I could hear the emotion in her voice, I asked, "how can more hands help push?"

"No, pull silly! It's not like with lambs where you can grab both legs and pull. With calves you tie ropes around them then pull each time the cow pushes. It's hard work and can take a few people." She parked the car at the end off the sheds and we both jumped out.

We could see which barn they were in due to the bright light so without wasting a moment, we headed in that direction. We found that the farmer had already tied the rope to the calf and his farm hand was trying to pull. The farmers at the front end of the cow tried to keep her standing and told the helper when to pull but the calf didn't seem to be budging.

Lizzy took over from the farmer at the front and started to calm the cow down, stroking her and trying to make her as comfortable as possible. The farmer shouted for me to help with the ropes as he got to the back of the cow while trying to examine how the calf was stuck.

After another four or five pushes, the cow was exhausted and her legs were wobbly.

"Come on," Lizzy said, "you can do this. I know you can, just like your mummy done for you."

It was no use though, and the cow dropped to her knees. We all stopped for a bit to catch our breath.

"I think we should call for the vet now." The farm hand suggested.

"Hold on a minute." The farmer said clearly thinking something through in his head. "Run to the fridge and get out the large stallion that's sitting in the bottom." I didn't know what he meant but the farm hand clearly did as he dashed over to the fridge.

The farmer then poured in a solution. "The vet left this on his last visit to give the cow if she got too weak. It might give her the boost she needs."

The cow didn't seem to want to drink so the farmer starts putting a tube into the back of her mouth.

I think it's safe to say that this is nothing like lambing and I'll thank my chickens never to have to do it again. I think to myself. Also realising that one fall from the cow and the massive burger meat could kill me! But I try to hold back my fear and the worry I felt that this might end bad.

Lizzy was still at the cow's head talking gently to her and telling her all will be ok. I suppose if you were in a bad situation then Lizzy is the person you would want. She keeps her cool and never seems to show any fear or doubt.

After a few minutes, the cow was back on her feet and seemed to have a second wind.

"Pull!" The farmer shouted as he manages to pull a leg free.

"Pull." He shouted again and there did seem to be a little movement. On the third pull, I give it my all and suddenly I was flying backwards into the side of the barn and the farm hand landed on top of me.

I lifted my head to see the calf was out and gave out a big sigh of relief. Everyone was quiet for a couple more seconds until the farmer shouted, "IT'S OK."

Everyone started laughing at the sight of me and the other guy who thankfully took the majority of the fluid that came rushing out the back end of the cow. I was glad he fell on top of me. The farmer rubbed the calf down with the dirty straw and placed it in front of its mum which encouraged her to start licking and the calf to started moving. I stood there admiring the view and feeling thankful that both were safe and well.

As the farmers said, we were not out of the woods yet, but this was enough for me right now. Lizzy caught my eye and I watched as she stood there gleaming with pride and I felt the same pride. She saw me looking and a huge smile appeared on her face and I felt one stretching on mine too but I caught myself and broke the stare.

The car journey back home was peaceful until I heard an alarm coming from my phone. *SHIT! It's four thirty, fuck off! No way!*

Lizzy jumped at the noise. "Why the hell do you have an alarm set for this time in the morning?"

"Sorry I meant to set it for half past 7 but still getting used to this phone."

Lizzy had given me her old phone just a couple months ago, saying it was for business reasons so I needed a reliable one. Besides it was her old one and she didn't need it.

She laughed. "Well, at least I know you won't be late for work anytime soon. I'll give you a lesson on the phone tomorrow if you like?"

"Thanks, but I'm not that old! I'm sure I'll get used to it."

We pulled up outside my house. "Thank you again for coming to help Rab."

"It was my pleasure. I care for the animals a lot too." With that we bid each other good night.

I stood in the hallway for a minute wondering if I had time to get changed. I decided to just change my jeans and wear a hoodie over the t-shirt. I didn't have the time to have a shower but also didn't want to leave a mess in the van. I grabbed the old tank that I didn't need and popped all the little babies' tubs inside. I carefully got all the boxes down to the front door and just hoped that Mum didn't wake or come investigating. To be fair, I could still hear her snoring and so I was a bit assured.

I creeped back outside and grabbed my bike that I'd left and the side of the house and headed off to the garage, going past the shop to throw the tank in. No one was going to look in there and even if they did, they could think it was from a florist maybe. I was surprisingly not that tired, pulling the calf must have woken me up good. I whizzed down the black streets and I made it to the garage at 5 a.m. *Thank God! First goal done.*

I pulled away the little stone that Derek was using to hold the window shut and did my body bop moves to get in. Trying my hardest not to scream, I placed my hand down on some jaggy tool. I was in but I could see blood dripping from my hand and onto the floor. I searched around looking for a first aid kit which I was sure was a legal requirement as we had to have one in the shop but found none. I made my way into the toilet daring not to take a breath and grabbed some bog roll from the top of the cistern. *OMG man! At least fucking clean the toilet once a year! In fact, just set fire to it! Kim and Aggie wouldn't even venture in there.*

I found a lighter and by the tiny flames, I wiped up the little droplets of blood that have escaped my hand. I then found the keys in a lock box, that was clearly not locked, while wondering how this guy ran a business for so long. Getting out the window was much easier than getting in but still I was careful not to drop any more blood. I rammed the dirty bog roll in my back pocket and clenched a new piece into my hand. I got out without too many problems, gently pushed the stone back in place and jumped into the van. It took me just over ten minutes so I still had time to make it work.

The drive to the post office was without any issue since there was not really anyone else on the roads. The farmers would be up soon and in their fields, but not many cars used these roads. Even though I was being shit crazy and doing so many illegal things at the same time, I actually found the drive very peaceful and relaxing. It was not too bad an experience at the post office either. The young guy behind the desk was clearly hating life and was not up for a chat other than a few grunts. Just like that, forty-two minutes later I was out the door and £184.70 lighter. I nearly fainted when he said the due amount without even blinking but I didn't have another choice. It was already Thursday and forty-eight hours was the quickest service you got here so if I had gone for anything less, it would have meant the poor wee buggers dying in a warehouse somewhere until Monday. It would have been easier to hand over that amount if the guy had even said thanks. *Doesn't matter now, it's done and another goal achieved.*

I jumped back into the motor and noticed that after sitting for a bit the petrol showing thing had gone right down. *Will it be able to even reach back? Is that how these things work? Can I risk it?*

I'd seen a petrol garage just off the road on the way here but it wasn't open. *Should I risk going there?* I thought hard and then knew that I needed to, even if it got me home later. Derek might notice the missing fuel. I brought £200 with me so I had £15.30 left. I'd need to just put in the £15 and hope for the best. I made it to the petrol garage and the sign on the door showed it opened at seven.

For fuck's sake, it was only 6:35!

I banged my head on the steering wheel while I tried to think what I should do. Do I just sit here like a sitting duck waiting to be caught or attempt to drive back and run out of fuel? Yeah! Try and explain that one.

When I lifted my head, I saw an older lady walking towards the garage. She didn't have a uniform on but she was also not driving a car so why else would she be there if she wasn't an employee? I opened my car's door and approached her slowly. She didn't seem surprised or scared to see a young man heading towards her in the dark but then I saw why.

In her other hand she was carrying a baseball bat. I called out to her to try and show her I meant no harm. "Hi, there! I'm so sorry to be here so early but is there any chance I could fuel up now?"

"What?" She clearly couldn't hear me from a distance so I stopped in my tracks and let her come closer. She seemed slightly nerved but also looked like she would stomp my brains out in one whack so I tried to remain calm.

I repeated my question and she yelled back, "okay, but you'll need to pay through the window as I'm not having you in my shop."

I agreed to myself that I didn't want to be in her shop anyway so this worked best for me too.

She turned the pump on and I put in £14.50 worrying if I go over a little and she might kill me because I was one penny short. My heart stopped as I was walking to the window and noticed the police car pulling into the spot behind the van. He got out and was coming straight over to us so clearly, he didn't need fuel. I didn't know who I was more scared of if I'd have run and didn't pay, the old woman or the pig.

I kept walking even though I heard the copper calling. He caught up with me as I reached the window and I started worrying that the old codger had pressed the alarm.

"Alright Jan" the officer says. "Bit early for you to be serving is it not?"

"It's alright. This young man is just in a hurry, as all youngsters are these days." She replied directing the last part to me.

"Why such a hurry?" I heard him say to me.

192

I turned around not realizing I have unzipped my jacket and there's blood on my hoodie.

He took a step back. "I said what seems to be the rush?" This time in a more demanding tone.

"Oh" Looking down and realising there's a bit more blood on me than I thought. "I have just been at a farm helping a struggling calf and would very much like to be getting home now."

"Ah! I see." Relief cleared in his voice automatically assuming I was a vet. "Oh! Sorry, young sir," he continued, "was the calf and cow ok?"

I tried to use words that I could remember hearing from the farmer to try and sound more *"vet-ish"*, "yeah the heifer was too small for the calf but after some oxytocin and a good few hands they are both now resting up."

He placed his hand on my shoulder and I nearly crumbled from the weight. "Ah thank God for people like you Sir. Right, you be on your way and drive carefully if you're that tired."

"I will." I said heading back to the van while trying to stop my legs running like the clappers.

The drive back took longer, thanks to the fucking inconsiderate farmer twats that the tyre took the same amount of time to do one full circle on the tar as the moon took to go round the earth! But it was ok as it was quarter to eight when I got back to the garage so I was only slightly running behind. I managed to squeeze my ass back through the window and found the lighter I used to guide myself around last time. The lighter was running out of gas so I searched for another but couldn't find any.

I found a tall candle though, like one of them you see at the front of churches on TV and again wondered how the fuck this guy stayed in business. I lit it as it would be only a few seconds that I needed to be there, and I placed it down balanced on the table next to the locked box. I placed the keys on hook number eight where I found them and turned to head back to the window. I felt a nudge against my hip and then everything seemed bright and hot. I was lying on the floor but didn't know why, so I scrambled to my feet and headed back to the window. I managed to get out but then heard a mighty bang which threw me past the clustered trees and onto the far side of the stoned parking lot. I realized how tired I was and everything was so warm so I decided to have a small nap before heading back.

"Rab", "RAB", "RAAAAAAB."

Shit, did I miss my alarm? Am I late for work?

I was looking around but I seemed to be outside. What the hell? I could see people all around in yellow and orange jackets. There were flashing blue lights and it took me a minute to realize what was going on. Shit! I must have set fire to the place. There was a loud buzzing in my ear so I was struggling to hear what the person was saying to me.

I blurted out, "those boys." I didn't know where that came from but I went with it.

"What boys, Rab?" the woman responded.

"Lads... on dirt bikes." I found myself saying.

"Let's just give the lad a minute to rest before asking any more questions." A woman said emerging from behind the other woman. I was being lifted to my feet and taken over to what I guessed, was an ambulance and given some water. It didn't take long for the ringing to stop and for me to realize how deep in a shit I was.

"Right, son, how are you feeling?"

"Fine." I said after a coughing fit that made me feel like I was going to throw up.

"Do you think you are well enough to speak to the police officer or will we get you to hospital first?" I shit my pants when I heard that but the last place I wanted to be was stuck in a Dettol white room with my mum worrying at home. *Fuck!* What the hell was I going to say? There was nothing left to do but admit it was me but then there would be questions as to why I was there. I think I might faint, maybe I should go to the hospital.

The same woman that was draping over me when I woke up walks over. She introduced herself as PC Dragas and explained she was there because of the fire. I sat quiet and waited for the questions that were going to expose everything.

"You said about some boys?"

"Eh?"

"Some boys you said when you first came round."

"That's right! Some boys on... eh... dirt bikes. I was heading to work when I saw it was very bright over there and knowing Derek was on a stag, I came to check it out."

"So, is it common knowledge that the owner is out of town?"

"Yes, he's been excited about it for weeks, missing out the part that he couldn't wait to get away from his bat shit crazy wife."

"And what did you find when you arrived?"

"Some young lad, they were wearing helmets so no idea who they were, jumped on the back of the bike and they headed off. There were just the two of them that I can see. I then saw the light coming from inside so I climbed in the window that was open to have a closer look."

"Then what?"

"Then I saw you."

"Ok, so do you remember anything else about the scene when you arrived?"

"No, sorry it all happened so fast." She gave me a card and told me to call her if I remembered anything. Then, just like that, she was gone.

I sat in disbelief that I was not already in handcuffs and on my way to the single jail cell we had in the village. The ambulance woman was trying to convince me to go to the hospital but I kept repeating that I was fine. She finally gave in and asked how I was at least getting home. "I have my bike so I'll be fine." She turned and headed off.

"Where is it?" I heard her shout and realised she was headed off to find it. She reappeared within seconds round the back door smugly saying "This bike?" As she held up a frame with a bent wheel.

"Damn! It's fine I'll just walk home!" I snapped.

"We will take you home." she said shaking her head and popped the bike into the back of the ambulance with me.

How the hell does she know where I live? I think but then recognising it was the nurse from the Doctors who dealt with all my mum's treatments.

Mum was still passed out and I asked the woman, whose name I couldn't remember, to leave, but she insisted. "Can't just leave you on your own, in case, you have a head injury."

"Fine! I don't mean to be rude but the sooner everyone is gone the better." I headed up the stairs to shower but it seemed all my energy had gone. I slid down so I was sitting on the stairs and gave myself a minute to get myself together.

"Oh! Rab, honey, are you ok?"

Great, here comes mum!

"Yes, I'm fine. I just need to get ready for work."

"Don't you think you're going to work, you silly boy. You get to bed and I'll call Lizzy."

I didn't even argue. I could feel my whole body aching and desperately it just needed to sleep.

The ambulance woman helped me up and off to my bed, helping me onto the bed and she started pulling off my T-shirt and jeans.

"Easy, Rapist!" I shouted, and then immediately apologised when I saw her expression.

"I'll give your mum some codeine to help with your pain and chuck these clothes in your machine but if you start coughing heavily or feel unwell then please just call us back asap."

I nodded and she was out of the room. I didn't have the energy to think about what happened. I didn't even remember closing my eyes but within seconds I was asleep.

I dreamt Dad was here holding my hand and singing to me. I thanked him but then heard a giggle. I opened my eyes to find Lizzy sitting there next to my bed.

Cheeky git!

"I'm not old enough to be your dad!"

I gave her a puzzled look but then realised I must have said it out loud.

"Sorry, I just thought…"

"It's ok." She said rubbing the back of my hand. "I just wanted to come to make sure you're ok. Your mum seemed quite frantic on the phone so I said I would keep an eye on you to convince her to attend her Doctor's appointment. It took a lot but I got there."

"Thanks!" I said in a wheezy voice. "But what about the shop?"

"It's not going to go under by being closed for one day. You get some more rest and I'll make some soup for when you get back up."

"Thanks Lizzy, honestly thanks. If anything ever happened to me, my mum I will need someone like you around."

She smiled and tucked me in. "Get rest. You're going to need it when you taste how horrible my soup skills are."

I managed a small giggle and fall back into the darkness.

Chapter Eighteen:

Breaking News

It took a couple days for me to fully recover but it was the weekend so I hadn't had to worry about work. Mum said the police called Derek and everything was going to be ok as he had got insurance.

Thank fuck! He'd done one thing right.

They still haven't found the young lads that started the fire but will keep looking. Derek had come over to say "thanks" for trying to put it out but I was sleeping so Mum didn't want to wake me.

Mum and Lizzy had been bringing me up food and drinks but I felt strong enough today to head downstairs. Lizzy came everyday so she could help Mum look after me and help with the house work. I was pretty weak on my feet from being in bed the last few days and my head was dizzy. With mum and Lizzy's help I made it downstairs to the main living room. Mum got me a blanket as I felt pretty cold and I snuggled up on the sofa with a warm bowl of soup. Mum advised me not to stay up for long and that they'd help me upstairs after a couple of hours. I knew Mum was just trying to help but I think my body felt like this from the exhaustion and fear of the last few days, not from the fire.

We watched "Pointless" which I was not a huge fan of but Mum likes all the game shows so I sat listening and answered any questions I could. Lizzy's actually really good at it and seemed to know an awful lot about olden day actors. She and Mum were sitting on the other sofa pretending they were a team on the show too. It was nice watching them, Mum really seems to like having Lizzy around and if it made her happy then that was all that mattered.

The six o' clock BBC news came on and there was a "Breaking News".

Five people were found dead in one business in the centre of London and two employees found dead in their homes. It seemed the ones in the office had laid there all weekend and not found until Monday morning. They were not ruling anything out yet but there was nothing to show that there had been any foul play. It could possibly be a suicide pack but again they were not putting any labels on it yet.

"Oh! How awful!" Mum exclaimed.

Lizzy nodded along in agreement. "Just seems like such a waste of life."

I, on the other hand, thought that seven deaths from three parcels was a win.

"Why are you smiling, Rab?" I heard Mum asking me.

"Oh! It's just nice to see how you both seem to act the same and have the same opinions most of the time."

"Oh! That's sweet, son."

I was smiling even more that I'd managed to dodge another bullet.

"Right, let's get you back upstairs" Mum said slipping her arm under mine.

"Good Idea." Lizzy said then turning in the direction of the kitchen. "You take him up and I'll go make his supper."

In no time, I was back snuggled up in bed. Just that little trip out of bed had actually wiped me. As Mum left the room Lizzy entered with the tea and toast on a tray.

"Thank you, I promise I'll be back to work as soon as possible."

"Don't be silly! There's no rush! I'll manage the shop while my mum's running the post office, so all is good for now. I'll pop back

199

over tomorrow evening after work. You just get some rest." She was already heading out the door.

I looked down to see two smiling faces on my toast and I couldn't help but laugh. Although Lizzy can be pretty annoying, she can also be alright.

.oOo.

The next evening, we were all back downstairs watching TV and my Mum bought us all a chippy as a treat. As usual, at 6 p.m. the BBC News appeared back on the box.

Another eighteen people were found dead in five other companies around London. They still couldn't seem to find the cause and with it being a bank holiday and two of the businesses being quite small, the bodies had laid for quite some time before being examined. They wanted to assure everyone that none of the bodies had any injuries or fatal wounds so it still looked like a suicide pack, just one a lot larger than they had considered. The toxicology report came back not showing any normal toxins used, but it did show an unknown chemical. They'd continue to research this while asking the public if they had any information. If someone wanted to contact them, they could call them on the read-out number.

Mum and Lizzy looked at each confused.

"What the actual fuck?" Mum burst out in anger and confusion. "Why the hell would different companies all come together and make such a sick pact like that? I know there's people that believe in that "doomsday" but it's not like any special date is near." She continued while shaking her head.

"Maybe they were in a pact?" Lizzy said trying to calm Mum down. "Maybe they just haven't found a note or book explaining why. Either way it's such a waste as they all seem to be very smart professionals."

Mum nodded in agreement.

I stared at them for a while seeing how Lizzy held Mum's hand in a comforting way and how they both did actually seem upset by the news. I didn't quite understand because it was not like they knew any of these people and they were certainly not highly educated professionals, so they didn't have anything to worry about.

I did feel a little guilty at how upset it had seemed to make them.

"It was probably some whack job that had made a cult and even though they might be smart people they probably just got sucked in?" I said in the most convincing voice I could. I was not tired but want to get back upstairs. I wanted to be on my own for a bit to try and make sense of their reaction. "I'm just going to head back upstairs for a lie down."

"Want me to help you get up there?" Lizzy offered.

"No, it's ok but thank you. I'm feeling much stronger today so I'm sure I'll manage."

She just nodded and headed into the kitchen to help Mum make some supper.

Mum seemed in a world of her own when she brought me up tea.

I asked if she was ok and she nodded, leaving the room without a word.

Luckily, I had moved Mary's tank into the bottom of the wardrobe the day I made the deliveries, so no one has seen anything. I was going back to locking my door as I couldn't keep risking them walking in. I'd need to get up tomorrow and try to spend most of the day out of bed so there was no need for them to come in. I only managed to feed Mary twice since the fire and she'd not had any daylight so I needed to get her back out of that wardrobe.

It was nice to see and be able to watch her again. I told her the plan had worked and her babies were doing their job. She didn't show any response as usual and was just excited to see her dinner. I gave her two crickets today and got her fresh water. I started to wonder what kind of life she must be having. Sleeping all day and wandering the tank all night. The only time anything changed for her was the time when she got dinner, no wonder she wanted to play with it a while first. It was not like I could release her in the wild, especially not here as she would die in that weather and there was certainly no way I would be taking her on a plane to get her back to her real home. The breeder bred her so I doubted if she knew anything different and maybe being released into the wild would scare her. I left her to enjoy her dinner and hopped back into bed, making sure first that my bedroom door was locked.

.oOo.

I woke up at eight the next morning and managed to get myself into the shower without feeling too dizzy. Mum had been running baths for me which was nice but it was not the same as having a shower. I could hear Mum up and about downstairs by the time I got out and called down that I'd be down for breakfast so she didn't need to bring any up.

She shouted back that it was fine. I got dressed and went downstairs just in time for the full breakfast to be ready. *Yum! I love when Mum makes a full breakfast.*

She made haggis and fruit pudding! Which everyone should have with theirs!

"Oh, turn around a minute Rab." So I do, but feeling confused as why she was asking me to. "There's a hole in the back of your hoodie."

Without thinking I replied, "it must be from the fire."

She looked at me oddly. "Why were you wearing a hoodie to work?"

Fuck! She knows I always go to work smart!

I couldn't really say I had the shirt on underneath as she'd have known I was lying. "I left a shirt at work and was wearing black jeans that day. I like to put the shirt on at work otherwise it gets crumpled from me cycling and that doesn't look good for the

202

business." She seemed to accept that and continued making herself a coffee. *Phew! I think I got away with that one!* But in my head, something was telling me she has always known when I was lying.

"Do you fancy a wee walk after breakfast?" I said just to break the silence, but she agreed.

"I think that's a great idea! Some fresh air will do you a world of good. I have a letter to post anyway so we can walk to the post office and back."

Not exactly what I had in mind but it will pass some time.

The sun was really bright outside and it actually took a minute for my eyes to adjust. Town was quite busy today but then I recalled that it was that bloody time of year again, the village fair! Well, I'd be doing my best to avoid that this year since Mum would be able to go herself or with friends.

I passed by the fruit shop and Lizzy spotted us through the window. She ran out. "It's good to see you on your feet but don't push yourself too hard."

"Is that because you care about me or care about me not being off work longer?"

She laughed and headed back into the shop so Mum and I continued our walk to the post office.

When Mum said that she had a letter to post I think, what she meant was that she had a lot of gossip to share with Lizzy's mum. I browsed the shop and heard the topic turning to the bodies being found in London. They both discussed their theories and I started feeling hot and finding it harder to breathe.

I turned to Mum, "I'll meet you outside." I left the shop and went to sit on the bench trying to calm down.

"There's the man of the hour."

It was a voice which jolted me back to the present and as I looked up, I saw Derek. He continued, "Man, I cannot say thanks enough for you trying to save my business but I'm just glad you didn't get hurt. Let me get you a beer to thank you."

"No, no, I'm ok. Thank you." The last place I didn't want to be sitting in was that dingy wee pub.

"Well, the offer's always there so if I see you in the pub your first is on me."

Mum finally came up and as soon as she saw me, she said, "there is going to be a special report on the London cases at 2 o'clock today. I'm wondering what they have found out." She kept going through everything she thought might have happened, what they might have found or even that they might have found a suicide letter. I was not really listening as I was trying to think of anything I might have missed that they could have found.

"What do you think, Rab? Rab?"

I snapped out of my own little bubble. "I've not got a clue. We will need to wait and see."

She pushed me in a playful way. "Trying to talk with you is like trying to chat to a wet mop."

We both laughed and started back in the direction of home.

As we reached the door, I said, "I may have to go and lie down a bit. I'm pretty tired but I'll be back down for the report at 2."

She suggested, "Oh! I might as well. The heat's killing me." We parted ways from the front door.

I had no intention of actually having a nap. I sat on the bed going through everything wondering what it might be that they had found. They might have not even found anything but giving us an update to show they were doing something. I felt myself struggling to breathe again and the heat taking over. I took a drink from the bottle next to my bed and laid down repeating in my head that they wouldn't have found anything and I was just being silly.

Everything had been going so well the last couple days that I had forgotten about the feeling of fear and panic. I switched on the computer and decided to see if I could find out what it is that they were going to be announcing. It was not like they were going to be bothered about me searching about it, as surely most people must be doing the same. I couldn't find anything anywhere as it all seemed to be quite hush hush. I gave up after about an hour and again reassured myself that it was nothing. If there was anything they would be at my door arresting me instead of messing about with an announcement.

I laid back down on my bed and realised how tired I now felt. Everything was such a stress today that it really took the energy right out of me. I decided to sleep for some time and set an alarm for half past one. It was already nearly twelve so I didn't want to miss it but also didn't want to be waiting too long for it to start so half past one seemed perfect. *It is going to be fine. They won't have anything and I can stop stressing again, I know it.*

I was awake before the alarm could ring so I just laid there for ten minutes composing myself and trying to come up with answers to questions that might come up if they have found something. I realised there were a million different things and I was actually just cluttering my brain trying to answer questions that hopefully wouldn't arise.

I stopped in my tracks when I saw Lizzy and her mum sitting at the sofa.

"Uh... Hey!" I said, "what's going on here?"

Lizzy quickly responded, "Well, we don't want to miss it. I'll go back to open the shops again after. We do get an hour's break after all."

I just smiled at Lizzy's mum and sat across the room on the other sofa. My stress levels hit the roof and I started wondering if there was a way out of me having to watch it with them. *Why didn't I just tell mum I'd watch it in my room with my door lock and time to think about anything that came up?*

There was no time to do it now, as the show was starting. The chief man himself was walking out to the reporters at Scotland's yard ready to spill his findings.

"Right, no talking." Mum said, "we can chat afterwards because I don't want to miss anything."

I took a deep breath as the copper opened his mouth.

"We have now gathered that in total sixty-eight deaths have happened out of which all seemed to have died in a similar manner. We haven't yet managed to make the exact link between them other than they were all professionals working in a handful of different sectors and all died either in their workplace or soon after arriving back home. There is one other thing that all seem to have in common. All received a fruit basket delivery on the day or shortly before we estimate their time of death. We are working hard to find out if this is a link at all in any way but urge anyone to come forward that also received a basket like this."

Lizzy gasped.

"Hold on," Mum hushed her, "let's see what else they have to say."

The copper continued on the TV, "We have however tested the fruit from many of these baskets and none appear to be poisoned in any way. We are trying to track the company of the baskets but so far have had no luck. If you recognise this leaflet again, we would be very grateful for any information to lead us to this company. Again, I just want to make it clear that nothing has been found on the fruit that may have caused any harm so the owner of the company is not in any trouble, we would purely like to have a chat to see if we can establish any other possible links. We have spoken to different members of family and friends of the loved ones but no one recalls them saying anything about ordering or waiting on a delivery of any fruit.

Secondly, we are in contact with the royal mail to try and trace where the packages were sent from and if there is any more information that can be learnt from them. The toxin that was found in the original test sent from the first body has shown up in all the others too. We have experts working hard to trace how this could be involved. The only other thing I can say for now is to just reiterate that there were no wounds or fatal marks on any of the deceased and that only bruising was found on different parts of each body. We are certainly looking more into this as it is very unusual for all to have a similar size and colour of bruise just before dying. We are taking this investigation very seriously but still haven't found any evidence to show anyone else was involved or that this was a pre-planned event. I thank you all again for your patience and encourage anyone with any information, no matter how small, to get in touch."

The copper gave the contact details and straight away went inside without answering all the other questions which were being shouted at him.

Mum turned off the TV and looked at us. I turned to see Lizzy starting at me with a puzzled look too.

I began to say, "they're clearly not our baskets. They had completely different leaflets inside."

My explanation seemed insufficient, and no one replied. I knew I had to cook a stronger story, "ok, ok," I said, "I saw this company doing it online. I realised what a good idea it was to get our fruit shop up and noticed. It wasn't my plan or my big idea, ok. They explained what fruit would be added and how this should be positioned to stop the fruit getting damaged in delivery. They had already done all the figures and it looked like a great idea. The only difference with this other company is that they were asking people to apply to win a free one instead of charging for them. I'm sorry I didn't tell you guys before. I just got swept away in the moment of feeling useful. Lots of people would have seen that and probably decided to do the same. We definitely wouldn't have been the only ones."

Lizzy interrupted me, "You should contact the police and tell them about this."

"There wasn't a company name. It was just an article on the idea like in a business type site so they couldn't be the producers."

She didn't seem convinced.

I proposed another solution. "I'll try to find the page again online and email the police with the link."

She seemed much happier with that response.

Everyone stayed quiet for a while not knowing what to say. There wasn't really any new evidence in the report but the coincidence of us just sending off the baskets had shaken everyone up.

Lizzy stood up. "Ma, we need to get the shops back open."

Mum interjected, "Can I grab a lift to the store with you. I need some ingredients for dinner."

Lizzy and her mum both agreed in unison. Lizzy said turning towards me, "I will pop over after work tonight. Is there anything you'd like from the shop?"

I retorted, "No, nothing." She headed off with both Mums.

Did I really get away with that? Were they suspicious? Were they all now having a chat about it in the car? Maybe they all realised and were heading to the police station now? I tried to calm myself down and told myself that I was being stupid. There was absolutely nothing that suggested I was involved and most definitely there will be other companies that would have done the same. Well, if they had also read the made-up article, then they definitely would have. I go to make a cuppa and decide the fish tank had probably not been cleaned in a while. I'd get it done, and hopefully that will pass some time and keep my mind busy.

Chapter Nineteen:

Mira, not Cupid

Lizzy arrived at six and found me just finishing up with the fish tank. Mum was away having dinner with the old codgers today but Lizzy must have forgotten as she brought three fish suppers. I saw the package in her hand and said, "You remember Mum's not here for dinner."

She widened her eyes and I replied, "Don't worry, it won't go to waste. Mum doesn't mind cold chips from the chippy."

We both make a disgusting face and laughed. She offered, "You finish off with this, and I'd make us a cuppa and get them plates ready?"

I nodded and she ushered herself into the kitchen.

The food smelled amazing. I didn't realise how hungry I was so maybe Mum wouldn't be getting her cold supper after all. I hurriedly tidied up and cleared the little coffee table for the plates and sat waiting for Lizzy to come back upstairs.

I put the little TV on to fill in some of the silence while we sit eating. Luckily, we'd already missed the news so I didn't need to go through that uncomfortable situation again. Cleaning the tank took my mind off things but now sitting there in silence, I found my mind wandering back.

"You, ok?" Lizzy's voice broke my trail of thoughts.

I looked at her with a gub full of fish and accidentally spit some on her while saying, "Yeah."

"Shit! Sorry!" I spoke covering my mouth this time.

She giggled, "it's fine. Next time if you want to share your food, I would prefer it on a fork."

"I'll try to remember that."

"You know Rab, I don't want you to feel bad about earlier."

I looked up to her in shock. "Earlier?" *Does she know. How could she know?*

"Yeah! I mean, about the parcels."

I was sweating so much at what she might say next. I could feel my balls sticking tightly together like they were trying to form praying hands.

She spoke, "I don't want you thinking that I think it was anything less of your plan. I mean, I know it was someone else's plan but it was still a good business decision."

My brain took a couple seconds to catch up but I'd missed my chance to speak and Lizzy continued. "The fact that you saw that article and thought about how you could adapt it to boost our business, that, in itself is a good plan. No one thinks any less of you or questions your achievement."

"Thank you. I'm sorry I wasn't more honest earlier."

"Well, I don't want you feeling bad about it. You've done so well and I wanted you to know how proud your mum and I am of you."

I think I actually blushed and grabbed a chip so I didn't need to say anything. I just smiled and went back to looking at the TV.

There was silence for a bit. I was not sure if it was because of us still eating or that we both felt a little embarrassment from Lizzy's words. I needed to think of something to break it as it was becoming too uncomfortable. "How's the calf?" I couldn't believe I had actually forgotten all about it and this was the first time it popped back into my mind.

"Yeah! Blessing and Mira are both doing really well. I go visit them nearly everyday, before work. I'm just glad that things turned out the way they did." She looked up and noticed the confused look on my face.

"Who's Mira and Blessing?" I sniggered.

"Oh! Sorry. That's what I've named them."

"Does the farmer know that you have been naming his walking dinners?"

She laughed hard before speaking, "the farmer knows. It's only those two I have named and I think the farmer is fond of them too." I laugh with her and she carried on, "I don't think I've ever told you about what happened with that cow two years ago. Maybe if I tell you then you won't think I'm so strange for naming them."

I joked, "I doubt that but am happy to hear it."

She nudged me for my cheek. Finishing up her last few chips, she started to tell me her story.

"I've been helping at the farm for a good few years now, probably about the same amount of time as you but I help with the cows instead of lambing. Two summers ago, as I remember it was the first week in June, the farmer called me to go help deliver a calf. For me it wasn't any different than other time so I got out of bed and headed for the farm. When I got there, there was this really strange atmosphere and the farmer seemed quite stressed. I didn't understand why as we had done this many many times before so what was different about this one? The farmer explained that this was quite late in the year for cows giving birth, which I knew but continued to listen. He said that he had already had the vet out twice and was starting to worry something was terribly wrong. The vet assured him the calf still had a heart beat and that it was probably just mated later than the rest. Again, what he thought that night which made me worry more.

The farmer had asked the vet if it was possible that the cow needed help to go into labour but the vet didn't seem to worry and told him to give it another couple of weeks. Another two weeks passed until finally the cow started showing signs of labour. She had gone into labour the night before so at this point, she had been trying for more than twelve hours. They had done everything they could think of but nothing seemed to make the labour progress. He had called the vet just before he had called me but was told that the vet was at one of the other farms helping with a sick ewe so the message will be passed to him as soon as possible. The poor cow just lay there looking tired and spent. Up to that point, all the cows kind of looked the same to me and I knew I was there to help with a job so not to get too attached but something in this cows' eyes were different. She stared at me urging me to help. I went over and lay her head on my lap. I clapped her and spoke to her to try and give her some reassurance, I think she could feel the tension in the room too.

The vet arrived about half an hour later and confirmed that the calf was far too big for the mother to deliver. He could see that there was already some internal injury from her pushing so much and the only thing left to do was a section. The farmer didn't even have time to answer. The vet injected the cow in the neck and started putting on really long gloves. He turned to me and said that I'd let him know if she stopped breathing and not to be alarmed if the head slightly moves as this sometimes happens when they are sedated.

I sat there in shock and horror. Could I do this? Could I watch this happen right in front of me? Could I be responsible of making sure the cow is still breathing? How will I even know if she stops breathing. I started to panic but the vet snapped me out of it. He said that it was ok. Just watch her chest expand as usual. If we don't do this the calf will die and, so will she. Every life matters no matter how big or small so I need you to stay focused and help me save them. He was right and I managed to pull myself together.

I'm not going to get into too much detail about how the section went, all I can say is, it's not as clean and easy as they show on TV. The vet said that the calf was pretty far down and he was struggling to pull it free. He told the Farmer that the cow would lose her womb so wouldn't be able to calf again. Once he had pulled the calf free, he passed it straight to the farmer and got on with trying to save the heifer. I kept my eyes strongly fixed on her chest trying not to fell faint at the sight of how deep the vet's arms were in her stomach. I was glad when the farmer shouted the calf was alive but I couldn't feel happy until I knew mummy had made it too. After the vet sewed her up, he gave her another injection and told me to move back. The cow might wake confused and he didn't want me being hurt if she started to stand up. She gradually started to come round but still just lay there slightly moving her head from side to side. I didn't care when the vet tried to stop me, I just got straight back over to her and told her everything was going to be ok.

The calf tried to suckle from its Mum but it didn't seem to be getting anything and just seemed to be causing her more pain. It was a tough decision but the farmer and vet decided it would be best to move the calf to another pen just now and to be bottle-fed to let the Mum rest up. He gave her another injection and told the farmer to keep a close eye on her but he had done everything he could. I looked back into the cow's eyes and again felt something warm and lovely about her. She was clearly scared and sore but it was like she was asking me not to leave her. I told the farmer I would sleep in the barn next to her and that he should go get some sleep before he has to start sorting all the animals again soon. He told me I didn't have to but I think he could see how much I wanted to. He said he would call my mum and let her know and would bring me out some blankets. I was grateful when he also brought me a cup of cocoa and a pillow. I assured him that I would come and get him if anything happened and he slid the farm door shut. The little lamp was still lit and finally there was a calm in the air. I lay down next to the cow and pretty quickly fell asleep.

When I woke the cow hasn't moved but I could see she was still breathing. Poor thing was shattered after such a horrible night. I lifted over the large bowl of water the farmer had left and tried to encourage the cow to drink. She seemed really reluctant at first but after she had tasted it, it was like she realised how thirsty she was and before I knew it the bowl was empty. The farmer told me that it would be best for me to go home now but again the cow looked at me as if urging me to stay. I tried to tell the farmer that I would rather not but he insisted and promised to keep a very close eye on the cow. We came to the agreement that if I went home for a few hours and rested up then I could come back later for a bit. I took the blanket that I had slept in and placed it over the cow telling her I would be back soon and not to worry.

I got home, had a shower and jumped into bed but couldn't sleep. Every time, I closed my eyes I could see her sad eyes staring back at me. I got back up and had a cuppa and some toast then settled down on the sofa putting the TV on even though I couldn't pay any attention to it. I lay down and managed to fall asleep with Mum waking me as she returned home from work. She asked for an update from the farmer and she told me that farmer said that I was very brave and helpful. I told her about everything that had happened and that I would be returning to the farm so possibly staying over again tonight. She didn't try and stop me. It was like she just understood that this was something I felt I had to do. She made me a flask of tea and packed a couple little snacks, telling me the apple slices were for the cow. I got in my car and headed back to the farm just hoping she would still be ok when I got there.

The farmer had seen me approaching and straight away assured me that the cow was ok. He said she had been up and been drinking but still was refusing food. They let the calf in with her after they fed it so she could be with it without it trying to feed. After a while of the calf bounding about and bumping into her, she looked quite tired so returned the calf to the other barn. All she has done since then was sleeping.

She lifted her head to see me when I walked in the barn like she was happy to see me again. I sat down beside her and got the apple slices out my bag. She didn't really seem interested at first but I dipped it in the peanut butter my mum had packed and that convinced her to eat. She ate all the apple then again, I got her water bowl and she had a large drink. I snuggled back down beside her in the blanket and together we drifted off to sleep. I was woken by the cow moving about and realised she was moving her head closer to rest it on my chest. I gave her a hug and petted her as again we went back to sleep.

When I woke in the morning the air was so cold and her head lay really heavy onto my chest. I gently patted her and tried to get her to wake but she just continued to sleep. I shuffled from under her head, holding it and gently laying it on the floor. She was so cold and her eyes were closed, I didn't want to leave her side but knew she had passed away.

Trying to see through the tears built up in my eyes, I walked to the farmer's house. I had no clue what time it was but the farmer answered half asleep in a dressing gown so it must have been still night time. I didn't have to say a word as he could tell from my face and gave me a big cuddle. He guided me to the sofa and made me a large cup of cocoa. He told me that from all the deaths he had seen on the farm that she was a very lucky cow indeed. He could see the bond between us and knew she was happy and comfortable with me being there. I told him about how she moved closer to me during the night and he said she probably wanted me to know that it was ok. I was comforted by his words but still my heart was broken with the sadness. He told me to try get some rest and that I could drive home in the morning but he didn't want me driving right then. I agreed.

The next morning, he told me he wanted me to come help him with something before I left so I followed him out to the barns. I didn't know if I could go back in and see her lying there so was grateful when he turned into a different barn. Here you will be needing this he said and handed me a bottle. He then led me into the pen at the far side and there she was, the little calf. She was so happy and spirited, even nearly took my arm off trying to get the bottle. When she was calm, she was very steady on her feet but each time she got excited it seemed like she forgot how to use them. She had such a kind, beautiful face and the same eyes as her mum with long dark eyelashes. I started to cry, not sure if it was the joy of meeting her or the pain of losing her Mum. The farmer came back and told me he had to go up to the top field to gather the ewes so he would see me later. He said I was welcome to come any time to see her and that he will make sure to put that blanket over the Mum before she was collected. I was so grateful for his kindness and told him that this little girl was a miracle. 'Mira, it is then,' he said and that's what we called her from that day forward.

That night we were called to the farm, that was Mira giving birth. I was so worried that it was all happening again. The relief I felt when the calf finally came out was over whelming and I can't thank you enough for being there to help. After I brought you home, I went back to the farm and laid with her and her calf till morning, just to make sure they were both ok. The farmer came back in the morning and asked me of what I thought of the new calf and I said she was an absolute 'blessing'. We both laughed knowing that 'Blessing' was now her name and it didn't need to be discussed. Every time I go up, they are both getting stronger and stronger and soon they will be back in the field with the others. Those two cows mean so much to me and can't help feeling like Mira had done her mum proud. I think about that cow often but still never been able to choose her a name. That night when the vet said 'every life matters no matter how small' I knew I was going to do everything I could to keep Mira happy and healthy."

Lizzy lifted her head and looked at me with tears in her eyes and that's when it hit me. At that moment, it was like my brain and heart finally aligned and I realised I loved her. Before I could even think I leaned forward and kissed her. She didn't push me away but instead leaned a little closer. When our mouths parted our heads leaned together and with my eyes still closed, I thought, "I love you, Lizzy."

I realise I've said it out loud as I immediately heard her voice. "I love you too, Rab."

Chapter Twenty:

Reconsidering

I couldn't stop thinking about what Lizzy said, "every life matters, no matter how small it is."

Those poor little spiders I sent out, never mind, the human lives they took. Spending time with Lizzy taught me that some people are kind and caring and want to do the right thing. Some people are good at their jobs and get into that role because they want to make things better. Others just fell into their jobs, and do it to survive.

The business was going really well and even though I still couldn't imagine it, but if I was to become successful, would I just become one of those people I hated too? Not all people do the jobs they do for the reasons I thought.

Thankfully, no more deaths had been reported.

I worried that Lizzy would find out about what I'd done or even that she might get in trouble without even knowing she'd anything to do with it.

I can't have that. Maybe, I should come clean to her? I don't think she will ever be able to understand though. She always sees the very best in people no matter what walk of life they come from.

I decided on one thing though—I was sending Mary back. It was too risky to keep her as a pet as someone would eventually find her and I won't be mating her again. Lizzy left a boxed tank at my house and I told her that I'd got one a little bigger and better which she could have as I no longer needed it. I will send hers back and she could get a refund for it. It'd be easier to send Mary back in that box because it already had the packaging and was a bit smaller. I didn't want to send her off in a plastic tub because in all honesty, I did love her and had grown to her presence. I changed Mary over to that tank last night and made changes to the packaging so she could breathe. I cut the polystyrene away from the top corner and popped holes in the box. That was directly above where the little vent was, so she'd be able to get air but not get out. I'd put it on top of her tank back in the bottom of the wardrobe as an actual courier was coming to collect her on Saturday morning.

I needed to remember to remove Lizzy's address label off it and to have her boxed up by 5 a.m. I went for the 6 a.m. collection and they better come on time as I'd to get ready for Saturday evening.

Lizzy and I were going on our first official date. We were going for a meal at four and then Lizzy had bought us tickets to go to the cinema. She didn't tell me the name of the movie, but she assured me that I'd like it. I was just hoping it's not a chick flick. Then we would grab a couple drinks in that dingy bar, which Lizzy quite likes, and she will be staying over at mine. I needed to get the room in some better order. I ordered a new chest of drawers, wardrobe and bedding from Amazon that should be arriving on Friday so I'll get them built up after work. I didn't want to spend the only night I have with Lizzy in my broken dingy room and also preferred to leave it in good shape for Mum. I planned to just break down the old ones and burn them in the garden but probably won't have time on Friday so will need to go in the living room till I can.

I knew I was being really selfish but I just wanted this one night with Lizzy. I should be honest and tell her first, but I wanted us to have happy memories of each other even if it was just for once. I wanted to lay next to her as she slept and wake her with breakfast. I wanted to try and cram everything into those twenty-four hours with her before I lose her away for probably the rest of my life.

It didn't even matter how long I go away for—she will probably never even want to hear my name mentioned again. Why didn't I realise everything before? Why didn't I stop being a child filled with hate? I regret it all but remorse wasn't going to make this all better. I knew I had already lost what I wanted, before I even knew what it was. I just hoped she could move on and have the amazing life she deserves. This is why I shouldn't go ahead with Saturday's plans but it was the only thing I'd be left with to hold onto the rest of my jail bird ass so I just couldn't give it up.

Not only am I selfish but I'm also a coward. What a catch you've caught here Lizzy.

I'd like to think I'd sit down with Lizzy on Sunday to try explaining everything to her and admit everything I'd done, but I won't. Looking back there were so many things that tied Lizzy to my awful plan—using her leaflet company, her supplier for fruit and the packaging. I should never have put her in that position. I had to make sure everyone knew she had nothing to do with it.

When the police opens up again on Monday, I'm going to go and confess everything. I would tell them of how the whole plan was mine, no one knew about it and even now they are the only people that know. I thought about writing it all down in a letter but I got too scared that someone might find it earlier. That would be worse, as it would look like I was caught instead of handing myself in. I didn't really care what happened to me after Sunday as long as Mum and Lizzy are ok.

On Sunday night, I'd be writing a couple of letters and then popping them in the post box on my way to the station. Just so, they wouldn't find them beforehand. I already bought a book of stamps and packet of envelopes.

First, I'd write a letter to Mum saying how sorry I am and how much I love her. I knew she'd be devastated. It was not her fault I turned out the way I did and wished I had been a much better son.

I would also write a letter to Lizzy's mum to ask her to keep an eye on Mum and be there for her as she usually is. I don't need to tell her to watch over Lizzy as she will do that naturally as her mum.

Then, I will write a letter to Lizzy. There was no point trying to explain everything or declaring my love for her as it would be nasty of me to try convincing her to ever see me again and need her to be able to just let go. The letter will be about business only. What orders I'd made on the Friday, apologies that I won't be able to work there anymore but will write names of some people I think will be a good replacement for me. The most important thing I needed to write was me giving up all rights or shares in the shop. I knew Lizzy had talked about making me an official partner and I was not sure how that was done. I decided it's best I gave my consent to make it easier to remove just in case, she has already put it in place.

I had considered organizing a company to come take away the tank and the fish so mum didn't have to be responsible for them but then I know how much she loves sitting watching them so I thought it would be better for her to make the choice. Maybe, I'd put a contact in my letter to her of someone that will remove it if she did decided she wanted them gone. I'd been to the hole in the wall to empty my account leaving only fifty pounds in it to use for Saturday. I'd hide the money somewhere in the kitchen and tell Mum in the letter where to find it so the police won't take it when they most likely search my room. It was not much but will see her good for a little while. I wanted to make sure everything was in place for when I'd be gone as I didn't want Mum having to deal with anything.

It was Thursday night and I'd just been through all my clothes and junk and got everything I didn't need into black bags. I'd take them to work with me tomorrow to put them in the large bin in town. I didn't really know what you get to take to prison and didn't want Lizzy or Mum wondering why all my stuff was gone so I'd kept some clothes, little trinkets, photos and books to make everything look normal.

These were easy things, Mum could just chuck out if she decided she wanted nothing to remind her of me. I cleaned the room the best I could and hoovered the floor. I was going to take down the units tonight so I just needed to build the new ones tomorrow but then remembered that I needed to keep Mary hidden, in case, Mum came in. Also, I was just too tired. The units didn't look like they'd take long to do and my old ones were so old that they'd probably just fall apart anyway when I tried to move them. Thank God! That screw would be gone as I wouldn't want to think of Mum being hurt by it like I was, hundreds of times.

I chose a shirt for my very last day at work tomorrow and quickly ironed it downstairs. Mum went to bed already as she wasn't feeling very well and it was already 9 p.m. I'd spend Sunday with her, maybe even take her for lunch, trying to show her how much I love her before my chance was gone.

I made a cuppa and some toast as I knew I was really going to miss that. There was nothing like supper before getting a good night's sleep. I wondered if they got supper in prison? The nearest prison is on the main land so I didn't really know much about them. Luckily, I'd be far enough away for Mum not to need an excuse, not to come see me, or be reminded of me by seeing the building I'd be in.

I snuggled up in bed and appreciated how warm and comfy it was. I wanted to try and enjoy every last moment and take memory of everything to look back on. I was not scared anymore.

I actually felt relieved that everything was going to be out and I won't need to lie to anyone anymore. I deserved to be punished and I was ready for it. I closed my eyes and drifted into sleep finally feeling that all the weight of fear and guilt has been lifted off my chest.

Chapter Twenty-one:

Karma really is a bitch!

Lizzy ran into the shop at lunch time looking a bit worried.

"What's wrong?" I asked as soon as our eyes met.

Is she going to cancel our plans? I don't have time to reschedule! Or is she going to chuck me completely? Not like I could blame her.

"The tickets for the cinema. . ." she began.

Oh shite! She really is going to cancel or maybe the movie has been cancelled.

She had panic in her voice, "I got them in the post this morning and realised I've booked the movie for tonight, not tomorrow. I'm so sorry. Could you manage it tonight or is that too late notice? Sorry, I shouldn't even ask as you probably have plans. It's ok, I can cancel them and try booking for another time as tomorrow's fully booked with when I checked."

"Lizzy, stop!" I rested my hands on her shoulders to stop her pacing round the room. "It's ok, we can go tonight, I don't have plans. I'll call the restaurant and change it to tonight but what time will I make it as we won't be finished till five or would you prefer to just skip the meal?"

"No, I don't want to skip the meal. I've been looking forward to a big greasy burger." She laughed.

She grabbed a blank piece of paper and took the pen from the top of the till. *What the hell is she doing?*

She turned around holding the paper up for me to see what she'd written. In large bold letters it read:

CLOSED EARLY AS SOMETHING IMPORTANT CAME UP.

She headed towards the door and after picking off the 'open' sign, with a bit blue tac she stuck it to the door. It reminded me that the new sign I'd ordered still hadn't shown up yet and having to use Blue-Tac was driving me mad.

"Come on then," she said, "chop, chop, and I'll give you a lift home. Wouldn't want you turning up to a date in your work clothes and un-showered."

"I'll let you know that I actually showered this morning!" Lizzy giggled.

She started turning off the lights in the fridges and covering the fruit so I grabbed my jacket.

"Wait! I'll have to cycle home as have my bike here." I called out to Lizzy.

"It's cool, Rab. We will just put it in the car like before."

"No, because I have the trailer with me too."

She went to ask why I had the trailer with me but then it was like she decided it was not important. We kissed goodbye, "Don't worry. I promise I will be ready for half three for you coming to pick me up."

"You sure it will still be ok for me to stay over? Just so I know if to pack a bag or not."

"Yes." I told her, "unless you snore then you will need to sleep in the garden."

"As if you would be able to hear me over your mum! But luckily no, I don't snore."

She had a good point there, maybe I should make Mum sleep in the garden tonight as she might keep Lizzy up! I cycled home and detached the trailer so I could get it back in the garden and covered up. *Won't be needing you again old chap but grateful for all the loads you've lugged.*

Mum was busy tidying up the living room and I went through to find her trying to work the new carpet cleaner that she got at the charity shop.

"Mum, why are you doing all this?"

"Well, we have a young lady staying with us tomorrow night so I just want to make sure everything is right."

"Mum, Lizzy has been here plenty times and has never bothered that the carpet has not been washed."

"I know, but I'm just excited."

"We probably won't even be coming in here as we will be home late and would want to get to bed." I quickly added in, "to sleep," as I saw her snigger.

"I know, but she will be down in the morning and I would just feel better knowing everything is done."

"Well, you better get your skates on as she's coming to stay tonight."

Mum looked at me confused.

"She messed up the movie tickets and accidentally booked tonight and can't change it to tomorrow so we have re-arranged for tonight. Hence, why I'm home early."

Mum looked even more panicked and I assured her, "everything looks fine."

She started to struggle with the cleaner, so I helped her work it out how to use it. I left her talking to herself about how shocked she was about how much dirt there was coming out and that she might have been better just buying a new carpet. I could hear her continuing her conversation with herself and headed upstairs to shower and change my attire.

It was already half past one by the time I'd tidied the bits in my room. I hadn't finished, I grabbed my clothes for tonight and got in the shower. Glad I ironed them last night with my work shirt and hung it up as time seemed to be running away from me. The water was nice and cool against the summer heat. *Summer heat to us Scots means it has stopped raining for a bit and the sun has popped out to just show us it's still alive.*

I closed my eyes and enjoyed the feeling but then my heart stopped. *No, shit, fuck!*

I'd been so caught up in the excitement of spending time with Lizzy that I hadn't thought it through properly. Mary wasn't leaving until the morning and I needed to be up early to get her packed up and ready. Maybe, I could wake before Lizzy and get it done but how was I going to get her from the wardrobe and out without risking Lizzy waking and seeing her? I couldn't move her to the living room and there was nowhere to hide the tank. We might even go in there for some drinks when we get back. I couldn't take her downstairs as I couldn't risk Mum finding her during her big clean up! What was I going to do?

I was sweating while standing in a cold shower and tried to calm myself down. I'd just have to risk it and get up at five and sort her without waking Lizzy. I'd tell her that they are collecting her tank in the morning so I need to get up for a bit as I couldn't risk her mum asking questions about why I was sending stuff in Lizzy's name. *Yes, that will work, it will just have to work.*

I quickly showered, got out and threw my clothes on. I popped a cricket in Mary's tank hoping it will either be too exhausted by tonight to make noise or Mary will get up early and have it killed before we get back home. I grabbed the tub and opening my bedroom window, I chucked them out just hoping no one sees it. I grabbed a thin blanket that Mum sometimes used in my living room while watching the fish and draped it over the tank, in case, Lizzy peeked in. I was dashing about mad that I realised I might be sweatier now than before I got in the shower. I sat down and tried to convince myself that it was all going to be ok. Lizzy had already said that when she drinks, she ends up always sleeping late the next day so hopefully, she'd be in a deep sleep. I double checked if there was nothing else lying about that might need to be removed and then found there was nothing left to do.

I ran out the bedroom realising it was 3:25 p.m. and with soaking feet I ran into the living room. "Mum, you know there's a sucky up bit on that thing!"

She shouted back from her bedroom, "I can't hear you," so I squelched through knowing I didn't have time to change my soaks.

"Mum, where have you put my shoes? Lizzy will be here any minute and they are not at the bottom of the stairs where I've left them."

"Not to worry, son, I cleaned out that wee cupboard under the stairs to keep the shoes in like we used to. About time we finally get back to taking pride in this place and maybe wash the carpets more often as the stuff that came out of them was revolting. I forgot the carpet was cream and not charcoal."

I knew she'd made a massive step as the only thing that sat in that cupboard under the stairs, has been Dad's shoes, work boots, a tool bag and his lunch box that he used every day.

I didn't ask what she'd done with them but I was happy to see she'd taken that step. At least, it meant I won't trip over any shoes again coming down in the morning or when heading to bed late.

I was just slipping on my shoes when Lizzy chaps the door. I grabbed my jacket and shouted to mum not to wait up.

I pop Lizzy's bag behind the front door and we headed off. There was a small parking bay near the cinema so we parked Lizzy's car up there for the night and made our way to the restaurant. Lizzy seemed disappointed that there were no burgers on the menu.

I asked her, "what did you expect from a restaurant called La Trattoria."

She thought about it for a second and laughed, "true, I might have missed that hint."

We decided to get one pizza and one pasta dish and share. The atmosphere was lovely and the light seemed to highlight Lizzy's beauty. *Shit! I forgot to tell her how good she looks, isn't that a date comment 101?*

I took a deep breath before saying, "Lizzy, you look beautiful. I'm sorry for not telling you sooner."

She laughed and a bit of pasta flew from her mouth onto my cheek. I grabbed the opportunity to give her the line she told me when I spat fish at her.

Lizzy was trying all the different flavoured gin on offer as the pub didn't really stock many but I sticked to beer and watched as the gin started to take effect.

"You better not fall asleep on me in the cinema as I can't promise I won't stick popcorn in your hair."

We laughed and giggled throughout the meal, having to remind ourselves of the time so we didn't miss the movie.

I can't describe how I feel when I'm with Lizzy. It's like I can be me and don't even notice that others are about.

We skipped desert when we noticed on the menu that the restaurant had tried to be inclusive and offered spotted dick but translated it wrong. Once we have managed to control our fits of laughter, I grabbed the bill and we started the five-minute walk to the cinema, although it took at least fifteen minutes as Lizzy kept stopping to laugh.

She said she can't walk while she's laughing as she's too clumsy and will fall over. This sent us into a roar of laughter again.

We reached the steps of the cinema and Lizzy pulled the tickets from her bag. She had a huge smile on her face as she passed the tickets to me so I could see what we were going to watch. I didn't know what expression came on my face but suddenly the laughter was gone and Lizzy was all serious.

She asked, "Are you ok? You hate it, don't you? I'm so sorry. I made a joke to your Mum about how you had all the James Bond VHSs but no tape player and she laughed and said she didn't care as they were not hers. I assumed they must have been yours but now I'm not so sure."

"They were my dad's. He used to watch them all the time even though he knew every word to every movie."

"Oh! Shit! I'm so sorry."

I hadn't heard Lizzy swear very much so it sounded funny coming out her mouth. I began to laugh, "its ok. This one will be totally different so doesn't matter. I will probably even enjoy it if you don't fall asleep."

"You sure?"

"Yeah, come on, let's get popcorn before we miss all those amazing ads." I winked and she smiled, grabbing my arm as we headed inside. It looked like Mum and I were both making a big step forward today.

The movie actually turned out to be really good and we agreed that we should try watching some of Dad's older ones together. We decided to grab a taxi home and had a couple drinks there instead of the pub and found Mum in her jammies watching TV when we reached home.

"Oh! Sorry guys. I expected you home a lot later than this. I'll get myself off to my room and give you guys space."

"Don't be silly." I told her. "Have a drink with us, nothing better than spending time with two of my favourite women."

Mum laughed, "I think you've already had enough to drink."

But I didn't feel drunk, well, I did feel drunk with happiness and not alcohol.

We decided to have a game of Cluedo but it only ended up with us all getting it wrong and pretty much giving up. Lizzy went to the loo and declared when she came back, "My tights seem to be wet under my feet."

Mum and I roared with laughter again. We told her about Mum's fight with the carpet cleaner and that she nearly washed away the whole carpet. We had a few drinks together and spent the time laughing and just having a good time before Mum declared it was past her bedtime. She winked at us, "Both of you don't stay up too late. I will see you in the morning."

We decided to head upstairs too and Lizzy went in to the bathroom to get changed.

I couldn't miss the opportunity to have one more glance round the room making sure I had not missed anything but all looked good. I stripped into my boxers and put on the lamps on the bedside cabinets, jumping into bed.

228

I made sure I left out the massive book that Lizzy gave me on my cabinet, promising I would start on it soon. I made it look like that was my intention. Lizzy was through soon after and nearly killed me by jumping over me instead of having to walk the whole way round the bed.

We giggled as Lizzy landed on my body and I think she might have punctured one of my lungs. Our eyes met and our faces came closer.

"I don't know why you got changed in the bathroom as I'm about to see all now anyway." I said lifting my eyebrows and looking at her to make it seem more of a question.

With that she started to remove her night shirt. *Her skin is so soft and radiant!* It's weird as I didn't even feel embarrassed as she pulled the covers back and started removing my boxers. I pulled her close and whispered, "Sorry, I'm a virgin so might need some direction and help".

She laughed and whispered back, "so am I. So, we will need to work it out together."

"Kept myself for the one! And I'm confident that that's you." I gulped knowing that I was just about to let her make a massive mistake but then I was overcome with what she was doing and I couldn't find the breath to even speak.

We collapsed on the bed beside each other and I pulled her closer. We stared into each other's eyes. We didn't need to say a word. We could both feel that the other was satisfied. I laid on my back and Lizzy rested her head on my chest. I wished I could stay in that moment forever. I wished I could even be with her forever but I tried not to think of leaving her just now and enjoy the time I'd got. Lizzy drifted off to sleep quickly and I laid awake for a little while longer listening to her breathing and soaking in the feeling of her skin next to mine. I didn't want the evening to end but then remembered about my 5 a.m. alarm and let myself drift off to sleep.

.oOo.

I woke up feeling like I'd rolled over onto a knife and pulled the covers back to see where the hell the pain was coming from. It took a minute for my eyes to actually tell my brain that I was seeing right. It was Mary! She was standing there, staring at me like she has plotted this all along. Getting back on me for Silver, for taking away her babies and using her to do such horrible murders. I quickly kicked out my leg and she fell onto the floor. The next thing I knew, I grabbed the large book and whooped it on top of her. She didn't move and I was sure I'd just killed her. I hoped I had not woken Lizzy or Mum up and turned to see Lizzy facing the other way. She seemed to still be fast asleep. I thought fast and remembered that the antidote injection that I'd purchased was in the drawer on Lizzy's side.

I gently tried to reach over her and managed to retrieve it from the drawer but something was not right. Lizzy's body felt really hot and when I turned the lamp back on, she looked grey and foam was slowly seeping out her mouth. *Fuck! Mary must have got her first.*

I didn't even need to think about the choice in front of me. Mary was dead and I needed to save Lizzy. I grabbed my phone while trying to pull the cap of the injection and managed to type in 999. I was feeling really sweaty and drowsy. I couldn't seem to focus my eyes on the buttons to find dial and my arms started to feel really weak. It was like my mind was telling the wrong finger to move but I finally think I managed to hit the call button. With the last bit of strength I had in my arm, I rammed the jag into Lizzy's thigh and tried to push the syringe down.

Everything started looking dark but my eyes were still open. I couldn't hear ringing or anyone on the phone but I hoped that someone was there. "Help, girlfriend sick", and I think I managed to get out my address on the phone. Or maybe not. Darkness filled the room and I couldn't feel my mouth anymore. I think I slumped over the edge of the bed but I couldn't feel my body or even think which parts were where. I hoped I pushed the syringe down. I hoped I pressed dial. I hoped someone was there.

Chapter Twenty-Two:

The power of a mother's love and dangerous secrets
Robert's Mom, Three hours ago

I was going to tell him tonight but now with Lizzy coming over that was not an option. I didn't want to ruin the first time she stayed over. I hid everything for all these years but waiting one more night feels like it might kill me. I knew everything had to come out one day but with Billy leaving Rab over three million and his amazing house in Inverie, he'd going to want to know why he's getting all his belongings. How do you tell the boy that adored his Dad so much that in fact, he wasn't his Dad but now his real Dad had died?

I know once I tell him, I'll lose him forever. Things were so much simpler back when we were at college. Peter, Billy and I decided to run off to finally be with the people that understood us. I married Peter here, and then married Billy once we arrived in America. We found the polygamist settling in that we agreed to move to but then we realised the grass wasn't much greener on this side. The other polygamist families looked at us funny too because I was a woman with two husbands instead of the other way about.

We gave it our best shot and pushed through three long years but nothing got better. Then one day, I found out I was pregnant with Robert. I longed to be back home. When I called Marie and she told me she was pregnant with Lizzy it just made me want to return more. Marie and I met at school and I always told her everything, never once did she judge us. She told me that she had been disowned by her family because she had married a Muslim man. She told me over the phone, "I had moved to this original village. The people here are so accepting and rarely have any visitors. Maybe, you guys could come here?"

It didn't take much convincing and one day we left everything and found ourselves on a flight back to the UK.

After speaking to Marie, we spent a few days organizing how we'd make our return work. Because in the UK, I was legally married to Peter we decided the best thing to do would be for us two to move into one house and for Billy to move into a remote house where I could still visit him every other day. Billy came from a very affluent family and after a few calls he bought us two houses in the same village as Marie. He had to make offers to the current owners that they couldn't refuse. We had agreed that it would need to remain this way until Robert was older as we couldn't risk him being taken away and us being put in jail.

Polygamy is illegal in the UK but Robert was our number one priority so we had to just do the best we could. Peter and Billy didn't have a sexual relationship and I never slept with both of them at the same time so Peter stayed at home with Robert on the nights I spent at Billy's.

Once Robert started getting older, he started putting up questions on where I was. It was then that I put an end to me staying at Billy's. I spent time with him whenever I could but as the years passed by it was harder and harder to hide it. We all knew we needed to make sacrifices so I had to just get on with it until the day came where we could tell Robert.

A few years later I went to the Doctor for help as we had been trying so hard for another child but it just was not happening. My results came back fine and the Doctor suggested she should test my husband too. I spoke with Peter and he gladly went for the test but it wasn't good news.

Apparently, he had the lowest sperm count they had seen. He was practically infertile, and they kept telling him what a miracle it must have been that we conceived Robert.

Peter took this really hard as it showed that Billy was the biological father. We had never considered even finding that out because to us he had two Dads and one Mum and that was all that mattered. We only went for help and would have never imagined this would be the result.

Peter grew bitter and jealous, saying Billy had started treating Robert different and making it obvious he was his dad. This wasn't true. If anything, Peter distanced himself a little from Robert and was struggling to come to terms with reality. I desperately wanted to have another child but for Peter's sanity we agreed we wouldn't. Peter left that day and didn't return for eight months. I begged him constantly to come home, telling him how much Robert missed him and that we could work it out. He finally came back but things were never the same.

Peter would get jealous any time I tried to go to Billy's so my love life with him became next to nothing. He didn't seem to mind as much when Billy came to us but he couldn't stand the thought of us being off together while he was left with Billy's kid. Billy was so understanding and kind. Even though he was paying for everything he tried to give Peter as much space as he needed. He promised me that no matter what, he would be there and would wait until I was ready. No matter how long that would be.

It was clear where he got his kindness from because when he told his family everything, they completely respected our wishes by seeing Robert whenever they could but never telling him the truth. The years seemed to just fly by but we finally decided it was time. We had arranged to go away for the weekend, all three of us, and decided the best way to tell him but we never made it to the resort because of the crash. Billy tried to visit me in the hospital but I didn't want him to see me in the state I was in. I didn't want him to see how much I was grieving for Peter but he was the one I had spent all the years with. Then, when I finally got home, I told him I had to concentrate on Robert and I couldn't tell him that Peter wasn't his dad with everything being so raw. Billy kept his distance but continued to pay money into my account, in case, I needed anything but I eventually took my name off that joint account as it didn't feel right taking his money.

Billy was such a kind-hearted loving person. He would have done anything I asked of him and now I'd waited too late. The least I could do is to come clean with Robert as it's not fair the way he speaks of him. It's going to be hard since I've lost both the men I loved my whole life and I was just about to give up the last one I have but it's a choice I have to make.

I regretted now not letting Robert know sooner, as Billy was the best father he could have had. Tomorrow, I'll definitely tell him. Tonight, I'll let him have fun with Lizzy as he's very excited about it.

With Lizzy coming over tonight unexpectedly, I popped upstairs to make sure he'd cleaned up everything. He'd left his room unlocked again, and I never went inside but I was sure he didn't want her to see his dirty clothes thrown across the floor.

I was actually surprised at how tidy and clean it was. Clearly, he wanted to make a good impression. I saw that his wardrobe door has been left open and go over to close it. It won't close at first but I hear Lizzy's car so I slammed it hard.

Shit!

I heard something smash and the door creaking back open. It must be broken. I think I might have broken something lying in the bottom, but I was sure that will be the last thing on his mind after I speak to him tomorrow.

After enjoying a couple drinks with them, I say goodnight to them both and tell them I'd see them in the morning. Rab looks so happy. I'm glad he's finally getting his life together, even if I know I won't be allowed to be part of it after telling him the truth.

Acknowledgment

Whenever I read a book, I always wonder why there were so many "thanks" and people mentioned at the end, but writing a book myself, now I know why. It's not possible without the care and support from others.

Firstly, I would like to say a massive Thank you to my sister Natalie Whyte! From the first letter I put on the paper to the last she has read every change and listened to my ideas to the point of knowing the book as much as I do. Also supporting me with every step, from understanding what the next step would be to helping me find my editor. I couldn't have done this without her.

Secondly, my editor herself. What can I say? It's difficult to put into words. Yes, it's her job and she was paid but she went way over and above what she was required to do.

My dyslexia, affects my ability to spell and my grammar. Kriti basically got pages with writing on them. No dialogs, real structure or any punctuation in the right places. Kriti made this into a book. She also taught me lots about writing styles and continued to be there for me even when her part was completed. She had so much going on with her life while doing my book, but still she made me feel she was truly there for me and believed in me.

My day-to-day job have been absolutely fantastic and supportive. Kirsty Love for allowing me to share and discuss my book at work. Erin Jackson for reading my very original draft to give me feedback and Jessica Hunt for encouraging others to read my book. My wonderful colleagues Caitlin Everett, Kerry Buxton, Deborah Chard, Jennifer Duncan, Ryan Mitchell and Pamela

Strickland for reading my book and giving me that much needed feedback.

To some of my "best neighbours ever", Dawn, Gail and Alistair Clark, Gayle Brown and Steven Hardie for listening to me each time I wanted to share ideas and thoughts. Stacey Gibson for looking through my first printed copy and giving me her thoughts. Then there's my best friends, Kate and John Wood, Nina, David and Harley Craig, Louisa Dawson, Kirsty Wellburn and Karlyn Moughan for not only giving me their thoughts but letting me off for being a bad friend and abandoning them a little while I was writing.

There's a fantastic Facebook page called "Scottish (Slightly insane) Reptile and Invertebrates fans" that is full of extremely knowledgeable and incredibly welcoming members. I just want to thank all of them for letting me join and letting me ask the most bizarre questions. Special thanks to, Scott Vtec Glen and Dave Maguire for their direct input, for not only answering all my questions but sending me photos, links and videos for me to get the information as accurate as possible.

Thank you to the extremely talented Jonny Liver for my amazing book cover. There was a good bit of to-and-fro but we got there in the end. Jonny can be found on Fiverr, have a look at his fantastic array of work.

Last but certainly not the least! My Hubby Andy and my two girls Bethany and Coral. There are no words to express how much I love you three and how grateful I am for enabling me to write this book. Letting me escape into my own little world to get into the characters' minds and being understanding when I declined to join in family days outs, movie nights or games. You girls are nowhere near old enough to read this book, but I hope when you are then you know I couldn't have done this without you.

About the Author

Norma Fraser, author of Killed by Mary, brings dark humor and colloquial wit to her characters and to her commentary on life in small-town Scotland. Norma writes about people that are both familiar and surprising, leaving the reader feeling uncomfortable with their own empathy. She brings this ability to merge comedy and unrelenting honesty to her real-life professional and family roles.

Despite being dyslexic and suffering some health challenges, Norma keeps her spirit of creating quirky characters alive. Killed by Mary is her debut thriller and she intends to keep creating similar characters in the future. She lives in Fife with her husband and her two beautiful daughters. Whenever she's not writing, she loves to spend that time with her family.

Printed in Great Britain
by Amazon

12024183R00140